I was angry, hurt, and frustrated, but I couldn't know the guilt my actions would bring...

He looked around the room, and I waved a finger to get his attention back.

"I looked her up a few months ago," he went on. "I shouldn't have. Some things should be left alone. She and her son are after me. They'll never stop, now. I opened up Pandora's Box for myself, and now I can never go home again. They're violent people. I don't know what they'll do to me."

His eyes continued to search the room.

"What are you looking for?" I asked.

"That woman," he said. "Could I have more pie? She said they have some kind of berry. I want to try it."

"I need to know where you come into this story, Dad. I need to know what you did. Why are they after you?"

He looked at me owlishly. "You *need* to know?" he asked. "Since when do you *need* to know about me?"

I was hugely irritated. I wanted to tell him that he didn't own the world. I wanted to tell him that he couldn't just land on other people's doorsteps, disrupt their lives, and not tell them the whole story. I wanted to tell him that I was worried sick about him.

Instead, I walked him out to the jeep and said nothing. I ignored his request for a second piece of pie.

Days later, I remembered my small cruelty and wept.

During the summer of 1946, a group of children play a kissing game behind a general store in rural Georgia. It's just kids having fun, until one innocent kiss leads to the brutal beating death of a ten-year-old boy. The horrific hate crime shakes an entire town. It spawns a series of murders, and a secret that is hidden for generations.

Mike Latta follows the story back into the heat and humidity of a sixty-five-year-old Georgia summer, back to dirt roads, wooden bridges, and muddy-water fishing holes, back to a single kiss that has killed, and killed again. It's a kiss that has slept for decades, but now it's awake. Learning its secret may cost Mike his life.

Fiction inspired by the real-life Emmett Till murder, *Deadly Kiss* is the story of loves that won't stay lost and ghosts that just won't sleep.

KUDOS for *Deadly Kiss*

"Bickford seamlessly weaves the past and the present. A ripping good mystery." ~ Peggy Blair, author of *Hungry Ghosts*

"The book is well written, a chilling tale of spirits who can't rest, due to the consequences of a childish prank almost seventy years before—a thought-provoking story that will make you sit up and take notice." Taylor Jones, Reviewer

"Bickford skillfully navigates through the past and the present to create a thrilling tale of murder, the corruption of innocence, and a serial killer bent on erasing entire families, if necessary, in order to protect a shameful secret. *Deadly Kiss* is a page-turner that will catch and hold your interest from beginning to end." ~ Regan Murphy, Reviewer

DEADLY KISS

BOB BICKFORD

A Black Opal Books Publication

GENRE: PARANORMAL THRILLER/GHOSTS/MYSTERY

DEADLY KISS
Copyright © 2016 by Bob Bickford
Cover Design by Dawné Dominique
All cover art copyright © 2016
All Rights Reserved
Print ISBN: 978-1-626945-15-9

First Publication: AUGUST 2016

Published by Black Opal Books **http://www.blackopalbooks.com**

For Jane and Sam
Never closer than now.

PART I

ECHO ISLAND
ONTARIO, CANADA

CHAPTER 1

My earliest memory was of a merry-go-round. I was perhaps three or four years old, and I had no way of knowing the circumstance that placed me on it. It was a part of a county fair perhaps, or a travelling carnival. No doubt the contraption was very small, not a grand, glittering European carousel, but just a dusty thing trucked in and parked by the side of a two-lane southern highway. That ride was as clear in my mind as if it happened this morning.

The horse was alive. I could close my eyes and smell his warm horsey smell, hear the creak of leather, feel the thump of his hooves as he stirred and danced beneath me. I looked down and saw my small hands twined in his mane. I held on for dear life as he bolted and carried me away across dirt tracks and green, green grass. The wind in my face forced tears from my eyes.

Most of all, I remembered my father. The world rushed past, and he was standing beneath some trees, holding a camera and waving to me. He was a young man, slim and dark-haired, and he was all by himself. It was perhaps my greatest sadness that I couldn't wave back at him. I was too small, and the horse was too big. I was afraid to take my hand from the great neck, terrified that the air currents would pluck me off and I would fall.

I wished that I had waved to him, even now. I wished that I was braver.

Though I had stood with a cold wind blowing grit into the first of my gray hairs and watched a silver hearse carry him off, I was still that tiny boy, and my father was still looking at me from under the trees, holding his camera, waving and waving.

CHAPTER 2

Sam Latta,
Cobb County, Georgia, Tuesday, July 2, 1946:

The boy reached into his pocket and checked for his single nickel. It was still there, along with a rabbit's foot, dyed green, on a small chain. He rubbed its tiny claws across his fingertips, unaware that he was doing it as he walked on the edge of the dirt and gravel road.

It was hot. The trees on the verge, hung with Spanish moss, gave him the illusion of shade, though they kept their darkness to themselves and shared none of it with the roadway. An old pickup, colored a dusty shade that had once been blue, slowed as it drew abreast of him, but he didn't look up. It ground its gears, a metallic ratcheting sound, and left him behind.

The general store came slowly into his view, weathered gray wood with a roof that sloped into a large veranda across the whole front of it. A nearly-new station wagon was parked by the steps, beside a low-slung black Ford Deluxe whose chrome V8 emblem shone from beneath a layer of dirt.

It was dark inside. Overhead, two large fans mixed the

stifling air, which smelled vaguely spicy. Bare light bulbs struggled with the dimness; after the brightness of the day outside he was nearly blind, and had to wait for his eyes to adjust.

A pallid young woman stood behind the counter. The boy knew that she and her husband had taken over the store from the old couple who had owned it before them. The old man could generally be depended on to slip a free sweet to young patrons, but the new people never seemed even to smile. The store smelled the same as it always had, but now it was different. He saw the young husband, in short white sleeves, standing in the rear of the store and talking to another man.

"Grape Nehi, please, ma'am?"

She turned and bent. He heard clinking as she stirred the bottles in a metal cooler filled with ice. "Got none," she said, straightening. "Orange, RC, and ginger."

The boy hesitated. He had imagined the cold purple fragrance the whole long hot walk here.

A husky young man back in the dim wooden aisles eyed him suspiciously and then returned to his conversation.

"Orange please," the boy said.

The woman pulled out a clear bottle and paused with a church key in her hand. "Five cents."

The boy put his nickel on the counter. She opened the bottle and pushed it across to him. He went back out into the hot sunlight and took the first small sip. Bubbles stung his nose, and he was flooded with the icy, too-sweet essence of orange. When he lowered the bottle, he saw a girl about his age standing at the end of the covered porch. She was blonde and barefoot, wearing a soiled cotton dress.

"I know you," she said. "I seen you at the school. I'm one grade ahead of you."

He didn't respond.

"How old are you anyway?" she asked.

He told her that he was ten, and she sniffed dismissively, allowing that she was eleven, almost twelve. She started to go and then turned back.

"Wanna see something? Come back here," she said.

He reluctantly followed her around to the rear of the store. The girl unsettled him, but he was well brought-up, and, so trapped by his courtesy, he followed. She was unkempt and a little bit wild. Although his parents had little money, they made him aware that they differed from their poor white neighbors in the matter of breeding.

The dooryard in back of the store was packed dirt. It was here that the coloreds knocked, cash in hand, and were served. The store did more custom at the rear than the front, but its best clients were not permitted inside. In the midday heat, there was no traffic at the door. A black child about the same age as the two of them sat on the ground with his back against a hand pump, idly holding his pale palm under the drips from its spout. He wore denim overalls with the knees torn out. A yellow dog sat beside him, worn out from the heat.

"What d'you want to show me?" the white boy asked, a little bit impatient.

She turned herself to him and made a show of closing her eyes. "I like you," she said. "You can kiss me if you want to."

The boy was thrilled. This was a bad girl. He thought about it. "No, I don't guess I will," he finally said. "I don't kiss girls."

Her eyes flew open. "You crummy little creep," she shouted. "I ought to tell on you for trying."

He took a few steps back, and she turned to the Negro boy. "You!" she called, and gestured imperiously. "Come here!"

The black child hesitated and then got to his feet, clearly unwilling. He shuffled over to where she stood. He kept his eyes down. When he was close enough, she grabbed his chin and kissed him hard on the mouth, an exaggerated smack.

The back door flew open and banged off the wall with a sound like a gunshot. The shop owner cleared the three steps and grabbed his daughter roughly by the arm. The Negro boy was already fifty yards away, his yellow dog running at his heels.

"Wanda! You dirty little bitch!" the man screamed, spit flying. "What the God-damned hell are you doing? Did I just see you kiss a nigger?" He shook her violently, and she shrieked in fear and pain. The man caught sight of the white boy and stopped, staring at him.

"Oh God," he said. "Who're you? Get over here!"

The boy dropped his bottle of soda pop in the dirt and ran.

∽∾∽

Present Day:

Another warm season was beginning. I hammered home steel retaining pins that held the dock to a natural rock pier jutting out from my island. When all of the anchors were seated securely, I straightened and felt the muscles in my back protest.

"Getting old, Bill," I said. "I'm aching."

My friend and business partner stood watching me. We restored small boats together in the off-season. I stayed at his marina at the other end of the lake during the winter months, when ice made the island inaccessible.

"Wait. Just wait. You'll be my age in about twenty years," he said. "If I'm still around, you can tell me about it then."

He paused, looking at me intently. "You're not staying out here tonight, are you?"

"Sure," I said. "Lots to do, getting this place back in shape after the winter."

"Really? Better not have an accident, Mike. This end of the lake's awful deserted still."

"I'll be fine, Bill."

"You haven't been out in these woods long enough," he said, shaking his head. "I've told you before. Hollow Lake's got a mean streak."

"I've heard the stories." I needed to change the subject. "Won't be lonely for long," I said. "Couple weeks, the early birds will be opening up summer cottages, and you'll be getting boats back in the water. Need help this year?"

"I hired on a high school kid from town for the heavy stuff, but if you want to take a turn on the forklift now and then, that'd suit me."

I nodded. My divorce had left me with some money and no burning desire to spend it. I worked on old boats because it was interesting, and because I sometimes needed the human contact I got at the marina.

"I've gotta get back," Bill said. "Diane's thinking I'm off somewhere smoking cigarettes by now."

I laughed. "You do smoke cigarettes every time you're out of her sight. She's right. You ought to be ashamed."

"Oh, bullshit," he said. "The two of you make me crazy."

We stood in companionable silence for a moment. The sun was nearly balmy, but every now and then a cold spring breeze from across the lake blew away the warmth.

"You're sure about staying out here?" he asked again.

I nodded.

He looked up at my hundred-year-old cabin, tucked in

among the jack pines that towered over it, and shook his head. "You and the ghosts."

"It's fine, Bill," I said. "There are ghosts everywhere."

He waved over his shoulder as he headed for his boat. I watched him as he reversed away from the dock. He completed a slow sweeping turn away from the island, and then the boat hunkered down in the rear and kicked water out behind itself, roaring out into the reach, headed for civilization.

The phone startled me. It vibrated in the front pocket of my jeans like something alive. I pulled it out and peered at the display in the red shimmer of the spring sunset, cupping my hand to cut the glare. It was Angela.

"Mike? Where are you? I've been trying to get you for almost two hours."

I hadn't heard my ex-wife's voice in months, but as always the effect on me was immediate. I was never sure when I spoke with her if I yearned for an ending, or a beginning that had never happened. I could feel the weight of her on the other end of the connection—cool, blonde, and blue.

"I'm back on the island," I said. "You know there's almost no reception out here. Sorry." I wasn't sure what I was apologizing for.

"I can't imagine how you can set foot on that place again," she said. "Anyway, I'm calling because…it's your dad, Mike. I just got a call from him. We were on the phone almost an hour. He isn't doing well."

"He hasn't done well in years. What's the problem now?"

"I haven't phoned him in a few weeks," she said. "I feel bad. He called me because he needed to talk to family, which I guess I still am, in his mind. God knows you aren't."

"Easy, Ang," I said. "What's going on?"

"I don't know, but he doesn't sound good. He wants to fly up here for a visit."

I was stunned. "Put him off," I said. "I'll give him a call. Maybe I'll fly down this summer and visit him."

"Too late, Mike. He's coming. He says he *has* to come."

"Has to," I repeated, shaking my head. "Terrific."

I looked out at the lake. The water had an amber tint, residue from the spring melt. The opposite shore had dressed itself in green, but it was still easy to imagine the ice and snow that had covered it until a few weeks ago. I wasn't sure how to handle this.

"He hasn't left Atlanta in years," I said. "You need a passport now to get into Canada. Do you think he even has one? He can't come up here if he doesn't."

"He's an old man. They'll accommodate him."

"He's really not that old," I said. "He's what...hardly even seventy. Seventy-something."

"Seventy four," she said.

I had never been close to my father. He was bitter and silent, even in my earliest memory of him. Since we had lost our daughter a year and a half before, Angela had gravitated toward the old man at the same time that I drifted away from both of them. Perhaps she found in him a sense of familial comfort that was lacking in me. She had flown from her home in Toronto to see him in Atlanta several times and spoke to him on the telephone regularly. I hadn't seen or talked to him in over a year.

"Well, I guess it's good he's coming to visit you," I said.

"Me? He's not coming to visit me. He wants to see you. He needs to talk to you."

I was dumbfounded. "What the hell could he possibly want to talk to me about?"

"Don't snap at me, Mike," she said quietly, her voice

tense. "I'm telling you what he told me. I'll pick him up at the airport and get him to you. Maybe he'll stay with me for a day or two before I drive him up north."

"I don't really want a house guest right now, Angela."

"You'll probably have to meet us in Huntsville. I don't want to go to the lake. I'll call you when he's here, assuming you'll answer your phone."

We hung up, and I stood and looked at the planks beneath my feet. The wood was raw and slippery. The lake beneath me was still, and I could see the smooth rock bottom sloping down into the deep. The freezing water looked warm.

I stayed that way for a long time. Finally, I sighed and went back up through the trees to the cabin. After months away, I didn't feel entirely comfortable here. I didn't feel entirely comfortable in my own skin either.

Problem was, I had to be somewhere.

CHAPTER 3

Sutton family,
Marietta, Georgia, Wednesday, July 3, 1946:

Two men sat at the kitchen table, illuminated only by a dim light bulb. Each of them held a jelly glass; the bottle between them was already half empty. The store owner had his elbows on the table. His hair was greasy with sweat. He pushed it back from his brow and rested his face in his palms for a moment, and then he gripped the edge of the table top.

"Jesus," he said. "I don't know what the Christ to do. I really don't."

His pale young wife stood in the corner of the room, her hip against a peeling sideboard. "You're her father," she said. "You better do something. She has no chance of a decent life, of getting married, nothing. These niggers'll have it all over town. You know they will. We won't be able to walk down the street the way this is."

"Decent?" the man asked sourly. "Like you?"

She crossed the room in an instant, and the sound of the slap was like a pistol shot. The man stood up, his cheek reddening. The other man, her brother, raised a hand to separate them.

They stopped and looked at him. He laid a pistol on the table.

"We're gone do what we have to," he said, one index finger resting on the gun. "No one's doing any talking about this family."

"You can't shoot someone over a thing like this," the store owner protested.

"You shut up!" his wife hissed, leaning over the table. "Thank God there's at least one man in this house."

"I never said we were shooting anyone, or not shooting them," the brother said. "I did say no one's going to be talking about this. That's what I said."

Standing, he picked up the gun and tucked it behind his belt. He looked at the other man. "Let's go."

☙✍☙

Present Day:

In the morning, I brought my breakfast out to the front veranda and set it down on the steps. I sat next to it. When I picked up my coffee, the cup left a dark wet ring on the old wood. Early May sunshine filtered down through fresh leaves and stained the clearing in front of my cabin a bright new green. The sky was mirrored in the bits of lake I could see between the trees in front of me. It was chilly, but the patch of sun on the porch was warm.

I watched the big yellow dog nosing through the pine needles on the floor of the clearing. He wasn't mine, and he didn't look at me.

"Hey, stranger," I called. "Where'd you come from?"

I tossed a piece of toast in his direction. He ignored it, and me.

His owner must have come in by canoe. The sides of my island sloped so steeply into the water that the dock was the only place to land a boat, and I had seen no one arrive. It seldom occurred to summer explorers that the island was private. The infrequent appearance of picnickers or hikers didn't bother me, though. I sometimes welcomed the company.

My Echo Island was a seven-acre egg. It sat in Hollow Lake, thirteen miles of cold water, a couple of hours north of Toronto. It was mostly covered with tall pines, and the interior stayed dim and cool, even in the summer time. A single dead oak stood by itself on the north shore. It looked like an enormous scarecrow, put there to guard the conifers.

My cabin was a century old. The living area and kitchen were part of the original structure, made of wide boards and rough-cut beams. I had built an addition on at the back, which housed a modern bathroom and my bedroom.

There were two larger islands that were my neighbors. Duck and Long Duck Islands swam side by side, with a passage between them. On misty mornings they appeared to hover above the surface of the lake.

The southern shore had a gravel road running along it, with a few summer cottages sprinkled along its length. Most of the vacation homes on the lake were on the north shore, accessible only by water. The people who summered here valued privacy.

There were only a handful of us who lived here all year, and we stuck together. Molly Bean lived in a small white house on the south road. The MacMillans, Bill and Diane, owned the small marina at the other end of the lake and lived upstairs, above the office.

The yellow dog put his head up and stood still. He listened to something that I couldn't hear and then trotted off, headed for the trail that led behind my cabin. I was curious, so I finished my coffee and stood up to follow him. The pine canopy overhead kept the path free of undergrowth, and the soft loam underfoot deadened foot-steps and imparted a deep hush.

Down the trail, the dog joined a small boy, who was peering intently at a tree trunk. He appeared to be carving something in the wood. I walked toward them. The boy was black and very small, probably eight or nine years old. He wore too-big denim overalls that were cut off at the knees, different from the standard brightly-colored bathing trunks or shorts that were nearly a summer uni-form among the area children.

He spotted me, waved happily, and skipped off. The dog followed him over a rise in the path and they disap-peared. I walked to the tree and saw most of a crude heart scratched in the trunk. I started to trace the heart with my finger and was stopped by the sound of a boat approach-ing across the reach. I changed direction and walked back and onto my dock.

The sun was bright on the water, and I squinted through a million sparkles. The morning wind was warm and smelled fresh. Molly Bean's red and white boat emerged from the light, headed toward me.

The dock rose and fell underneath me as the boat came close, and I caught the line she tossed at me. I took her wet hand as she jumped out.

"Little early for wearing shorts, isn't it, Molly?" I asked. "You're freezing."

She smiled sweetly at me. "If summer won't come to me," she said, "I'll go to summer. You have to believe in it."

Dark-haired, with clear skin and strangely amber eyes, Molly made the day bright. I had met her the summer be-fore. The first time that she had turned her head and looked at me, I was head-over-heels, just-like-the-fifth-grade in love with her. The past year had only deepened my feelings, and I had no idea what to do about her.

She lived part of the time with her estranged husband. I wasn't clear on their relationship or on what his role in her life was. He appeared for a week or two at a time and then vanished again. He seemed to dismiss her, and I never saw any gesture or word of affection pass between them, yet I knew that Molly was still in love with him, because she had told me so.

She loved me too, but it was not with the same hopeless fascination that she felt for him. Occasionally, she spent the night at my cabin. Each time it happened, I woke up in the morning believing that we had bridged a gap, and then each time she moved away again to a safe distance.

We were in love with being loved. Romance was the excitement of being reflected in the mirror of someone else's adoration. I didn't think I was going to have that from Molly. Still, she was my best friend, my sometimes lover, and I'd made a decision to settle for what parts of her she was willing to share.

"Summer's almost here, and winter just left," I said. "I've hardly had time to even notice spring yet. It just came and I miss it already. Funny, every season makes you miss it when it's gone."

"The trick is to kiss them while they're here," Molly said.

"Kiss them?"

She nodded.

"You might be right," I said. "Want coffee?"

We walked slowly up toward the cabin.

"I still miss your damn dog," she said. "I keep looking for her to run out to the dock every time I come here."

"I do too," I said. "There's another dog around here this morning. Might be a lost one."

"Doubt he's lost, unless he's a good swimmer. Someone's probably here for a walk."

"I mean a really lost one, Molly. I didn't get too close, but there was something odd about him. He was with a boy."

She looked at me, surprised. For a couple of years, I had seen things that weren't really there, in the normal sense. I saw people who had died, and sometimes scenes from events that had happened a long time ago. I didn't know what caused it and had never been interested in those things until they started to happen to me. I considered myself almost painfully average. Sometimes I figured that everyone saw things that weren't quite there and didn't realize what they were seeing.

"A ghost dog?" she asked.

"Sure. I think so."

She looked away. "Well then," she said. "If he's not real, then I guess you can't keep him."

I smiled. Molly saw ghosts, too. We didn't talk about it much. We didn't always see them, we didn't always see the same ones at the same times, and we didn't quite experience them the same way.

We didn't seek it out and took no pleasure in it. We didn't play with Ouija boards or hold séances. We seldom discussed it with each other or with anyone else. It wasn't an important part of our daily lives, and we were usually both able to ignore it. We just lived with it when we couldn't.

Molly's aunt ran the post office in Ansett, the nearest town. Kate Bean was Molly's *de facto* mother and a good friend to me. She sometimes saw things too, and she put it down to an Irish quirk that was passed down to the females in their family line, from mothers to daughters. She once hinted that her younger sister had been driven a little bit crazy by things that haunted her before she died. Molly didn't talk much about her mother, and I didn't ask.

I didn't see ghosts until I divorced and moved to the

island, or if I did, I didn't recognize them for what they were. Molly saw living spirits, entities acting in the here and now. She was more comfortable interacting with them than I was, and, on the occasions that we had been together and witnessed a visitation, she was as kind and natural with them as she was with everyone else. I admired her for it. In contrast, I seemed to be more prone to seeing past events, or strongly symbolic scenes connected to the places that I happened to be.

We've all been in a crowded room or a subway car and felt someone else's eyes. We look up and our glance immediately homes in on the person who is looking at us. It happens without thought or hesitation. We sense their presence, and even if they are in a sea of a thousand faces, we lock their gaze immediately.

So it is with ghosts. More often than not, you feel a gaze and look up at...nothing. Your reliable radar has malfunctioned, you think, because there is no one there. Sometimes the feeling persists, and you have to tear your attention away. Where other people saw a vacant room or an empty street corner, Molly and I saw who was there, staring at us. It was that simple.

Usually, they looked like anyone else. It was often something inappropriate about them, something jarring about what they were wearing, or the things they said or did, that alerted me to what they were. Molly claimed that they missed the shine that living eyes had. I couldn't say if that was true or not. I was usually too scared when I saw something ethereal to sort through details like that.

"Come here," I said. "I'll show you."

I led her up the path to the tree where the little boy had been. She looked at the carving in the trunk. "It looks like a heart," she said.

"I thought so, too."

"Do ghosts draw things on trees?"

"I don't know," I said. "I just had a feeling about him. He seemed…wrong, not real. You know what I mean."

"Well, I think it's very sweet, whoever he was."

We went back to the cabin, and I made coffee. She sat at the table and watched me. When it was ready, we took it out onto the porch.

"So what's new?" she asked. "You said your dad is coming to visit?"

I sighed.

"Guess so. No idea why—we don't even talk on the phone any more. He told my ex that he needs to tell me something. I really don't know why he couldn't just tell her and get her to pass it along to me."

"There's more to it than that, right? More is bugging you than the inconvenience of having a visitor."

"An island is pretty close quarters when you don't really get along with someone, Molly."

She sipped her coffee and looked out at the lake. "This is good," she said. "I don't know why I make such shitty coffee, no matter what I do. I can't even drink my own, mostly I don't even bother. What's he like anyway? You never talk about him."

"There's not much to talk about," I said. "I hardly know the man."

CHAPTER 4

Tull family,
Marietta, Georgia, Wednesday, July 3, 1946:

They followed the dim glow of headlights off of the road and onto the packed dirt of the front yard. The house squatting in the darkness wasn't much more than a shack. The roof sloped into a covered porch that sagged at one end. A rusty sedan rested on its belly in front of them. It had not moved since before the war. They bumped forward until the lights were aimed at the door. A figure came out and stood on the step, one hand raised as a shield against the glare. Holding the wheel in one hand, the store owner turned and looked at the small figure in the back seat.

"Stay here, y'hear? Don't move. Had enough trouble from you."

The girl didn't answer. She sat huddled in the darkness.

"Let's go," the uncle said. He opened his door and got out.

"Who's that?" the man on the porch called.

"Got to talk to your son. Bring him on out."

"He sleeping, sir. Talk to him about what?"

The men from the car sounded nervous and impatient.

"Never mind," the uncle said. "We'll get him our-selves."

He bounded the steps and took the black man by the shoulders. He moved him aside and went inside, stopping briefly to hold the screen door open for the girl's father, who had come up behind him.

In contrast to the outside of the dwelling, the front room was swept and tidy. A single oil lamp burned on the table, and shadows danced around the room, whirling into and then spinning out of, the corners. A woman stood in the gloom, wearing a cotton nightdress open at the neck. She twisted her hands. Her skin shone with sweat.

"Go put something on," the store owner said, his nervousness rising. "Shit. Never see a white woman say hello to company like that."

Her nipples were defined under the thin fabric. Both of the men noticed them, and the evil in the room increased, as if a feral cat had been let loose and was climbing the curtains. The uncle pulled his pistol out. The dirty chrome reflected the lamp light dully. All eyes in the room settled on the gun, and, at first, no one saw the boy enter and stand by his mother. The uncle was the first to notice him, and the spell in the room changed.

"You, boy," he said. "You know we got to talk to you."

The boy was fast and moved to run, but the man was faster and had him by the arm. There was a struggle.

"Help me with this," the uncle grunted, his hair in his face. The girl's father moved in, and the three of them moved in jerks toward the door.

The small boy began to scream and throw himself backward, straining to reach his parents. Finally, the two men picked him up and carried him out. At the car, the uncle pulled open the rear door and shouted something.

The door on the other side opened, and the girl scrambled out and got into the front. The uncle piled into the rear seat, his arms wrapped around the wailing boy, and the girl's father slammed the car door behind them.

The headlights came on, and the car turned around in the yard. At the road, the clutch was disengaged too fast, and the engine stalled. The starter ground, and to the three people standing on the porch it seemed for a moment as if a divine hand might work to save all of them, but then the engine caught and roared. The helpless parents stood with their remaining son and cried, watching the single red eye of the tail light turn through the trees and disappear, taking all of their lives with it.

The man's whole body was shaking. His wife hugged herself and stood apart from him. The other boy was motionless, eyes wide, staring at the spot his little brother had vanished into. After a time, they went inside, because there was nothing else to do, but some parts of the three of them stood on the porch and stared into the darkness that was the road for the rest of eternity.

୧୬୧୬

Present Day:

"I don't think I've ever really known my dad. Not like you'd know a father. It's not that he was abusive to me or anything—it's more he didn't know what to do with me. Like someone had given him a cat, and he wasn't interested, but he figured he'd better take care of it."

I heard a noise behind the cabin, stood up, and walked to the end of the porch. I looked up the path. I realized that I was looking for the dog, but I didn't see him, so I came back.

"It was worse after my mother died. He seemed to

withdraw. He taught high school and I always figured the kids in his class knew him way better than I did. I was never in any of his classes—didn't want to be, but sometimes I wish I had been. I might have some idea what he was like."

"I don't know if that's so weird," she said. "I never had parents, just Kate. I've only seen pictures of my mother when she was staying here, on this lake. No one talks about her anywhere else. She doesn't exist except as a girl younger than me, water skiing here. My father could be anyone, could even be some old man from around here that I know now."

Her shoulders were hunched, and she seemed dwindled by her memories. She was always lovely and, usually, self-assured. This was a side of her I had never imagined. Her hurt made my heart feel heavy.

"Bill's enough of a father figure for me anyway," she said. "Between him and my Aunt Kate, I could have done a whole lot worse."

She shook the mood off. "How did your mom die?" she asked.

"Car. Someone broke her car window. My dad covered it, and she couldn't see out of it very well. It caused an accident. They thought it might have been a kid in her class, but they never proved it. Didn't really matter anyway."

She had died before I graduated from high school. She came out to her small blue Volkswagen one morning to find the passenger window shattered. A rock lay on the front seat. My father taped a sheet of translucent plastic over the window opening, and she left for work. She crossed a highway on her route. That morning she pulled into the path of a semi-truck, which hit her before the driver could even touch the brakes. Pieces of her car were scraped into the asphalt for almost a quarter of a mile.

The police confirmed the truck had been behind schedule and speeding. She had miscalculated the distance before she pulled out, likely due to her hazy view of things through the makeshift window. They said my father should never have improvised that way. For a long time, I sifted the events that led up to her accident and speculated on who had actually killed her. In the end, I decided that a lot of people had."

"She was a teacher too?" Molly asked.

"Yeah, same school as my dad. We all acted like we didn't know each other. She could have ridden with him that morning, but they never went together. She was only in her late thirties, maybe early forties."

"God—that must have been awful for him. For you both."

"I think he blamed himself," I said. "I know I blamed him. What a stupid thing to do, taping the window that way. I think that's when he started drinking more. He hardly noticed when I left home."

"There must be some good things that you remember," she said. "There's always some good."

"You always think there must be some good, Molly." I smiled. "I guess he was a good teacher. They said he was, a lot of people seemed to think so. He cared about the world, and politics, and poor people. He loved animals more than people. He was always good with them."

"Like you?" she asked, eyebrows raised.

"Maybe." I thought for a minute. "He loved baseball. The Red Sox. I believe he always secretly dreamed that he could have played in Boston. He loved Angela, from the day he met her, even though he wasn't at our wedding. Mostly, though—"

Suddenly I was breathing shallowly, and my eyes stung. "He loved our daughter, I guess. I'll give him that much."

Molly slid over closer to me and put an arm around my waist. "It's good you'll get a chance to see him."

I shook my head and slowly let my breath out. I dreaded the whole thing. She put her hand on the back of my neck.

"I'll be here. Call me if you need to. I'll make you guys dinner when he's here."

I walked her to her boat. When she had roared away across the water toward her own shore, I stood and looked at the cottages dotted here and there in the forest on the other side. They would soon begin to fill up and the area would get on with the summer season.

Even in the brightest summer sunlight there was a curious dimness about Hollow Lake. She was dark, and she was haunted. She exhibited none of the party mood that was evident in many of the vacation communities in the lakes around her. There was something muted about her celebrations and her tragedies, something that suggested the present was seen through the frosted glass of the past. She accepted few visitors, and there had been no new construction on her shores in decades.

On summer evenings, fathers of years past stood among the pine trees with the fathers of today as meat was turned over hot coals. Clusters of women on verandas sat and sipped drinks in warm twilight. Some of them were not easily visible and did not join conversations. Children, splashing in the shallow water alongside docks, were sometimes joined by playmates; small children from long ago who had left, grown up, gotten old, and then at last returned to play again. Mothers who had gathered broods in for the night leaned in lighted doorways, looked into the deep gloom under the trees around them, and wondered what it was that they sensed. They felt as though there was something they had forgotten, something just out of reach.

The elderly were troubled by memories as they looked into her waters. Old loves and forgotten sins returned to them with a vividness that stole their breath. They were briefly gifted with the knowledge that we were all born with and learned to deny. As we looked forward, we also looked back.

CHAPTER 5

Elijah Tull,
Milton County, Georgia, Wednesday, July 3, 1946

It was too hot in the shed, and the smell of human sweat was overpowering. They dragged the boy to a rack that was used to spread and dry something or other and tied his wrists to it. He had squalled and fought the entire way from his house to this place in the back of the car, and Willard Davis was glad to be quit of him. His arms ached from restraining him.

The building was long and low. It had been shut and disused for years, and, even this late at night, it retained the day's heat. They had brought one oil lamp with them. It illuminated them, but outside of its yellow circle there was nothing but shadows. The far end of the building was completely black. The darkness at that end felt occupied, as though things were hidden, watching what transpired and whispering about it.

Sutton showed the gun straightaway, holding it near the youngster's nose and cuffing his chin with it. "You look at this, boy," he said. "You look at what I have for you, if you don't listen, and listen good."

He set the pistol down at his feet and slapped the child

hard, forehand and backhand. The sound of flesh on flesh was horrible in the narrow space. The boy continued to wail and struggle against his bonds.

The girl had been pushed into a corner when they entered, and she looked from the gloom into the lamplight, chewing on a knuckle.

Davis stepped in and grabbed the boy by his throat. "You—stop—your—squalling," he shouted. "Hush up!" With his other hand, he turned the small head toward the corner. "Do you see that girl? Do you want to know what we're willing to do to any nigger who lays a finger on her? Apologize to her right now! Beg her for us to leave you be!"

"I've never seen her before! I don't know who she is!" Eli screamed.

Elijah Tull was ten years old. He was, at the heart of it, not a symbol. He was neither black nor white. He had not shed the innocence of childhood. He had never hated anything or anyone. Every morning was still a miracle to him. He wasn't very big for his age. He liked almost any kind of pork and didn't get it often enough. He had a cigar box with no lid on it under his bed. It had a red feather, four or five cicada shells, and the scratched lens from a magnifying glass. He thought that it came from a telescope and made up stories about its origin that he never told to anyone. He loved his mother and his father and his dog. He idolized his older brother Roy. Although he quarreled with him, he secretly wanted to be just like him.

He had endured rough handling from these men, but the slaps were different. They evoked parental discipline. His mother slapped him when she was angry. For the first time in his ordeal, he felt like a child in the hands of adults.

Like any ten year-old boy, he cried. His angry shrieks

dissolved into tears, and that was his undoing. That was the end of him.

"I never saw her before!"

"Take that back!" Sutton screamed. "Take it back, you little bastard! Liar."

Eli stared up at him, his small chest heaving, his voice all gone. Tears streamed down his face. His nose ran, mixed with blood from his mouth. His silence broke the last of Sutton's reserve, and he fell on the boy. The sound of his heavy fists on the little body sounded like meat being hit with a mallet.

When Davis pulled his brother-in-law off two minutes later, Elijah was semi-conscious. His body was beyond repair. His jaw was shattered and turned at an impossible angle. One eyeball rested on his cheek. His left arm and four ribs were broken. Inside his skull, his brain was already beginning to swell.

Davis was furious. "What's wrong with you?" he hissed at Sutton. "We can't never go back from this now."

He pulled a knife from his pocket and cut the ropes that held the child up against the drying rack. The boy collapsed onto the dirt floor of the shed. His right lung had been punctured by a rib, and his breathing bubbled, hitched, and sounded as if it would stop.

"There ain't but one thing I can do for this nigger now," Davis said. He picked up the pistol from the floor.

Elijah Tull lay there and looked up with his remaining eye. He thought he was in his own bed at home. It had been a good day, and tomorrow would be better. He was going fishing with Roy. The yellow dog jumped up and settled himself on the end of the bed, and Eli could feel its bulk with his feet. His father came into the room and stood over him. His hand was warm on the little boy's forehead.

Eli's ruined mouth could not form words, nevertheless he heard his own voice. "Night, daddy. Love you."

His father bent to kiss him.

Willard Davis pulled the trigger and Elijah Tull was gone.

Present Day:

I got to the restaurant in Huntsville early. Angela had no patience with people who were late. I backed my old jeep into a space near the entrance, sat, and looked at the rain running down my windshield. When I was tired of that, I watched the line of cars inch through the drive-through.

Right on time, her white BMW turned into the entrance. She glanced over at me as she passed, but didn't wave. I got a glimpse of my father sitting beside her, staring straight ahead. She pulled up to the building and let him out at the door then pulled ahead to park. I got out and walked across the puddled pavement to meet her. She stood and waited for me, impervious to the wet.

Up close, she smelled expensive, even in the rain. Same Angela.

"How was the drive?" I asked.

"Fine," she said, impatient. "He's inside."

"Are you coming in? At least for a minute?"

"Why? Are you scared of him?"

"Scared?"

I looked through the window and saw that he had found a booth. He sat, hunched and smaller than I remembered, staring into a cup of coffee. I was nervous. I felt as though I faced some sort of cosmic punishment. A vague feeling of guilt, the weight of unknown sins, pressed on me.

I turned to go in, and Angela caught my arm. "There's something you have to understand, Mike. He isn't going back to Atlanta. He isn't going back home."

"What the hell are you talking about?"

"I've had him at my house for three days," she said, "and I'm telling you there's something wrong with him. He isn't himself. I got him in to see my doctor, and you know what she told me?"

I was shocked to see her tearing up.

"Trauma. She suspects he's had some kind of trauma. I thought he was showing Alzheimer's. She said it's one of the tragedies of old age that people are always suspected of and ignored. She thinks something bad has happened to him. Something recent."

"What kind of bad thing?" I asked. "He must have said something to you, for God's sake."

"He's terrified of something. He's a closed book, just like you, but something's wrong. Even taking him to the doctor—he normally fights me on that, and he didn't. He was practically meek."

I looked in at him again. He sat, staring at a cup of coffee on the table. It seemed nearly impossible that he had gotten so old. It was unthinkable that in spite all of his stubbornness, he was being brought down. I thought of my mother and about her relatively young exit almost thirty years before. I wondered if this elderly man had missed her for all of these years.

"I'm kind of surprised he even bought himself a coffee," Angela said. "He doesn't do much on his own. Listen. Visit with him a few days, and then I'll pick him up, and we'll decide what's best. He isn't going home, though. I'm definite on that."

"He's *my* father, Angela."

She flushed, and the hurt was instant in her eyes. She was so cool, so impervious, that I was always shocked when something I said actually mattered to her. She had been a better daughter to my father than I had been a son, and I hated myself for the remark. I held the door for her and followed her in. We went to the booth. My dad glanced at me and then looked to Angela.

"They gave me a black coffee," he complained. "It isn't what I asked for."

"You have to put your own cream and sugar in, Sam," she said. "It's on the counter."

"Want me to fix it for you, Dad?" I interjected.

He didn't immediately acknowledge me, but I looked into his eyes, and, after a very long moment, he nodded once. I looked over at Angela. Her lips compressed, she shook her head. I fixed his coffee for him. For some odd reason, I thought again about my mother.

My parents met in Berlin. After a stint in the army, my father had a lifelong aversion to all things military and later said the posting that led him to my mother was the only good thing that had come of his enlisted time. Daughter of a wealthy southern family, she had lingered in Europe after her expected post-university cultural tour and stayed on a work visa to take over the ownership of a small cafe-bistro in the slowly rebuilding city. Her parents were aghast, and even more upset, when she married my father, whom they considered socially far beneath her. As a consequence, she had drifted permanently away from them.

Ironically, the loss of financial support from home had doomed her business, and the couple returned to the States. They armed themselves with teaching degrees and settled outside Atlanta. They eventually took teaching positions in the same high school. They embraced the liberal activism of the 1960s with a sense of destiny and fervor. The recession of that tide had left them stranded, vaguely betrayed, and without purpose. I supposed both of them lived in the hope that a new decade would bring another movement, another anchor for their lives.

From my earliest memory, my existence seemed to befuddle them, and they appeared perpetually surprised to return from classroom skirmishes to find a single soldier from the enemy forces living in their home. They were never unkind to me, but their drinking in the evenings occasionally caused minor issues with me to explode into furious rants and extravagant threats of punishments that never happened.

Between themselves, they fought almost constantly, without passion, usually with wine. I moved as a child phantom through the dry smoke of their exchanges.

My father was angry, literate, and aware of all the small nuances of the international stage. He was incensed by events in China and Granada and Cuba, scornful of those who missed all of the complexities, but was baffled by what went on in his own home. He bitterly approved of rebellions and uprisings across the world, but had no empathy for his own teenage son.

He still lived in the same house in Marietta where I had grown up. It would not have surprised me to find that he still walked the rooms, glass in hand, and argued with the shadow of my mother. My move to Canada was perhaps the one event in my life that had caused him to feel paternal pride. He viewed me as a draft dodger who came late to the festivities. To disabuse him of this would have been unkind.

After my mother's death, we lived in mostly anxious silence. I remembered him as perpetually exhausted and bewildered, and a sort of general disapproval seemed to be the limit of fatherly interest and affection. When I left his house after my eighteenth birthday, he shook my hand at the front door. I didn't remember if he asked where I was going.

CHAPTER 6

Elijah Tull,
Cobb County, Georgia, Wednesday, July 10, 1946:

Dead was dead, and done was done. The Negro boy never came home.

A body was found six days later in a muddy field. The corpse was a featureless lump, red with Georgia clay. No attempt at concealment had been made. It had simply been put there. It was the awful smell that led to its discovery, and, when the sheriff rinsed the face, it was sent immediately to the colored funeral home.

The clothes it wore matched the missing boy, but definite identification was impossible. A merciless beating had obliterated most of his features before a gunshot to the head caused enough cranial pressure to distort what was left into something only vaguely human. His mother was physically restrained from seeing him. Six days in the hot Georgia sun had actually performed a kindness, as his father allowed himself to believe that it was decomposition that had transformed his son into something that looked like the remains of a small monster.

He was ten years old, and he would never kiss another girl, white or otherwise. His name was Elijah Tull. The

yellow dog that he shared with his brother grieved him
and had known the very moment that he died.

His parents' hearts broke, and broke was broke.

Dorothy and Jacob Tull buried their son in the tiny
cemetery beside the Negro Baptist church. More than two
hundred people attended the funeral, packed onto wooden
benches and spilling outside the open doors, stoically ig-
noring the stench that seeped from the closed wooden
box.

Jacob Tull identified the two men who had taken his
son. The storekeeper, Floyd Sutton, and his brother in
law, Willard Davis, were arrested. They were brought to
trial eleven days later without having spent a single night
in jail. The two men admitted to having driven away with
Eli, but claimed that after a warning he had been dropped
off in his dooryard, unharmed.

The impossibility of the positive identification of what
was left of the boy made the proceedings nothing more
than empty ceremony. The gate of reasonable doubt
yawned open wide enough that the defense attorney barely needed to stir from his table. The all-white jury did
their duty and acquitted without much deliberation, which
caused tears to flow on both sides of the courtroom.

There was little celebration in the community. The
atrocity was seen as unfortunate and distasteful, and the
storekeeper's family was marked and shunned to a greater degree than gossip about a children's kiss would have
caused. Most of the white families who had attended the
general store quietly shifted their custom to one a little
farther away.

The little girl was condemned. The details of what had
transpired behind the store were known only to Wanda
Sutton's family, and the absolute truth of it only to the
white boy who had witnessed it, but the vague sense of it
was enough to stain her in that society for the rest of her

life. She had crossed a line that was never spoken of and stirred the fears of the uncontrollable change that was approaching.

Oddly, the most scorn shown to her came from the blacks in her community. They continued to patronize her father's store because they always had, and their open contempt for her was far more stinging than the whispers and averted glances that came from the whites.

Floyd Sutton might have saved his daughter. He had served his country for two years in Europe, and it was his Colt pistol that Willard Davis had used. It had made the trip home with him from Italy and France to dispatch Eli, who was a different sort of enemy.

Because of the war, Sutton had a larger sense of the world than most of his neighbors, and had he sold his store and taken his family north, things might have turned out differently than they did.

If he ever considered it, he wasn't given the time to act.

The Negro child rested in his grave outside the small Baptist church, tranquil through all of the winter rains and summer suns that should have marked his lifetime. As decades passed, the church fell into disuse but was not torn down, for the land had little value. For the next sixty or so years Eli Tull remained there, waiting. It wasn't time for him to go.

On warm summer afternoons that buzzed with insects and heat, a passerby who was alert might spot him and not find it remarkable.

He was only a small black boy, loitering in the high grass, amusing himself in the shade of the oaks that surrounded the property, wandering among the grave markers and passing the time.

ოჲო

Present Day:

I pulled the throttle back and cut the engine to idle. The boat came down off its plane and slowed, pushing a wash of water in front of it. I looked over at my father, who had one hand on his hat and was smiling, perhaps in spite of himself. We were stopped in the middle of the sound, opposite my island. The drizzle had stopped, the sun was out, and the lake was calm.

Echo Island sat on the horizon, freshly washed by the rain, ready for company.

"You good, Dad?"

"I haven't been on a boat in years." He grinned. "When did you learn to drive one? It doesn't seem like something you'd do."

"When I moved here, I had to learn fast." I smiled back. "At first, I pretty much just slammed it into whatever dock was nearest when I needed to stop."

I looked around me, seeing the lake and its bordering forest as he must be seeing it, for the first time. It was all beautiful. "This part of the lake is unique," I said. "The water's about seventy-five feet deep, except right here beneath us. We're sitting over a kind of underwater canyon. The bottom's almost four hundred feet down. The people around here call this the 'Hole.' There's all kinds of stuff down there—boats, even an airplane."

He peered over the side. "Why?"

"Anything that sinks and ends up down there stays down there. It's too deep to even try to bring it back up."

A bomber on a training mission from the old Muskoka air base crashed into the lake one night in 1943. It took its crew with it to the bottom of the Hole and was never recovered. There were also a couple of boats that I knew about down there, and other things as well. It was not a part of the lake that I liked.

I pointed ahead of us. "That's my island," I said. "The small one."

"How can you live out here alone? What does Angela say about it?"

"Angela hasn't thought much about what I do in a long time, Dad. If she has an opinion about it, she doesn't tell me."

"Lonely," he said.

"People can be lonely in the middle of a city," I said, thinking about it. "Sometimes it's lonely, I guess. I have friends, and I go into town to shop or work at the marina almost every day."

Another small boat passed by, headed west. It was moving fast, and the wind-whipped people on board waved, holding onto their hats.

"If I want to see some lights, Huntsville's a decent-sized city. It's less than a half-hour away."

"Doesn't seem like much of a life," he said. "You never stop running away from things. You're just living off your wife's money."

"She isn't my wife anymore," I said. "That's what divorce is. I took what she gave me. I was entitled to half and didn't take it. I never asked for anything. She didn't want the island any more, and that's what I settled for."

"If you didn't drink so much back then, you'd still be married to her."

I felt a flash of hatred for him. "I haven't had a drink in years. Guess I came by it honestly, Dad." I was stricken by the instant hurt on his face. As quickly as it had come, my anger fled. "I'm sorry," I said. "I didn't mean that."

We sat in silence for a few minutes. The boat rocked gently. I heard a light plane overhead; I squinted but couldn't pick it out in the glare.

"You don't even work, do you," he finally said.

"As much as I need to. I restore old mahogany boats now. I built this one," I said with some pride. "It's more than seventy years old."

"That's a hobby. It isn't work." He crossed his arms and slumped in the pilot's chair across from me, refusing to enjoy the day anymore.

"I have something to tell you," he finally said. "I can't go home. I don't know what I'm going to do."

"You can stay with me, Dad," I said. "You can always stay with me."

He waved his arm around him. "Here? In the middle of a lake in the middle of nowhere? You've found the end of the earth. I might be running, but I don't have to run this far."

"Just tell me, Dad," I said, as gently as I could. "Just tell me what's going on."

We sat in silence for a long time. I looked over the side of the boat. This early in the spring, the water was amber with tannins close to shore, but out here in the deep it was a cold dark green, opaque with sediment from the melted ice. When I was just about to start the boat, he finally spoke.

"I have to tell you about the summer when I was ten years old," he said. "The summer of 1946. None of it makes sense otherwise."

"I'm all ears, Dad."

He sighed, not looking at me. "There was an old general store about a mile up the road from our house. Old gray wood building, covered with soft drink signs, had a big veranda out front. It's still there today, but it looks different. I used to walk up there about every day, to pick up things for my mother, buy some sweets for myself if I was lucky."

A cloud bank went across the sun, and the air was instantly cooler.

"Out back of the place the black pickers and share-croppers hung around. If you wanted to pick up day labor, you went back there, pick from the dozen or so guys hanging around, playing dice, cards, shooting the breeze."

"You getting cold?" I interrupted.

He shook his head. "The day I'm talking about," he said, "there was no one back there. We had the back of the store all to ourselves. I don't know why."

He talked for the next twenty minutes and then trailed off. I didn't see a connection with his childhood memories and whatever was bothering him today. He resisted my efforts to probe deeper and gazed at the shoreline across the sound, lost in thought. After a few more minutes, I shrugged, started the motor, and took us across the green water to my dock.

After a late supper that he had only picked at, we sat in the cabin's main room. I had a fire going in the wood stove. The old iron pinged and hissed and creaked. He had told me about himself and his little friends in fits and starts throughout the day. The little black child, Eli, grieved me.

"Sad story," I said.

"Sad story," he agreed. "Seems funny you have to heat this place in May."

"Springtime in Canada, Dad. We get some warm days, but nights are cold."

The interior of the cabin was unfinished white pine that had aged to dark gold. Although I had electricity by underwater cable, the service was fragile and unpredictable. On nights like this, I liked to use the gas lanterns. In their warm flickering light, the wooden walls glowed, and shadows danced and gathered to whisper in the rafters. The room looked exactly as it had a hundred years before.

"Get me a drink, would you?"

"I was just going to put the kettle on for tea," I said. "Something hot sound better?"

"Drink'll do."

When I came back and handed him his rum, he continued to tell me about his tenth summer. I had a hard time picturing the man sitting across from me as a small boy.

I tried to remember if I had ever seen a photograph of him at that age, and couldn't.

"The girl, Wanda," he said. "She always bothered me the most. I've crossed paths with her for the last fifty or sixty years. Every time I think I've seen the last of her, she turns up again."

"Why does she bother you?" I asked.

He looked up at me. "She's ruined my life. She's after me, her and her son."

"She's after you? What does that mean?"

"Her life has been one long mess," he said. "One unending, ugly story of misery. She lost any chance and a lot of it's my fault. She has every reason to never forgive me."

"What did you do? You weren't responsible for anything that happened to her."

"Her mother hung herself in the store. She couldn't go on. Wanda found her, and that was the worst. No kid should find a parent dead. I think for a girl to find her mother like that—something got broken that no one could ever fix."

"That isn't your problem, is it?"

"The boy, Eli," he went on. "I still see his brother Roy. He wasn't there behind the store, but he saw them take his little brother away to kill him. He's suffered too, all these years. He did okay for himself though, became a doctor. My doctor these last few years, matter of fact."

I thought back. "Clarke was always our family doctor," I said.

"Retired. He retired, and I looked up Roy. He's as old as I am, but he still practices. Better shape for his age than I am, that's for sure." He set his glass down and stood up. "I'm going to bed," he said. "We'll finish this another time."

I gave him a hand up from the deep armchair, and he went off to the spare room. I sat up for a while and nursed the fire, enjoying my tea and the quiet night. I thought about Molly in her warm, lit house across the windy sweep of cold water. I considered calling her, but it meant walking down to the dock to get reception for my phone. She was probably asleep, anyway.

A long time ago, this island had been a sanctuary. Algonquin Indians had hidden women, children, and old people here while the men battled enemies somewhere else. Tonight, I sensed those old spirits moving around in the dark forest outside.

Sometimes, the island was a scary place, a doorway to somewhere else. I had been drawn to it, perhaps because I needed healing, or perhaps because I was so damaged that I belonged in a lost land.

Tonight, it was refuge again, though. It was a haven that had accepted my father and sheltered and hidden him from whatever was chasing him. The black water that surrounded the island was more security than any locked doors could ever be.

I drained my tea. I could see into the kitchen from where I sat. I looked at the red kettle on the stove and thought about boiling more water. I looked at the ranks of slightly dusty bookshelves on the far wall and thought about getting down a book. I listened to the stove pop and hiss, and my eyes closed. An hour later, I half-woke up, turned down the lamp, and went in to my bed.

I came awake in the middle of the night. The wind had picked up, and the old cabin creaked on its foundations. I blinked in the dark. There was a figure standing in the doorway of my bedroom. I lay still, my breath stopped. It didn't move.

"Dad?"

"They're going to get me," he said. "I have nowhere left to run."

"No one's going to get you, Dad. I'll keep you safe. I promise. Go back to bed."

He stood quietly. "Could I get a glass of water?" he finally asked.

"Sure, I can get you some water."

The floor was cold on my bare feet. I padded out the kitchen and handed him a plastic glass on my way back. I slipped back under my blanket. "Go back to sleep, Dad. I won't let anyone or anything come to get you. You're safe here."

He didn't say anything else, and, after a moment, the dark doorway was empty. I was flooded with a vague sadness, a feeling of forever loss. "I promise," I mumbled. "Cross my heart."

I slid back into sleep.

CHAPTER 7

Sam Latta,
Marietta, Georgia, Saturday, August 3, 1946:

The boy pulled open the door and walked into the store. The man and the girl were behind the counter. She sat on a high stool, a book open in front of her, looking bored and defiant. Her expression brightened when she saw the boy. She sensed diversion. The man stared at him.

"I know what you did," the boy said. He addressed both of them. His voice seemed very small, and he tried again. "I know what you did."

The woman emerged from the aisles on his right. Her voice was shrill and angry. "You get out of here, boy! You got no business coming in here. You got no business at all!"

The girl smiled, her eyes shining. The man stood still. His hands rested unmoving on the counter in front of him. His face was expressionless, eyes dark holes in his ruddy face. Although he looked the same, some part of him was gone, and he was less than he had been. His suspenders were slack over his beefy shoulders, as if the portion of his spirit that had left forever had taken some of his physical presence with it. He was becoming a void, and a void was dangerous, because it rushed to be filled by those things that lived in the darkness and waited for human despair and the abandonment of light.

"I know what you did," the boy said for a third time, "and I'm telling."

The sound of the slap filled his head. He felt the skin on the side of his face sting and flood with red. Tears betrayed his vision, but he didn't take his eyes away from the man, even as the woman moved close. She pushed him violently. He lost his feet and went to the floor. His knees and elbows knocked on the bare gray boards.

Slowly, he got to his feet, went back to the screen door, and stood for a moment with his hand on it.

He was ten years old and slightly small for his age. In that moment, he was more than a boy, and far more than the man he would become. He stood for a moment, looking at them, and the three of them looked at him. Finally, he turned his back and went out into the hot, bright day.

⌘

Present Day:

I parked on the street and crossed to the passenger door to help my dad from the jeep. Traffic crawled along the main street. The town was packed, and I was lucky to have found a spot. The pizza parlors and ice cream outlets that lined the street were coming out of their winter hibernation.

Tiny Ansett was a summer town. It was almost deserted during the winter months. Most of the five hundred permanent residents did their regular business in the small city of Huntsville, twenty miles to the west. The locals looked on their own downtown area as a transient carnival, too crowded in summer and too deserted in winter to bother much with.

The main drag was dominated by Robertson's Market, a rambling log structure that was a supermarket, hardware store, garden center, and souvenir stand under one roof. Robertson's shared a parking lot with the liquor store.

The Echo Island Pie Company was only coincidentally named after my island. Kate knew the place and was drawn to it long before she met me. Crammed into a tall, narrow old building, it was hard to get one of the six or seven tables inside.

Though the summer crowds passed it by, Kate Bean's coffee shop stayed moderately busy all year, perhaps because it also housed the post office. People came in to pick up their mail and stayed for pastry and conversation. Her tables were usually full of gossipers, eating pie and drinking coffee.

There was no attempt to discourage summer trade, but the cottagers who came to town were looking for summer fare—beer and paper plates, watermelon and suntan oil. They saw the boats under the main street drawbridge and long-legged girls in tank tops. They heard the exhausts of fast cars and motorcycles, and the summer's hottest hits blasting from speakers that seemed to be everywhere. They didn't see a quaint, dim storefront, and they weren't there for pie and coffee.

I pulled open the door for my dad. We went in, and I breathed the dim perfumes of nutmeg, cinnamon, fresh coffee, and old wood. The space always made me feel as if I had stepped backward a century, to a time when the essence of life in the area was grim survival rather than summer holiday, and people clung to basic pleasures and simple treats.

The bell over the door rang, and Kate looked up from

behind the counter. Well past her sixtieth birthday, she was beautiful. While Molly had clear, creamy skin and dark hair, Kate was auburn, with blue eyes and faint freckles. She didn't look like her niece, but they shared a directness and honesty of manner, a basic integrity that marked them more deeply as family than hair color ever could. She came around the counter and gave me a stiff hug.

I introduced her to my father, and she took his arm and led him to a table. When he was seated, she turned to me and spoke in a low aside. "Has he met Molly?"

I shook my head. "Not yet."

"Keeping her a secret?"

"Something like that," I murmured.

My dad was attached to Angela, and I had avoided thinking about his inevitable introduction to Molly. She and I weren't nearly as much a couple as I wished, but we were obviously close enough to make things uncomfortable. I didn't know if he entertained an idea that my ex-wife and I would reunite, or if he cared, but it was a discussion that I didn't want.

Kate went off to get our coffee, and I sat down and looked across the table at the old man. "So tell me about the little girl," I said. "You never finished."

"Poor Wanda," he said. "She really didn't ever have a chance at all. By the age of twelve, she was a ward of the state of Georgia and was sent away. Marianfield Training School for Girls. I imagine it was a horror. About 1948, she joined a group of girls who tried to burn it down. They set fire to the main building and ran away. They were rounded up in a couple of days, except for two girls who drowned trying to cross a river."

"These were all kids?" I asked.

"Girls sixteen and younger, yes. They were jailed in two separate counties, depending on where they were picked up. Twenty girls in total. They either developed a taste for fire or they had it planned, but in both facilities they tore up their jail cells and lit the bedding on fire. In one of the jails, they attacked the firemen who came to rescue them."

"Nice girls."

"Some of them probably started out nice. Back then, arson was still a capital crime in Georgia. It carried the death penalty."

"Arson? Seriously?"

"Sure," he nodded. "Lots of funny old laws on the books, even now. Especially in the South."

"What happened to Wanda?" I asked.

"In just a couple of years, this girl had lost her whole family, been abandoned to strangers, and now she was facing the death penalty. Any chance of a happy, normal life was gone for good."

Kate brought a tray, and we busied ourselves for a minute with the coffee ritual. My father fixed his own coffee, and I wondered if he was getting better. He seemed stronger, more sure of himself, and I was relieved. I thought that telling me his story was lifting some of the stress off him.

"No one really wanted to hang a bunch of young girls, I imagine," he went on. "Eventually, they all got commuted sentences."

"Good to hear they didn't execute little girls."

"The youngest was nine. I've always thought the really little ones were the most dangerous. The thought of a nine-year-old attacking a fireman gives me the horrors."

"Did you know about all this when you were a kid?"

"Some of it," he said. "Some I found out later. Wanda's drifted in and out of Marietta her whole life. We're not from a very big town, you know."

"I don't remember you ever mentioning her."

"No reason to. Your mother never met her. We hardly ran around in the same circles."

"What happened to her? How'd she end up?"

"Pretty sad and predictable," he said. "She supported herself with prostitution. I heard she was arrested in every state in the South, through the '50s and '60s. Later, she came home to Marietta, and it was more of the same. She was in jail as recently as ten years ago. I assume she's mostly retired by now."

"She's the same age as you!"

He cocked an eyebrow. "I don't imagine she has trouble finding customers, Mike. You think hookers are showgirls?"

I gestured to Kate for the check, and she waved it off. I pantomimed my insistence, and she shook a fist at me, smiling, and wandered back to the kitchen and out of sight.

"She has a son Arthur, a few years younger than you. I taught him for a few months when he was a teenager. I felt an obligation to him, because of his mother, but I don't think I ever got through to him."

"Is he still around?"

"He still lives with her, far as I know. Interesting to me because of her age. Late thirties is a little old for a lady of the night to have a kid, unless she's left the life and is trying to start over. Abortions were usual enough, even back then—no reason to keep one you don't want."

"Maybe the father meant something to her," I said. "Being a prostitute doesn't mean you can't have feelings for someone."

"He's black. At least his father was. There's no doubt about that."

"So? Things like that don't bother you, Dad. Who cares?"

"It occurs to you," he said, "that her father killed a

black child for taking liberties with her, and then she has a child who definitely has a black father."

I thought about it. "Ironic, maybe," I shrugged.

"There's only one more thing, and it's not worth telling you how I know about it, but it's important. Her prostitution career was really only broken by one significant jail sentence. She had a lesbian affair that cause a scandal in Florida, in 1966. She was over thirty, the girl was sixteen. The girl's parents found out and pressed the matter. Eighteen is still the age of consent in Florida. If the partner is over the age of twenty four, it's a felony."

"It's important that she's a lesbian?" I asked.

"No, not at all. Let me finish."

"You sound like you did her biography."

"I made it my business to find out what I could. Know your enemy."

"Your enemy?" I asked. "I thought you felt sorry for her."

"I do feel sorry for her. She hates me, though, with good reason, if I'm fair about it." He looked at me, peeved. "Can I finish about the girl in Florida?"

I waved sorry, and he went on.

"If Wanda had been a man, it would have been statutory rape. Because she was female, she was charged with corruption of a minor. She did two years in women's penitentiary. Her next charge was in the '70s, in South Carolina. Same situation—she was in her forties and the girl was in her teens."

"Another minor?" I asked. "What gives?"

"This time it was worse. Much worse. The parents didn't stumble across it this time. Wanda approached them. Wealthy father, farmer, politically connected. She hit them up with pictures. If the parents didn't want their debutante exposed as a budding lesbian, they had to pay up."

"She's a blackmailer?" I asked. "They turned her in?"

"No. They tried to pay," he said. "In fact, they did pay. Two hundred thousand, a fair bit back then. No unmarked bills, it wasn't clandestine. They paid her with a bank draft."

"So then how did she end up in jail?" I asked.

"I have no idea what went wrong for her, but the cops got wind of it and Wanda eventually was sent away for extortion. She did eight years. The money wasn't recovered. The parents didn't cooperate in getting it back. I guess they were scared of her—didn't want to risk a visit from her or her son when she got out. She's not a nice person, pathetic or not."

He looked around the room, and I waved a finger to get his attention back.

"I looked her up a few months ago," he went on. "I shouldn't have. Some things should be left alone. She and her son are after me. They'll never stop, now. I opened up Pandora's Box for myself, and now I can never go home again. They're violent people. I don't know what they'll do to me."

His eyes continued to search the room.

"What are you looking for?" I asked.

"That woman," he said. "Could I have more pie? She said they have some kind of berry. I want to try it."

"I need to know where you come into this story, Dad. I need to know what you did. Why are they after you?"

He looked at me owlishly. "You *need* to know?" he asked. "Since when do you *need* to know about me?"

I was hugely irritated. I wanted to tell him that he didn't own the world. I wanted to tell him that he couldn't just land on other people's doorsteps, disrupt their lives, and not tell them the whole story. I wanted to tell him that I was worried sick about him.

Instead, I walked him out to the jeep and said nothing.

I ignored his request for a second piece of pie. Days later, I remembered my small cruelty and wept.

CHAPTER 8

Sheriff Ben Early,
Marietta, Georgia, Sunday, August 4, 1946:

Sheriff Early wheeled his radio car off the county road and onto the packed dirt lot in front of the general store. He felt a small shock in his chest when he saw the size of the gathered crowd. He edged the cruiser forward, and faces looked back through the windshield at him before they moved reluctantly aside. When the wooden steps were directly in front of him, he set the brake and shut the Ford's engine off. He picked up the heavy microphone from its chromed hook under the dashboard and keyed it with his thumb.

"Shirley, I'm going to need help out here. There's got to be a hundred people outside the store and more coming. Mel Schmidt should be out on 41. Get him here fast. Get hold of Dicky at home and tell him to come on out here too."

"Is Willard Davis dead, Sheriff? Caller said he's dead."

"I have no idea," he said drily. "Looks like somebody is."

He pushed open the car door and got out, adjusting his hat and belt as he stood. He ran his fingertips along the butt of the gun on his hip. He pushed the people lining the steps of the store back with his eyes and climbed to the front door.

"Stay where you are, folks."

Tin tobacco signs were nailed up on either side of the entrance. Nails bled rust from the top corners onto the red-and-green lettering. Ben pulled open the screen and the smell of shit and blood boiled out. He stepped in.

Floyd Sutton was curled up just inside the doorway. The wet trail on the wood floor showed that he had dragged himself from the middle of the store before he expired. His eyes were open. Early stepped over him and stopped for a moment to let his eyes adjust to the dimness. The store's center aisle was littered with cans and boxes.

Willard Davis lay amongst them, his body looking somehow small and childlike. Ben allowed himself to be momentarily grateful that the man's face turned was away, but then he moved carefully and leaned over the corpse.

The halo of blood around Davis's head covered the width of the aisle and spread under the shelves on either side. The top of his head was gone, but enough of his features and blond hair remained to identify him.

Ben walked back to the door and leaned out. "Who called this in?" he asked, certain that no one would answer.

"I did, suh," a voice said. "I called you."

The owner of the voice stepped forward and stood diffidently, turning his straw hat in his hands.

"Jacob Tull?" Ben asked, incredulous. "You? What— come here." He walked to the end of the covered veranda, as far from the wide eyes and ears of the crowd as he could get. Jacob followed him. "What telephone did you use, Jacob?"

"I used the one in the store, suh. They's one behind the counter. I've used telephones before, lots of times."

"What were you doing inside the store, Jacob? The nig—the colored service is out the back door."

"I know that, suh. There was something wrong, though. I had to go in. I had to."

"Why did you think something was wrong?" Ben's feelings were going from bad to worse. This was a disaster.

"She told me. I saw her standing on the porch and she told me. I found these two—" Jacob glanced back at the door, eyes flashing momentarily with hate. "—these two, inside, on the floor. She told me where they keep the phone. She wouldn't go in."

"Who told you, Jacob?" the sheriff asked, his dread building. "She? Who's she?"

"The little girl, suh. The little girl told me."

❦❦❦

Present Day:

In the morning, I went out on the veranda and was surprised to find my father already up and sitting outside.

"I'd like to sit where I can see the water," he said. "Can I do that?"

"Sure. We can sit on the dock. Want coffee?"

"You're on a damn island, and you can't see water," he grumbled. "Just trees. If you cut some of the damn things, you'd have a view. You could sit on your porch and look at the lake. Isn't that why people build on the water, for the view?"

"Probably," I said. "Don't forget I have to go every-where in a boat, though. I see lots of lake water. I like the privacy, and I don't much like cutting down trees."

I dragged a couple of canvas chairs down to the dock. When I came back up, I found him in the kitchen, splashing rum into a glass.

"Where do you keep your ice?" he asked, popping open a can of cola.

I opened the freezer and handed him a tray. "Why don't you mix that with orange juice? At least you'd get some vitamins."

He peered sideways at me. "Is that a joke?" he asked, handing me the glass. "Carry this. I need my hat."

He stopped by the door to put on a white cloth fishing hat, pulling the brim low over his ears. It accentuated his tan. A cord dangled jauntily around his neck. Despite his years, he was still a good-looking man.

He followed me down the front steps and onto the path that led through the trees. I turned back twice to check his progress over the uneven ground. The second time, he made a shooing motion with his hand. When we were settled, he sipped his drink, then leaned down stiffly, and set it on the boards at his feet.

We sat and looked at the day. The sound of a marine engine echoed over the lake. The morning was fresh and lovely. The long Canadian winters made the arrival of spring more acute—the new warmth and green brought an aching beauty. The air smelled like a kept promise.

"Have you thought about what I told you last night?"

"Yes. It's a pretty wild story. Did Mom know about this?"

"She knew," he said. "All of it. The only one I ever trusted enough. When she died, she took it with her, and I never expected to tell anyone else."

The dock moved gently beneath us whenever a boat went past. I leaned back, lulled nearly to sleep by the softness of the air and lapping sounds of the water.

"Are you going to tell me the rest of it?" I asked. "What did you tell Wanda that has her so pissed off?"

"It's not what I said. It's something I did, a long time ago, when I was a boy. I was part of Eli Tull's story, and no one ever knew. It got hushed up." He shifted and held out his glass. "Get me another one, would you?"

"You might want to take it a little bit easy, Dad," I said, taking it from him. "It's still pretty early."

The year's first real heat was on the way, and I figured that we'd need to move into the shade soon.

"Save your advice. I need a drink," he said simply. "I can't tell you the rest of it otherwise, about my part in things. It's the most important part, and I want a drink to tell it with."

I nodded, resigned, and took the glass. "Now's the time to tell me, Dad. I'll be right back."

I walked up the finger of granite that anchored the dock, through the screen of trees, and into the shady clearing in front of my cabin. The yellow dog was lying in front of my steps, and he scrambled to his feet when he saw me. We looked at each other for a few seconds, and then he trotted around the side of the cabin and was gone.

"This is beautiful," Dad said, when I came back. "You shouldn't forget how lucky you are, seeing something like this every day."

"I try to remember that," I said, setting his drink down.

"It's easy to forget what's important. You look right at it and you don't even see it anymore. Do me a favor? Leave me alone for a minute. Let me think."

I watched a water skier in the middle of the reach. She skipped the boat's wake and tumbled. Her head popped up, and the boat turned to come back for her.

"Don't you want to just get it done with?" I asked.

"I'm going to," he said. "I just need a minute to get my thoughts together. This isn't easy."

"Sure," I said, and stood up. I figured that he needed to get the drink in him. "I have some stuff to move from under the porch. I'll give you a few minutes and come back."

From time to time, I glanced along the path down to the dock, where he sat motionless, looking out at the lake. His ankles were crossed beneath the canvas chair. The sun was bright and stinging, and his hat looked very white. Its brim cast a shadow over his face. After a while, I left the trees and walked down to talk to him.

"You doing okay?" I asked. "Hot out here."

He didn't answer, and didn't move. His hands rested on the chair arms, relaxed and very tanned. The last slivers of ice in his rum and coke moved slightly, stirred by the breeze. All at once I knew.

"Dad?"

We were perfectly, finally, still. The lake sounds faded away, leaving only the silent two of us in the brilliant spring light. I looked at him, and he looked at nothing that I could see.

Later, I most remembered the ice that hadn't yet melted, and the twin tracks of tears that were still drying on his face. It wasn't a look of pain. It seemed more the expression of a man who had endured a painful mystery for the entirety of his life, and at last wept at the beauty and simplicity of its revelation.

CHAPTER 9

Jacob Tull,
Marietta, Georgia, Sunday, August 4, 1946:

Jacob was arrested for the murders of the two white men in the afternoon of the same day that they were killed. He was taken from his home in the hot afternoon, cheating the mob that would have taken him by nightfall. He was not treated roughly or unkindly.

"You know why we're here, Jacob," the sheriff said. "I'm taking you in for killing Floyd Sutton and Willard Davis."

"The girl knows I didn't do it, suh."

"The girl doesn't know who did it. You won't give me any trouble, will you?"

"I didn't kill them, but you're taking me anyhow?"

"I have to, Jacob," Ben said. "I have to take you. You know that."

"It isn't Christian to say it, but I'm glad they dead. Those men were trash, and they killed my boy. I wish it was me did it."

"Put your hands behind you."

When the handcuffs were tight, the sheriff straightened and looked Jacob in the eyes. "I'm a father, too. I might have done the same, but that don't change things."

"I know, suh," Jacob said. "I told you I don't mind."

"Where's the gun at?"

"I don't have any gun, suh."

"Doesn't matter, I guess," the sheriff said. "Let's go."

Jacob was glad that his wife Dottie, and surviving son Roy, were not at home to see him bound and taken. Once he was in the jail, they were not permitted visitation, and he never saw them again. His thirtieth birthday came and went during his trial and brief imprisonment.

Sixty-two days after his arrest, he stood quietly and waited. He was surrounded by uniformed men. He considered praying, but decided that it was unnecessary. He thought instead of his wife and his two boys as the waxed rope was drawn over his head and snugged tight behind his left ear. A rough hood was pulled down, and the world left his sight. It was hot underneath the cloth, and it smelled musty and old.

A constant pounding noise began, and Jacob supposed that people were stamping their feet. The rhythm became louder and louder and began to hurt his ears. He had still not realized that it was his own pulse that he heard booming in his head when the trap door opened and he fell straight down.

He felt a sharp crack through his whole body as the rope caught and his neck broke, and then he tumbled onto soft grass. It was an astonishing green, and he saw that it had been raining, although the cloud cover had that luminous quality that preceded the sun. He picked himself up and started running.

He knew he had to head uphill to get where he was going. He had been here before, although he couldn't have said when. He ran up the hillside effortlessly. When he crested it, the grass had thinned out and it was sandy underfoot. He stood at the top and was confused.

What should have been there was not.

A stunning vista of green hills stretched before him, but it was empty of what he had expected. Then he glanced to his left, and there it was. The rooftops were exactly as he remembered, although he had never seen them before.

Jacob turned his steps downhill toward home.

∾∾∾

Present Day:

The day passed in a blur.

The Simcoe County coroner, dressed for golf and mildly irritated, straightened from beside the deck chair my father still sat in, nodded his head, and got back in his boat. The police, with their flashing lights and noise of their radios, got ready to leave the island.

They put my father's body onto a stretcher and loaded him awkwardly for the trip down the lake to the marina. I followed in my own boat. A silver hearse waited on shore, backed onto the dock by the gas pump. Like an insane guest at a party, it spoiled the summer mood at the marina, and people passing on boats either avoided looking at it or else stared at it, open-mouthed.

From her living room window a mile across the water, Molly had seen the first strange boats landing at my dock and intuited the trouble. She met me at the marina and stayed, often with a hand resting on my arm or my back. Her touch was a profound comfort.

Eventually, I was able to call Angela from the marina office. I sat at Diane's desk and looked at a calendar that showed native turtles while I talked.

"Dead? What do you mean, he died? How could he just die? It happened this morning and you're just calling me now?"

"He was sitting on the dock. I went to check on him, and he was gone. I'd just been talking to him—he slipped away. It was fast. I don't think he felt anything."

Angela burst into tears. "Why didn't you call me?" she sobbed.

"It's been non-stop crazy," I said. "I'm sorry. It took a long time to get people out to the island. The police wouldn't move him until the coroner said it was a natural death. I haven't had even a minute to think since it happened. I feel numb."

"Where is he now?" she asked.

"He's on his way to a funeral home in Huntsville. I'm just heading over there now."

"You're burying him up there?" I could hear her tears dry—her practical side was stronger than her sentiment.

"No," I said. "I'm going to take him home to Atlanta. He was never even here before. This is a foreign country to him. No one should get buried in a strange place."

"Atlanta's the one place he shouldn't go, Mike. He was running from there. He ran away and now you're dragging him back. Don't take him to Atlanta." Her voice was rising. "He was scared and he came to you for some kind of help, or shelter, and look what happened. Look what it got him, and now you're—"

"Enough!" I snapped. I felt like she had punched me in the stomach. "Let me start over," I went on, my teeth clenched. "I have to go to Atlanta to sell his house and pay his bills, to close it and wrap up all the things he was running away from. He also left behind a body. Out of respect, I'm taking it down to put it with his wife's body. That's all."

"You don't even know where his wife is. Your own mother—and you don't know where she's buried. You told me that, years ago."

The worst part of divorce was that the person who liked you least in the whole world was the one who knew the most about you, knew all of your hidden corners and cracks and vulnerabilities.

"I'll find out where my mother is," I said. "There's a record somewhere."

"I'm booking a flight down there," she said. "I'll meet you, assuming you can get this much done without my help."

I was genuinely surprised. "You're going to Atlanta?"

"I loved him," she said. "He'd expect me to be at his funeral."

"Why don't you fly down with me? I'll—"

She hung up on me. I closed the phone and walked across the parking lot to where Molly waited in her pickup. I got in and related some of my conversation with Angela to her. I had no idea how to start looking for my mother's remains, but it was starting to feel important.

"It *is* kind of weird," Molly said. She started the truck and put it in gear.

"What's weird?"

"That you don't know where your mother is. I don't even remember my mother, but I know where she's buried. I still bring flowers on Mother's Day."

"I guess we weren't much into all that, my dad and I. I remember her funeral. I don't know what arrangements he made with her body afterward. We never talked about it."

She kept her foot on the brake and leaned her head on the steering wheel, looking sideways at me. Her eyes were luminous. Incongruously, I thought about kissing her. It wasn't the right time, and I shook it off.

"I'll find out where she is," I went on. "It shouldn't be hard. I'll put him with her."

"I'm coming with you," she said.

"No. Angela's going to be there. She can be…unpleasant. I'd rather you weren't exposed to that."

She straightened in her seat and looked out the window on her side.

"Who cares about the funeral? It's just a body, Molly. It's words over a body. You and I see ghosts. Of all people, you and I know it's meaningless."

She shook her head. Without replying, she took her foot off of the brake and wheeled the truck toward the road.

"Of all people," I repeated, "we know that the cemeteries and graveyards and funeral homes are all empty. You don't need to go to Atlanta with me."

CHAPTER 10

Sam Latta,
Marietta, Georgia, Thursday, May 20, 1948:

I s she going to go to hell, Daddy?"
Nathan Latta sat on the edge of his son's bed. He was
home from work early, because it was the boy's
birthday. There had been news, more bad news. It was
nearly summer again, and the window was wide open,
letting in the sound of insects drowsing in the afternoon
heat. The day was green and gold and flooded with sunshine, but the room felt dark.

"No, son. She was a sad woman. She suffered more
than she should for a thing that wasn't her doing. God
doesn't punish that. He doesn't lay on more weight than
someone can bear and then send them to hell because
they can't do it."

"How do people hang themselves?" the boy asked.
"She was way up high in the rafters in the store. How did
she get up there?"

The father looked up at his son, annoyed and alarmed
by degrees. "Who told you that? Who you been talking
to?"

"I seen Wanda—that's her girl. She told me she woke

up this morning and her ma wasn't in the house, so she crossed over to the store and found her hanging from a rope up by the roof. She said the face was black. She said the eyes and tongue were sticking out and it was wearing her mama's dress. She didn't know it was her mama until it started talking."

The man stared at the boy. "What do you mean, talking?"

"Her mouth was all swole up, Daddy," the boy said, "but she was still talking. She told Wanda it was her own fault that her daddy was dead, and Wanda should come up there and hang, too. She said Wanda was bad. Just really a *bad girl*. Wanda ran away."

"Hogwash, son. Hogwash. She didn't talk. I promise you that. I don't want to hear another word about this, y'hear?"

"She was dead but she could talk, and that's why I thought she was going to hell."

"Dead people don't talk," the man said. "That poor girl's in shock, is all. I feel bad for her, seeing a thing like that, her own mama that way, but I don't want you with her anymore."

The boy sat beside his father on the small bed and thought about it for a minute, looking at the floor. There was a rag rug on the wood, multicolored, and he liked looking at it, seeing the different designs and patterns in it. He looked sideways, up at his father's face. "She's glad her mother's dead. She says it was her mama's doing that boy got killed, that her mama made her daddy do it. Killing the boy was her mama's idea."

"Son, you haven't seen my hand on you much, but if I find you've been talking with that girl again, you'll feel my belt on your behind and that's a promise." The man stood up and went to the door. "Stay away from her, son. That's final. I don't like to talk to you this way on your birthday, but those people have poisoned my house enough, and I'm done with it. Listen to me, now. Your mother has a cake for you, and there might be a package beside your plate. Come downstairs."

෭ාෂ

Present Day:

I sat in the window seat and looked out, into the night. Atop the white fuselage of the plane parked next to ours a strobe pulsed, drowning the area in red. The windows of that jet were lit, and I could see people moving around inside, a mirror of what was happening in our own cabin. Yellow lights on the fuel trucks and baggage carts spun madly in the darkness as they hurried around the apron.

I had looked for my father's casket being loaded in beneath me, but hadn't seen it. I supposed they camouflaged them. People on board might see an occupied coffin as an albatross if they spotted it being put aboard their flight. I pictured a stampede for the exit and smiled wearily. If it happened, I'd have first-class to myself.

Almost all the people on my flight were busy with cell phones. They sent final texts before the order to turn them off. A nervous few checked the seat pockets in front of them, searching for reassurance in the routine presence of flight magazines and sick bags that had ventured into the sky and returned safely. Stragglers onto the plane smiled vaguely at the head of the aisle, as if in apology, while attendants slammed overhead bin doors with nearly excessive force.

It was ten o' clock, and the day weighed heavily on me. The coach seat was thinly padded but comfortable, and I closed my eyes and listened to the murmuring of the aircraft readying itself. I felt the gentle thump of large outside cargo doors being closed and latched. The round vent over my head puffed air softly into my face. There was a tiny bump and then we were pushed back. Jet engines began to whistle almost imperceptibly.

Now that I was on board, I realized how much I dreaded this trip. I didn't want to return to Georgia, I didn't want to face this funeral, and I wished I were on the island getting ready for bed. My thoughts drifted.

"Sir," the woman's voice said. "Sir! Excuse me."

I opened my eyes. With one hand on the seat backs in front of us, the flight attendant leaned across the two women who were my seatmates to address me. Older, she was probably senior on the flight crew. Her blue eyes were slightly puffy, and she appeared harried even before the flight was underway. Her front tooth showed a fleck of lipstick.

"You shouldn't be on this flight," she said. "You should get off now."

I sat upright, fully awake. "Isn't this for Atlanta?" I asked, alarmed. "The doors are already closed."

"You should get off," she repeated. She straightened and looked toward the front of the aircraft, her hand still resting on the seat back in front of us. She cocked her head and looked at me. "There's something not right," she said. "Can't you hear it?"

Another stewardess came down the aisle to us, and I waited for what would develop, but she continued past us toward the rear without pausing. The attendant was increasingly agitated as she looked up the aisle. She squeezed the headrest in front of me, and I saw that her hand was dirty. Three of her fingernails were broken off at the quick.

"I have to go. I can't do this again," she said and moved forward, shaking her head.

I twisted around to face my seatmate, an overweight

woman in glasses. "Is this not going to Atlanta?"

"Yes. Where do you think?" she drawled. "A little late to be asking now."

I sat back and buckled myself in.

"He wants to know where we're going," she smirked to the woman on the other side of her.

A voice came over the speakers overhead.

"Ladies and gentlemen, my name is Pam and I'm your chief flight attendant. On behalf of Captain Richardson and the entire crew, welcome aboard Canadian flight 1306, non-stop service from Toronto to Atlanta."

I sat forward, ready to stand up. The plane began to roll forward in its slow and clumsy search for the runway, an old fat dog following a scent. I unlatched my lap belt and turned in the seat, looking for direction, and realized that it was too late. I was going wherever the plane was going.

"At this time, make sure your seat backs and tray tables are in their full upright position. Also make sure your seat belt is correctly fastened. Also, we advise you that as of this moment, any electronic equipment must be turned off. Thank you."

The cabin went dark, and the plane left the commotion of the terminal behind and began to wander through the blackness of the airfield. We drifted past occasional blue lights that sat lonely in the grass beside the cement.

"Cabin crew; prepare for take-off."

The jet collected itself. The wing gleamed dully outside my window. The whistle of engines spooled up and up, into a shriek, and we began to roll. After the first hesitation, the jetliner gained momentum and I was pressed into my seat back. Lights on the runway went by faster and faster, and the wheels thudded a staccato beat on seams in the cement. The lighted terminal building came back into view far off to the right. As we passed it, the ranks of white aircraft on its flanks reminded me of nursing puppies.

The aircraft hunkered down and began to lift its nose. Unexpectedly, my window lit up from the outside. A huge flash of light was accompanied by a bang that shook the cabin. We skidded sideways into the air. My seat dipped and I threw out a hand to brace myself as the aircraft seemed to roll and yaw, threatening to turn its belly to the sky. The shuddering noise was deafening. We seemed to be aboard a freight train that was off the rails, its wheels rolling at speed across gravel and railway ties.

In unison, a hundred voices began to scream, a choir singing its complete terror, barely heard above the airplane's thrashing agony. The seat under me dropped hard. I was forced up against the belt and then back down, smashing my elbows on the armrests. Seat belt lights above our heads flickered and flashed, a rank of warnings stretching all the way to the front of the compartment. I focused on them. If they went dark, I knew we would lose our grip on the sky and fall.

Another explosion thudded against my window and the plane lurched. I looked out and back and saw flames expelled from the engine. The screams rose. The woman next to me gripped the top of my hand so hard that the bones ground together, and I struggled to free myself from her.

We passed strangely low and slow over a freeway, and I wondered if we would roll and drop into the river of headlights and orange sodium below us. I envied the people below. They were nearly close enough to touch, but worlds away from us, on their way home from dinner and headed to parties and factory night shifts. All the lost chances from my life gathered in the chaos, and I was nearly overwhelmed with sadness. I was going to die with a group of strangers.

By degrees, the plane steadied itself, and although the vibration continued, it was somewhat lessened. We soared low over the lights of the city, and I imagined people in houses and apartments below looking up at the unaccustomed harsh sound of a jet engine laboring over their neighborhoods. Voices in the cabin dropped off, with only an occasional loud sob or raised voice audible over the general throbbing of the distressed plane.

We stayed low, the wounded airplane struggling to maintain altitude. Beneath me, the city lights disappeared and it was completely black. I knew that the pilot had taken us out over Lake Ontario. I looked at the tops of heads above the seat backs in front of me. Three hundred people were packed into this small space. We were sitting close together, yet most were rigidly alone with what was happening.

"Ladies and Gentlemen, this is Captain Richardson. I am not completely satisfied with the performance of one of our engines, so we are going to head back to the airport and have it looked at. Please follow your flight crew's instructions. You can expect a safe landing."

Liar, I thought.

A stewardess stood in the aisle and scanned the rows of seats. She fell heavily into the passengers sitting beside her as the plane tilted and dropped into a crippled turn. A few isolated screams rose, but generally the cabin felt smothered with a crushing paralysis.

"Flight attendants, prepare for landing."

The fallen attendant got to her feet. She made her way shakily to an empty seat, sat down, and began to shout. "Heads down, stay down, brace, brace! Heads down, stay down, brace, brace, brace!"

From behind us and forward in first class, the voices of other crew members joined the chant, like a group of nuns performing a strange liturgy in the dark cabin, shouting the same words, over and over. People looked at their neighbors and then heads disappeared as they hunched over and stared at the floor. I felt the back of my seat shift when the person sitting behind me grabbed it.

"Brace, brace brace! Heads down, stay down, brace, brace! Heads down, stay down, brace, brace, brace!"

Noise from the remaining engine rose as we dropped lower, and the flight attendants were accordingly louder, sounding as though they were willing us to stay in the air. I risked sitting up, and looked out my window.

The lights of the city reappeared, even closer than they had been. We seemed to be far too low. Lit rooftops came up to meet us and then disappeared as we suddenly floated into the dark space over the airfield. The wheels touched and rolled. We were down.

I didn't hear the flurry of announcements after we came to a stop and were met by a flotilla of red and blue lights. Stairs were brought and we walked through the gathering of emergency vehicles and began the long walk back to the terminal building. It seemed that every muscle in my body hurt, as though I had badly overused them.

I numbly followed the line of people into the building, up a flight of stairs, and then down a long fluorescent-lit hallway. Noises were strange and muted. My ears seemed to be packed with cotton. A set of glass doors opened at the end, and we were back in the warm and quiet commotion of the concourse. Groups of airline employees stood, stopped in mid-conversation, and stared at us almost furtively.

The people in front of me headed vaguely for seats in the lounge or toward the information counter. I walked past them. A young couple sat on the vinyl seats with two small children; the parents stared straight ahead at the floor, not touching each other. There was no question that they had been with me. We were marked.

Leaving my luggage behind, I headed for Canadian Customs and re-entered the country, then headed outside to find a taxi and a hotel. I seemed to move in a zone of absolute silence, and I wondered if I were in some kind of shock. When I had checked into a room near the airport, I called Angela.

"Where are you?" she demanded.

"Still in Toronto. The plane had some kind of problem. We got turned around. I'll leave in the morning."

"Damn it, Mike. You need to be here. I'm down here alone. Have you even arranged a service yet?"

"There's a funeral home that's meeting the plane. I'm letting them make the arrangements."

When we hung up, I undressed and lay in the dark. After a while, fear came creeping in, and I got up and turned on a light. I was in a strange bed, in a strange room, in a building full of strangers that I would never see again. It was not a night that I wanted to be alone.

I turned the unfamiliar pillow and felt myself slide toward sleep. The flight attendant who had warned me showed me that spirits still moved around me. It didn't occur to me that her warning may not have been about the troubled flight, but what waited on the other end of it.

PART II

COBB COUNTY, GEORGIA

CHAPTER 11

Sam Latta, Wanda Sutton,
Marietta, Georgia, Tuesday, December 3, 1946:

It was a cold day, and the boy shrugged deeper into his wool sweater. The winter sun worked feebly against the grayness of the day and provided no warmth. Trees were bare and the road was mud. The red clay gave the world its only color. The cold season in Georgia was made more bitter by its brevity.

The boy spent the rest of his life in the area, and the general store would stand after he died, but he never again walked through its door. Today, however, he had been sent on an errand that took him past it. There simply was no other road to where he was going. He had little understanding of death, but he knew of ghosts and accepted their existence in the same way that all children did until the teaching of adults had hidden them away. He was also of a sufficient age to feel guilt, although he didn't know the word for what he felt.

When the structure came into view, the boy stopped in the road. It seemed to glow in the thin light. The shades of Floyd Sutton and Willard Davis did not visit from whatever place for child-killers they had gone to, at least not regularly. The building was haunted, nonetheless, by what they had left behind.

Sutton's widow, to everyone's surprise, clung to the store, and she remained almost reverent about the places on the floor where their blood had soaked into the old wood. After the first month of fretting over people's footsteps on the stains, she began to keep a display of goods over each spot. She pushed those aside when she was alone in the store to gaze at what remained of her husband and her brother.

Her daughter was neglected. People had died, and lives were altered and ruined for her honor, but her well-being became of no consequence. She came and went as she pleased and could have kissed a hundred black children, one by one, and it would have gone unnoticed by her mother.

There were no cars parked in front of the store. Its distasteful history aside, the girl's mother had little head for business, and her spotty ordering of new stock made the place an unreliable place to shop. The last of the regular white patrons drifted away. The Negro customers who attended the back door were more flexible about their demands, and the store's history was also of less consequence to them. The death of Eli Tull at the hands of the owner was no reason to condemn his widow, and even Eli's mother was seen at the back door as often as ever. Neither woman acknowledged what had passed between the two families.

The boy began to hurry as he drew abreast with the entrance to the store's lot. He could hear his own breath rasping in the cold air. The front door of the store opened, almost as if it heard him passing. It was exactly as he had imagined it. Dread flooded through him, and his steps slowed as the little girl crossed the porch, descended the steps, and crossed quickly to the edge of the dooryard.

She stopped there as if forbidden to enter the roadway.

"I know what you did," she said.

He stopped, and they stood and stared at each other. She was thin and pale. Her face was dirty and her blonde hair needed to be brushed. She had no coat and started to shiver.

"I know what you did," she repeated.

The spell was broken, and the boy took to his heels and ran.

"I know what you did!" she screamed, and her voice broke.

She began to cry and stumbled into the roadway to watch his retreat. Tears ran down her cheeks, but she stood in the cold and did not wipe them away.

ɛɔɛɔ

Present Day:

My ex-wife met me at the arrivals gate in Atlanta at lunch time the next day. She was clearly annoyed.

"Couldn't you have gotten another flight last night?" she asked. "Did you even try?"

"I wasn't in any shape to get back on a plane last night, Angela."

"Planes lose engines all the time," she said. "You needed to be here. Let's get your bags."

"Got it. Just this." I indicated my carry-on.

"Is that your way of saying you won't be staying long?" she asked. "Same old Mike. You haven't changed. Do the bare minimum you see as your duty and then get the hell out. Why didn't you have him cremated?"

"I might do that. I have no idea what he wanted. I have to find out."

She stared at me. "Drag a coffin thousands of miles and then cremate him?"

She turned and began walking toward the street exit, high heels tapping on the cement floor. Her legs were long, and I hurried to keep up. Trailing her, I caught her scent, exclusive and wonderful.

"I need to find my mother," I said. "I'll try to put him with her. I don't know if she was buried or cremated, so it depends on that."

She looked back at me sharply. She was slender and very pale, with a graceful walk. Long hands seemed to never stop moving from her hair to her purse to her buttons, alighting only for a moment on each thing, before moving busily on. In contrast, her lovely face moved little. When I talked to her, she often looked back at me with absolutely no expression and then looked away again without replying. She radiated a general sense of impatience with those around her, but displayed an occasional whimsy which charmed me.

She unlocked the car door for me. "Are you going to tell me about it?" she asked. She kept her eyes on the road as she entered the freeway that encircled the city of Atlanta. The traffic ran faster than most places.

"Yes. He told me a story. He didn't finish, and there are things I don't understand yet. Let's get the funeral home stuff done first, and then I'll tell you what I know."

A few hours later, I sat on the edge of the hotel bed and thought a little about my father, and a lot about drinking. It had once been so easy to know what to do at times like this, so automatic. There was a knock at the door, so soft that I wondered if it was at another door up or down the hall. I crossed and opened it.

Angela stood there. I took her wrist hard and pulled her into a kiss, closing the door with the side of my foot as we dragged each other toward the bed. She undid the button on her jeans, lay back, and looked up at me.

"Get the light," she said, stretching her arms over her head.

"No. I want to see you, Angela."

"But I don't want to see *you*."

When I came back, she was naked under my hands. The soft skin on the inside of her thighs radiated heat against my face. She smelled like withered roses, the fragrance corrupt beneath the sweetness, and she tasted like ashes and lost love. She rolled over and I kissed my way down her back. I found her most intimate places, but I couldn't get close. I had never been so lonely in my life and wondered if she felt the same.

When we were done we lay in absolute dark. I held her, my history, my past, my once-upon-a-time princess. My life was haunted by spirits of the dead. I lived alone on an island where the shadows of long ago came back to life and walked around. The warmth of her pressed against me was a bridge back to the safe and normal life I had lost.

"I'm sorry I ruined us," I said.

"You didn't choose what happened," she murmured. "Neither did I. It just happened."

She shifted away from me, just a tiny movement, and I pulled her back.

"So tell me the story," she finally said.

"Not now," I breathed. I was falling asleep.

"Yes, now," she said. "I want to be done with it."

I began to speak softly into the dark. The air conditioner hummed underneath the window as I took her into the heat and humidity of a sixty five year-old Georgia summer, back to dirt roads and fishing holes in the muddy water under wooden bridges and a single kiss that had killed four people.

It was a kiss that had slept for decades, but was now

awake. My father had passed out of the story and left me alone with it. The more that I knew, the more I resented him for it.

When I finished telling it, at least as much of it as I knew, she stirred.

"That's it?" she asked, her breath warm against my chest. "The little boy was killed. His father shot the men who did it, and then he was executed? That's the end?"

"No, there's more. I don't know what it is. I don't know what my father did, or what he knew. I don't know why it matters all these years later. I don't know why he thought he had to run away from these people."

Angela's breathing steadied and I felt her sleep. I lay awake for a long time.

"I'm going to find out, though," I told the dark room. "I'm going to end it and keep you safe, Dad. I promise."

In the morning, the bed beside me was empty. I showered, dressed, and walked up the hall to Angela's room. When she answered my knock, I saw the suitcase on the bed behind her.

"I'm not staying for the funeral, after all, Mike. I changed my mind. I don't belong here. I have to go. Right now. Sam would understand."

"How could you fly all the way down here and not go to the funeral? It doesn't make sense."

"Mike. Listen to me. I'm seeing someone. What happened last night is what doesn't make sense. I can't be around you. I'm sorry."

I was seeing someone else, too, so I could hardly explain the desolation that flooded me. I felt abandoned. "Are you at least having breakfast with me?"

"I had coffee," she said. "I'll wait for you if you want to grab some, but there's a flight to Toronto at ten. I want to catch it."

I drove her to the airport. I felt terribly alone, even

with her sitting beside me in the rental car. When she was checked in, I walked her to the gate. She kissed me brief-ly and walked away to find her plane. A few steps away, she turned back. "Did you mean what you said last night?" she asked. "About getting to the bottom of this? About keeping him safe?"

I was surprised by her question. She had been awake then, and listening to me. "Yes."

"You're going to keep your dead father safe?"

I nodded.

"You're a little bit fucking crazy, Mike. You know that?"

"Not about that," I said.

She stared at me for a long moment and then nodded once. She turned and walked away.

CHAPTER 12

Sheriff Ben Early,
Cobb County, Georgia, Friday, October 1, 1948:

Ben sat in his radio car. He pressed a fingertip to the chrome horn ring and then wiped the smudge away. He repeated the process several times before he slapped the white Bakelite wheel and looked out the window at the road. He was parked under a billboard outside the city limits, ostensibly to watch for speeding cars, but really to think things over.

He had served out a decade as sheriff, and this was likely his last term. Things had soured over the past few months, and while Georgia voters could generally be depended on to honor and prefer tradition, the flood of GIs returning from Europe and the Pacific meant that a younger man with military experience would likely hold his office after the next election.

He fished a package of Old Golds from his shirt pocket and lit one. He cranked the window down and made sure the blown-out match was cool before he threw it out. The tobacco smelled familiar and comfortable. He was settled contentedly back in his seat when the radio under the dashboard made noise. He leaned forward and adjusted a knob before he unhooked the heavy microphone. "Go ahead, Shirley."

"Sheriff, we have a caller reporting an incident past the four corners on Barne's Ferry Road. Call was made from the old general store."

"Incident? What kind of incident? Caller say if it was coloreds or whites?"

"Don't know, didn't say—just something bad happening."

"You have another car in the area?"

"No, sir. Leonard's on his break. He swung by home to take Mary to the doctor's office. You're the only unit in the area."

"Wait a second, Shirley. You said call was made from the store? That can't be right."

The dispatcher said something else that was lost in static.

Ben adjusted another knob. "Store's closed," he said. "No phone there, not one that works anyway. Where was they calling from?"

"I don't know, Ben. I thought they said they was at store. I couldn't even tell you if it was a man or a woman."

"All right, leave it. If you get another call on the incident, let me know."

He was puzzled. He couldn't think of a working phone anywhere in the area.

"Sheriff, caller said four people are dead. So far. So far, they said. Something terrible must be going on."

Shit, he thought. He was reluctant to leave his sanctuary of tall grass and red dirt underneath the billboard. He keyed the microphone. "I'll be out that way for a look directly, Shirley."

He sat back to finish his smoke. Odd to have a call like this when the weather was cool—tempers normally boiled in the heat. Generally, Negro problems sorted themselves out without white interference, and it was best that way. It was like dogs fighting in the yard—if you left them to it, they solved it their own way. Try to break it up and it lasted longer, and like as not you got bit for your trouble.

Regretfully, he butted his cigarette, adjusted his trooper's hat, and started the car. He drove slowly along the ruts that led out from under the sign. Once he was free of the scrub and onto pavement, he switched on his siren. It wound up slowly. He was about six miles away. With any luck the troublemakers would hear him coming and clear out. Less than ten minutes later, he turned onto the packed dirt in front of the old store.

The place had been shut only a few months, since Verla Sutton's suicide, but it looked like it had been abandoned for years. Trade had dropped off after Floyd Sutton and his brother in law had killed the Negro boy, and their subsequent deaths on the property had nearly doomed the place, although Verla had tried to make a go of it. The discovery of her body hanging by a rope from the rafters with a kicked-away ladder beneath it had been enough. There were no buyers, although the location was good. No one would touch it. Ben suspected that eventually the county would take it for taxes and the building would be torn down.

Already there were rumors that the place was haunted. The sheriff himself had heard that stock was left untouched on the shelves, because no one had been brave enough to clean the place up, and that the shades of the owners were inside, sitting behind the counter and waiting for customers.

"She hanged herself right over the spot on the floor where her men-folk died."

That was true, but what of it? She had to use a rafter

somewhere. He drove to the back of the place and set the brake. The rear area where black customers congregated still had a working hand pump for water, and there were usually people gathered there. Today it was deserted. Whoever had been there had heard the siren and cleared out. He got out of the car. The day was clouding over.

He did a quick survey of the area, specifically checking the ground for blood or any other evidence that someone had been injured. There was nothing. His police sense was many years tuned, and it didn't feel like there had been people there only minutes previously. At the same time, he felt like he was being watched. He looked at the building.

The back door and all of the windows were boarded up with gray wood. He tried not to imagine the dimness inside, empty shelves, the forsaken cash register, the smell of old wood, stains on the floor.

Walking once around the outside of the store, he confirmed that the place was shut tight. The ground under the hand pump in back was wet, and the cast iron spout dripped slowly, drops of water landing silently in the dirt. Ben went to the door of his car and pulled it open.

There was a muffled bang from inside the building, then a heavy thump as something fell. The sheriff started and then stood frozen, staring at the nailed-up doorway. A full minute ticked by and there was no other sound. He got into his car and started it. He had to jockey the car forward and back to point it at the road.

He didn't look in the rear-view mirror when he reversed. When he left the lot, the car spun a tire and rattled small stones against the front steps. The sound of his engine slowly faded up the highway and then the old store was quiet.

எஅஏ

Present Day:

"She left?" Molly asked. "How could she leave?"

"There was no reason for her to be here any longer," I said. "It was good of her to come at all. She cared about my dad, but the funeral is too much for her right now. Anyway, she and I probably had enough of being in the same place. I'm kind of relieved she's gone."

"Did you fight with her?" Molly demanded.

"Not exactly," I said. "But it was uncomfortable in places."

Was I unfaithful? I was stricken and fought the urge to tell her about the night I had spent with Angela. Although Molly was divorced, and she made no secret of the fact that her ex-husband drifted in and out of her life, I still felt like a cheat.

We had no commitment except friendship, and I had once spoken vows with Angela, but logic didn't help me.

"So, now what?" she asked. "You have the funeral—what else?"

"I guess I have to figure out about the house," I said. "Apparently there's a will, which shocks me, knowing my dad. I'll still have to deal with cleaning out his stuff no matter what."

She was quiet on the other end. I felt her smile. "I have something for you when you get back," she said. "A surprise. I'm having some second thoughts, so I hope it's the right thing."

"What is it?"

"Do you know me?" she laughed. "Can you even imagine I'm going to tell you? Really?"

"I'm going to be at least a week sorting this out," I said. "It'll have to wait, I suppose."

"Hang on a sec, Mike."

I smiled and held on while she put the phone down

and talked inaudibly to someone on her end.

After a moment she came back. "I'm at the marina," she said. "Bill's going to take me down to Toronto in the morning. I'm flying down there. You're not doing this by yourself."

The next morning, I walked through the airport concourse and spotted Molly standing at a luggage carousel. I stopped where I was for a moment and looked at her. She wore a light cotton dress in a floral print, high-heeled sandals, and a straw hat. She was elegant without a shred of sophistication, small town lovely, summer on the lake come to life. The women who stood in the crowd around her were faded to invisibility. Contained and serene, she watched for her bags and didn't look around for me. She knew I'd be along.

A yellow light flashed, a buzzer sounded, and the carousel jerked and started to rotate. When I glanced back at her, her eyes were on mine. As always, her smile erased everything around her. I needed to be near her, and hurried.

"You look terrific," I said when I got to her.

"My feet don't feel terrific." She laughed. "I always wear heels when I go somewhere I've never been to, because I think they make me look taller. I think they're pretty, and I never have a reason to wear them, but I can never wait to take them off."

She swiveled, bent to put down her carry-on, and then turned to hug me. She was warm and smelled wonderful.

"They are pretty, and they do make you taller," I said. "You don't need to be taller, though. Don't worry about taller."

"Yes, I do. You have no idea. I told you I got you a present. I wanted to bring it with me, but it wouldn't have been a good plan. You'll have to wait 'til you get home. Here's my bag. Get me out of here."

"This city's a little crazy," I told her on the highway from the airport. "The war. Sherman burned the whole thing down after it had no strategic value. The war was really over. The South was a shambles, and the geography around here made Atlanta impossible to defend anyway. The Confederates would never have tried to take it back."

"I know they burned it," she said. "I was always a little bit vague on why."

"At the end, the people were close to starving already, and the Union army came through and killed about fifty thousand civilians and left the rest utterly destitute. I wonder what the hell happened to all the children, the ones who survived. How dark and twisted did they grow up? What did they teach their kids?"

"Is it still haunted? Do you see things here?" she asked.

"I'm not sure," I said. "Maybe. A hundred and something years isn't enough to wipe out the horror. It's right in the dirt."

"It's pretty, anyway," she said, looking out the window.

I turned the rental car into my father's driveway. The house was large, brick and white wood.

"We're staying here, right, Mike? A hotel for a week is a little rich for me right now."

"Staying here. I want to get it done and get home."

"This is the house you grew up in?"

I nodded. At the front door, I pulled out my father's keys and sorted until I found one that fit. "He's probably got keys on here," I said, "for locks that have been gone from this earth for twenty years."

I pushed the door open, and let Molly enter in front of me. "Pretty big place for one person," she said, looking around her.

"They bought it when I was born. I think maybe they were planning a few more kids."

"But she died before they could?"

"No, I was a teenager when she died. I don't really know why they stopped with me. I think maybe they realized that they saw enough kids teaching. They didn't need to come home to it, too."

The entry opened left into a large living area, clad in the greens and gold that had been popular forty years before. There were vacuum tracks in the carpeting, and a visible patina of dust on every surface. The room was seldom entered and never used. I was nearly overwhelmed at the sense of long-ago that the room evoked.

"There are a few pieces of my mother's furniture that I probably want to keep," I said. "I'll have to check storage around here. For now, I mainly want to take any pictures of my parents or family documents that'll fit in a suitcase. I didn't bring much in the way of clothes with me so I can carry stuff back."

She looked steadily at me. "I'm glad. I'd hate to think you were just going to pitch everything."

I nodded at the cabinet stereo against one wall. "I spent a lot of time drinking beer in front of that thing," I said. "Probably find some milk crates of my records in the basement."

Molly trailed her fingers across the keys of an old upright piano that stood against the wall. The sound was startling in the silence.

"Did you play this?" she asked.

"A little," I said. "I took lessons for a while—didn't really like all the practicing. This was mainly my mother's thing. Her escape, I guess. She was good, a natural. Sometimes when I hear a piano playing, I remember her so clear I can smell her perfume."

We walked through the kitchen. Pale blue paint and

avocado-colored appliances were darkened by years of grease. In the den where my father had taken his meals and spent most of his time, a large black reclining chair faced an older television across the matted shag carpeting. There was a nearly full ashtray on the small table next to the chair, but the room didn't smell of tobacco. My father hadn't smoked in years.

A telephone on the table was hooked up to an answering machine; the red digital display indicated that there were unheard messages. I sat down in my father's black chair. I thought of the time he had spent sitting here, unthought-of by me, as my life had unfolded hundreds and thousands of miles away.

This was where he was on the rare, awkward occasions that I called him. I wondered what he had thought of me as he sat in this spot.

I reached across and pressed the button. I heard the tiny cassette rewind, and then the speaker hissed.

"I know what you did."

The voice was soft, androgynous, and the connection was broken immediately after the words were spoken. The machine moved to the next message.

"I know what you did."

I played through the rest of the tape. The messages were all the same. The background noise and timbre changed slightly from one to the next, but the speaker and the message were exactly the same in all thirteen of them.

"I don't get it," I said.

I was shaken. I looked up at Molly, who was leaning in the doorway. She shook her head. I rewound the tape and listened to the first message again.

"I know what you did."

"When did these come in?" Molly asked. "Can you tell?"

I picked up the machine and fiddled with it. "He

doesn't have the time and date thing set up," I said. "He wasn't much for gadgets."

"But these messages are all new, right? He hadn't listened to them?"

"They're new, yes. At least since he left for Canada, I would think. He didn't have much contact with people—he was fanatic about checking his mailbox and his phone messages. He wouldn't have gotten one and not bothered to listen to it."

"Should someone know about this, Mike?"

"This must be what he was so afraid of. This has to be that woman, Wanda. God knows how long this was going on. I wonder if he mentioned anything about this to Angela."

I pulled out my cell. Molly came in and sat on the sofa that was against the far wall. Angela answered. Her tone was guarded. After perfunctory hellos, I asked about the time she had spent with my father prior to my arrival.

"Did he say anything about being called?" I asked. "About someone harassing him on the phone?"

"Harassing him? How?"

"Leaving him messages. I found about a dozen, all saying 'I know what you did.'"

"That's weird," she said, "I don't think so, but let me think."

She was quiet, and I listened to us breathe. "God, Mike. It's hard to put my finger on. He said he had tried to set the record straight or something like that. He was tired of keeping a secret."

"Pretty much what he said to me," I said. "What the hell was the secret?"

"No idea," she said. "He was upset. I didn't push him. And old people talk, you know? I didn't listen all that closely, just tried to be there for him. I didn't think it was important. What does it mean?"

I didn't know yet. We hung up, and I sat with the phone in my hand.

"What are you going to do?" Molly asked.

We looked at each other, and I shook my head. My father's story was suddenly a real thing, not just the rambling of a frightened, confused old man. Some of the fear that he must have felt listening to these messages seeped into me, but I also recognized the beginnings of real rage stirring inside of me.

"I have no idea. I really don't. I guess I need to find Wanda, and see what she has to say for herself."

CHAPTER 13

Sam Latta, Roy Tull,
Marietta, Georgia, Friday, December 13, 1946:

The small stone bounced off the shutter and rattled the window glass. Sam Latta crossed his room and looked out. There was a small figure down in the dooryard, winding up to deliver another pebble. The movement was graceful and sure, and the shutter made another cracking noise. He opened his window and stared down. The shout came up to him.

"Come down here. I got to talk to you."

Sam said nothing. After a time, he closed the window then turned, left his room, and went down the stairs. In the yard he stood in front of the other boy, who was a little bit taller than he was and dressed poorly for the cold. "What do you want?" he asked.

"That girl told me what you done."

"I didn't do anything. That girl's a liar."

"Don't matter. I know what you done. I know it for sure."

"What do you want?" Sam asked again.

"My brother's dead, and now my daddy's dead too. I want to ask you a question, that's why I came here."

The December wind blew clouds across the dark sky. When they crossed in front of the weak moon, they were visibly tattered and falling apart.

"My mama says Jesus going to take care of us now. What do you think about that? Think that's true?"

Sam had nothing to say. The other boy puffed his cheeks and blew out. Sam could see his eyes roll in the darkness of his face. His voice was rising. "You don't think so neither? So then I got a question for you. Who's gonna look out for us with my daddy gone? Who?" He stepped closer, and Sam could hear his tears. "What am I supposed to do without my daddy? What am I supposed to do?"

Sam Latta turned and went up the steps and back into his house. He closed the door softly behind him.

ℰ⁄ℴℰ⁄ℴ

Present Day:

"Come here a second," Molly called.

She was standing on a chair in my father's bedroom closet. Only the bottom part of her was visible. I stuck my head in, and she looked down at me. "I found your mother," she said. "Careful. I'll hand her down to you."

I reached up and she put the urn into my hands.

I felt a tiny shock and my vision brightened. I stood on a gravel path bordered by lush green grass. The sky was warm and gray. I heard dripping on the leaves above me. Chimes sounded, I smelled rain, and then—

It was all gone. I stood again in the musty closet, looking up.

"I think you really did," I said. "I think you found her." I held the container against my chest and helped Molly down from the chair with my free hand.

"You never knew where she was?"

"I never did. I barely remember the funeral service. I know half the high school was there. Packed. I was in shock—I don't think what happened to her body occurred to me. I don't remember my dad ever mentioning it."

"He brought her home to be with him," she said, taking the urn from my hands. "He couldn't stand to be apart from her. It's very sweet. They must have been very much in love."

"I never noticed," I said. "Hard for me to picture my dad very much in love with anyone. They always seemed kind of…neutral with each other. Either that or fighting."

"You don't know a thing. What kind of a man keeps a woman's ashes in his bedroom? It's very romantic. She was perfectly lovely, and I think he was too."

She smiled sweetly at me and left the room, taking my mother with her. "You don't know a thing, Mike," she repeated over her shoulder. "You're in the dark when it comes to love, you poor man."

�’�’�’

"Belly full, no worries," Molly said.

"Beg your pardon?"

She looked at me across the table and burst out laughing. I felt my heart move. We were finishing dinner in a dark steak house outside of Atlanta, sitting in a sea of plastic Tiffany lamps and artificial foliage. Her dark hair was a cloud around her lovely features, and her eyes held mine and warmed me.

"When I was in university I waited tables," she said. "I hardly had time to study—my mom was dead by then and my aunt couldn't help much with tuition. I didn't think I could pay back student loans on a teacher's salary when I got out, and that's all I ever wanted to be. I was carrying the weight of the world." She picked up her glass and swirled the ice in it before she drank. "There was a guy I worked with, a busboy. Miguel. Older, not Mexican...Nicaragua or someplace like that. Probably illegal, raising a family on what he made in that place, God only knows how. Treated like shit, mostly. One night, we were on meal break, back in the kitchen. He finished eating and was rubbing his tummy and said 'Belly full, no worries.' He had his eyes closed. I don't think he knew I heard him."

I leaned back in the booth, interested. She brushed a strand of dark hair back from her cheek. The restaurant murmured around us.

"It was transcendent, Mike. I think I fell a little in love with him."

Her smile was dazzling. "Do you get it?" she asked. "He really did have the weight of the world on him, a thousand times my problems, but he *got it.* He understood the moment, and it was enough. Enough. 'Belly full, no worries.' It changed me. I would have followed him anywhere. You need a little of that, mister."

"I do?"

"Yes." She nodded slowly. "Yes, you do. I never forgot it." She reached across and took my hand. Her fingers were warm, and she rubbed the web of my thumb as she spoke. "I'm trying to think of the last time I heard you laugh, really laugh, or smile with more than your mouth. When I met you, you had just lost your daughter—your wife was gone, your home, everything. There was still something sweet about you. But what happened last year has made you, I don't know...just *haunted*."

I wanted to take my hand back and stopped myself.

"I know it's hard, and probably kind of stupid when you've just lost your dad, but, Mike, you have to see the moments that are there. You have to see the good when it's in front of you. There has to be enough just in the moment sometimes. Does that make any kind of sense?"

Our waitress hurried past the table, slim and dark. I caught her eye, signaling for the check. She nodded without pausing.

"I don't know how else to say it," Molly said. "I want you back. I want my friend back. Will you think about it?"

Her reference to me as a friend stabbed me, and I gathered myself to go. "I'll think about it," I said. "I really will think about it." I paused at the edge of my seat. "Before we go, I need to tell you something, and I don't even know why I'm telling you or if I should."

She reached across and put her hand back on mine. "So serious, Michael?" she teased.

I told her about the impulsive night I had spent with Angela. As I spoke, her smile faltered, and she returned her hands to her lap. When I was done, we sat in silence. From across the room, the waitress caught my eye and raised her eyebrows, Did we need something else? I shook my head.

"You didn't have to tell me that, no," Molly said. "It isn't really any of my business what goes on between you and your wife."

"Ex-wife," I corrected.

"Sure, whatever. Let's go, okay?"

She walked out in front of me. As I held the door for her, I saw that her cheeks were colored. I felt like an ass. I had intended to absolve myself, and I had only broken things further.

Back at my father's house, she asked where the clean sheets were kept. I didn't know, and we hunted closets until we found them.

"They're clean," I said, "but it might have been twenty years or so since they were last taken out of this closet."

She shrugged and gave a tiny smile. She didn't hold my look. She kissed my cheek and headed off to one of the spare bedrooms. I looked at the door when it was closed behind her and figured I should have kept my mouth shut. I turned and went to my own room at the other end of the hall.

It was the bedroom of my childhood and my youth, but there were no objects or mementos inside that reminded me of the years I had slept there. I lay down and was surprised to find that the contours of the walls and ceiling were as familiar to me as if they were an ancient map of a country I had once lived in.

I wasn't sleepy and reached over to the table beside the bed to get a book. I paused, thinking I had heard music from outside my room. I swung my feet off of the bed, padded over to the door, and quietly opened it. The hallway was dim, illuminated only by a light that had been left on in the bathroom. I went to the top of the stairs and looked down into the darkened space below, listening. There was only silence.

At the far end of the hall, Molly's door was cracked open and she was looking out at me. I started to speak, but she shook her head almost imperceptibly and gently closed it.

CHAPTER 14

Sam and Jenny Latta,
West Berlin, Germany, Monday, May 20, 1957:

"You sound American," he said.

"Really?" she asked. "What exactly is that, anyway?"

"Do you have menus?"

"I do," she said, "but I have a better idea. Let me tell you what you're going to have."

She told him what his dinner was going to be. None of it meant anything to him. He had come in here by accident, looking for somewhere else.

The restaurant was a single room of mismatched tables and chairs with an open kitchen at one end. There was a clock that said it was four-thirty in the afternoon. The place was nearly empty, but five or six people bustled around the kitchen. The air was full of excitement; the place vibrated with the evening that was coming.

He had wandered to the counter that marked off the kitchen when he came in. There was a stool beside it, and he pulled it up to sit down. He wanted to talk to the woman some more. She had dark hair and clear eyes, and he thought that he had never been around anyone as beautiful.

"My place can be expensive," she said, smiling. "Are you sure you can pay?"

He thought about it and nodded. He had cash in his pocket. He didn't much worry about money one way or the other.

"If you don't have enough, it doesn't matter," she said. "You'll run a tab anyway."

"I haven't tried anything yet. You think I'll be back?"

She nodded. Her eyes were luminous.

"This is your place?" he asked. "You're awfully young."

"I'm not young at all," she said. "I've always been here."

"What's your name?"

"Jenny."

"I'm Sam," he said, and she nodded as if she already knew.

Over her shoulder, and behind the concentrated activity of the kitchen, windows opened onto the ruined city. Anything that pretended permanence here had been erased by the bombers.

"What do you call your place?" he asked.

"This is the Blue Moon," she said.

She gestured to a piece of artwork hanging on the wall near her, as if to explain. She moved back into the kitchen to resume her supervision. The cooks seemed to move in orbit around her, conscious of her and, in the most casual way, eager to please her.

Behind him, a group of people came in, and he turned on his stool to look at them. Tables had been pushed together, as if by magic, of their own accord, not having needed anyone to actually touch them. While they were seating themselves, a man detached himself from them and came to the counter.

He wore the roughest work clothes, but called out instructions to the kitchen. The diner was very particular about the preparation of their food, but his manner was friendly and familiar, and he spoke as one connoisseur to another. The chef at last approved, and the woman nodded. Much of it seemed to have been for her benefit.

Finished, the man turned and spoke to Sam. "You're going to love it here."

Sam shrugged. He wished that he wasn't wearing a military uniform, but decided it wasn't important. He looked at the picture on the wall. It was a painting of a blue moon shining down on a scene below it. He squinted. The details were hard to discern, but he had a feeling it was a place that he knew. Across the room, the woman looked at him and smiled faintly.

His heart moved, and he thought that he would follow her always.

ℰↄℰↄ

Present Day:

There was no one at the funeral, really. *We aim to live long,* I thought, *and sometimes the reward for it at the end is that everyone we know has already left.* I knew that my father didn't care, but the empty seats made me acutely aware of my own loneliness. I sat on the aisle, a few rows from the front. Molly was quiet beside me, her hand resting on the back of mine.

The dim church echoed softly, emptily, with rustles from unseen movements that such spaces always have. A rack of small devotional candles flickered behind their colored glasses. We were early, and I closed my eyes and waited. When I opened them, there was a woman in the front row, kneeling with her back to us. The moment I spotted her, she rose and turned around. She looked back at me steadily through her veil and then went into the aisle.

She was in dark blue. Her calves and ankles were elegant in silk stockings. On her feet, she wore matching pumps with stiletto heels. Her face was largely obscured by the old-fashioned mantilla draped over her head and shoulders, but I knew who she was. I sat frozen and watched my mother approach.

She inclined her head toward me, and I saw the barest trace of a smile behind black lace. She reached out and grazed the back of my hand with her fingertips as she went by. Her touch was imperceptible, a tingle, the tiniest shiver. The sun from her caress hurt my eyes. I smelled grass, leaves, and plants. I heard running water and faint music.

Then as quickly as it came, it was gone, and so was she. I was back in the empty church. Candles flared and guttered as though all of the stained glass windows in the place had been thrown open to let in the wind. It was the only small sign of herself that she left behind.

I glanced at Molly beside me. I saw the startled look on her face and realized I was squeezing her hand, too hard. "Did you see her?" I murmured. My voice felt like I hadn't spoken in hours.

She nodded and then cast her eyes across the church, indicating that I should look at something there.

Another woman was being handed into a pew across the aisle from us. Heavy and stooped, she impatiently shook off the man who was helping her. Her hair was a bright shade of blonde, and her striped dress and heavy makeup were far too young for her. When she was seated, she looked fixedly at the front of the church.

"I think that's Wanda," Molly whispered. "Has to be. That's her son. What's she doing here?"

I shrugged. I felt a flash of rage. I had no idea of what

her role was in this, only that she had hated my father and scared him badly. I was baffled as to why she was paying her respects at his funeral.

The man who had helped her turned and looked at me.

His eyes were almost colorless, a startling pale that conveyed no hint of what was alive behind them. He was a light-skinned black, and the yellow cast of his features seemed to bleed into his hair and the whites of his eyes, making him appear curiously monochromatic. His shoulder muscles strained against the navy sport coat that he wore over his T-shirt in deference to the occasion. A blue tattoo crawled up from his collar, ending below his left ear. I watched him walk to the rear of the church and take a place against the back wall, arms crossed.

"Are you going to talk to her?" Molly whispered.

"Sooner or later. Not here."

There was noise as the coffin was wheeled in. The service was about to begin.

An older man appeared beside me. He placed one hand on my shoulder and shook my hand with the other without saying anything. His eyes and face were kind. He was well-dressed and smelled like soap. His kinky hair had receded into a tonsure, and the white still had some black shot through it. He released me and squeezed Molly's hand before turning away and taking a seat behind us.

The box gleamed in front of the altar. I had picked it out, not really paying attention. Seeing it now, in a different place, and knowing that it contained what was left of my father filled me with a breathless feeling, not quite panic. The transition from a man sitting in the sun, sipping a rum and coke, to this box in a cold church was too much, too fast.

"I forgot to ask you," Molly murmured in my ear. "How do I know what to do?"

"Do about what?"

"I'm not Catholic. You guys are really active. Isn't there some kind of program that says when to stand and kneel?"

"You're Irish. How can you not be Catholic? Does anyone know about this?"

"Just because—oh, my God—" She cut her sentence short and shook her head.

"Just sit there, Molly. It's fine."

"It isn't fine. It's your dad. I want to be respectful, and I can't just sit here. I'll watch what you do. Give me a nudge when we're about to do something so I can be ready."

Her face was intent and serious, and once again I was caught by how much I loved her, and how hard I worked to avoid the fact. My mood lifted a tiny bit.

"Fine," I said. "If you get it wrong, the ushers come take you by the elbow out to the parking lot. If that happens, wait for me, and I'll find you after."

She colored slightly and looked straight ahead at the front of the church. A moment later, she leaned over and cupped my ear. "You're an asshole, Mike," she whispered.

The laughter welled up, surprising me. I tried to choke it back and covered it with a cough. I had the fleeting that my father would approve of laughter at his funeral.

The priest began to speak the familiar words, expelling my father from his place on earth. It was over with quickly. There was no graveside service, and afterward Molly and I stood at the edge of the parking lot and watched the silver hearse drive away. A cold wind, startling in the early summer warmth, suddenly whipped grit against us. We raised hands to shield our faces, but it died away as quickly as it had come.

The older black man had come up beside me, and

when the hearse had disappeared, he offered his hand again.

"Roy Tull."

The name clicked. My father's doctor. Eli's brother; a boy from the story.

"His doctor, yes—when he was older," he said. "You folks had a different family doctor when you were a boy. More than that. I was his friend, on and off. We knew each other almost our whole lives."

"I don't remember you," I said.

"This is still the South, son." He laughed. His smile was gap-toothed and engaging. "Your dad might have been some kind of liberal school teacher, but we didn't golf on weekends."

I smiled. He looked absently at the road where the funeral home cars had driven away.

"We were more just aware of each other, I think, as years went by. It wasn't until we both got old that we talked much. I looked in on him from time to time and sometimes stayed for a drink on the porch."

"I'm a little upset about the last few weeks of his life," I said. "He came up to Canada to stay with me. He said he couldn't come back here again. There was some kind of serious trouble in his life. Did he talk to you at all?"

"Let's have the doctor for coffee," Molly interrupted. "Don't make him stand in the parking lot."

He smiled at her, and answered me. "I understand you're after some answers. I would be too. I might know a little bit. Follow me to my house, why don't you? You shouldn't have to make coffee for company on a day like this."

Molly looked around. "What about the other people? Not that there are many. Is that Wanda...what's her name, Sutton? Do you know her?"

"Yes, it is, and yes I do," he said, looking at the

church steps where the large man helped the older woman toward the parking lot. "Wanda Sutton and her son Arthur."

I decided to lie. "Any chance you could introduce us? My dad mentioned that she was a good friend of his."

He shook his head slightly. "I don't know about friends. Maybe a kind of friends. She knew your dad as long as I did, since we were all kids. I don't know that she'll want an introduction from me, though."

"Well, I'll do it," Molly said. "Let's invite them for coffee."

She started off and as quickly turned around and looked at the doctor. "I'm presumptuous, aren't I? I shouldn't ask them over to your house."

He laughed and waved her off. "Go ahead, by all means," he called. "You might get your hand bit though." More quietly he said to me, "Wanda Sutton's not likely to have coffee in my house, trust me on that."

I watched Molly cross to the couple on the steps. They appeared to bristle when she approached and then to relax as she spoke to them. I could see Molly's smile and her animation; she wrote on a scrap of paper and gave it to them. The older woman looked at it and put it in her purse. The group of them looked across at us. Beside me the doctor raised a hand in a greeting that was not returned.

Molly walked back and joined us. "She said no. She's not that bad, though." We headed for our cars. "Her caretaker is a little protective."

"Her son," Roy Tull said. "She's probably more his caretaker than he is hers. He's one of those men who are more comfortable in a jail than out. Sometimes if they go into the system early enough, the outside world is impossible for them."

We stopped beside his car, an elderly but immaculate

Lincoln. He got in and spoke to us from his open window. "Follow me. It's only a minute or two from here."

We followed his car as it made its stately way through the streets of Marietta's old section. Every turn was signaled well in advance and executed carefully. The black paint gleamed.

"I like him," Molly said. "There's something very...*decent* about him."

"The doctor? I do too. I never pictured my dad having any friends. Makes me glad."

A few blocks from the square in the middle of town, the doctor turned into a narrow brick driveway. I pulled the rental car to the curb, and Molly and I got out.

"What a beautiful old house," she said to me. "Something looks wrong with it, though, doesn't it?"

The building was terra cotta brick, with dark green shutters. It sat well back on a lawn of St. Augustine grass shaded by magnolias. The plantings were old and lush.

"What is it?" I asked. "What do you see that's wrong with it?"

"It's tilted, I think. It's slanted over."

I looked at the house. It did appear to tilt slightly to the right. The effect was odd.

"I think the lawn is just sloped, Molly, not the house. It is a bit weird when you notice it."

The old doctor crossed the lawn from the drive and met us at the front door. "Saw you looking." He smiled. "House is crooked. One end is sinking. Started having a problem about five years ago."

"Serious?" I asked.

"Yes, underground stream, or some such. Water table on that end rose up. I looked into fixing it, but it would cost more than building a new house. It'll need tearing down someday, but that will be after I'm gone. I waited a lot of years to get this place, and it will see me through the time I have left."

"It's wonderful, it really is," Molly said. "It's an absolutely charming house."

We followed him up the front steps. Once we were inside, the effect was immediately unsettling. Wood gleamed, the light was diffused and lovely, and a clean cool breeze moved the air gently, but there was a just enough slant to distort perception.

"You can't close the doors anymore. A while back the doors that were shut, closets and such, stayed shut. Couldn't get'm open anymore. Open stays open and shut stays shut. So I opened the ones I use and left them that way."

He gestured off to his left. "In through there is my office, consulting room, waiting rooms. There's been medicine practiced in this house for almost a hundred years now, and it ends with me. Shame. The doctor who built this house even did minor surgeries here. His son grew up and followed him into medicine and carried it on. Then it passed to me."

He was still talking when the ghost walked in. At first I waited to be introduced to her, but the old man ignored her completely, and then a sense of her oddness crept into the room. Molly gripped my arm.

The spirit was a black woman in her forties, in flat shoes and a shapeless cotton shift. She was tall, and the ripe curves of breast and hip under light fabric were at odds with her worn face, which was nearly masculine in its angularity. She stopped at the entrance to the waiting room, apparently blocking us from going in. Crossing her arms, she leaned against the door jamb and looked steadily at us.

"This was your family you're talking about?" Molly asked. "Your father and his father?"

Roy Tull laughed. "Not hardly. Not in this neighborhood. This was a white practice. The old doctor took me under his wing when I came back here, fresh out of medical school. Looking over my shoulder, teaching me, was charity at first, his gift to the poor blacks in town, but over the years it got to be something more. I lost my own father when I was young, and the doc never had a child. He never married, had no one else at the end. So he mentored me, and when he died in 1969, he left his practice and his property to me. It's funny, we talk about the 'bad old days,' but I don't think you'd see a gesture like that today. There was more bravery then."

The woman in the door stood still, her gaze switching from Molly to the doctor as they spoke. She didn't look at me.

"I went from poor to rich, just like that. Of course the practice he left me evaporated. No white folks were coming to see me, and I didn't want or need to see them. Not too many of my own patients were going to come into this neighborhood, so mostly I got in my car every day and practiced my medicine across town."

"It's good you kept the place, though," Molly said.

"Oh, I kept it all right. I opened regular office hours here every day for forty years, even if no one came in here until the '80s. Eventually, my mother looked after the front when she moved in with me, watched the phone and rode herd on the magazines in the waiting room. She unlocked the door at eight sharp every day. Times changed, and eventually I started doing most of my practice from here, black and white. This was her domain, though, right up until she died."

He smiled, remembering. "Talk too loud in the waiting room or come in with no shoes and my mamma sat right there behind the counter, glaring at you. I never could get a secretary in here. No one would put up with her."

"How long ago did she die?" I asked.

I felt the ghost's attention shift to me. I didn't look over, but her stare felt unhealthy on my skin. All at once there was a retinal image behind my eyes that popped brightly and then slowly faded.

I saw the branches of a tree with no leaves, a hanging tree, against a purple sky.

"Couple years ago," he said. "Ninety four years-old and she was doing for herself right up 'til the end. She thought she was doing for me, too. Maybe she was. Oh, well—c'mon in. I promised you coffee, and you should have something to eat, too."

We followed him deeper into the house. I looked over my shoulder. The ghost hadn't moved. Her dull eyes stared. She stood and watched us go.

CHAPTER 15

Louise Latta,
Marietta, Georgia, Thursday, June 24, 1948:

The array of bottles on the dressing table was large and varied, with tiny bows around necks, etched letters and cut-glass stoppers. There were small vials in ivory and mint green, clear flasks tinted in sapphires and yellows, crystal flutes full of white creams and amber oils. The boy's mother sat on her wicker stool and looked at them.

She held an addition to her collection, a squat transparent bottle full of a pale liquid that claimed it was "The Royalty of Perfumes." She didn't uncap it. It was enough to hold the thing, come by mail order all the way from Los Angeles, California. The label on the box said it had been sent from an address on Fillmore Street. She wondered if you could see the ocean from Fillmore Street, and if there were, right now, glamorous women going into and out of the door, while men in dark glasses watched and waited for them at the wheels of bright convertibles. People were going places and doing things that hadn't seemed possible before the war. The country was opening up.

She looked into the mirror behind the dressing table.

The solemn woman who looked back at her was never going to go to California, she knew that. She was dark haired and pretty, in a serious way, but at age thirty-three, middle age was encroaching hard, and the possibility of a movie star waiting for her at a curb lined with palm trees was probably gone. She had seen the ocean once, in Savannah, but it was a different ocean, dirty and brown, not the blue of the Pacific. She wished that things had been different for her.

She thought that she had loved her husband, and for the first years of her marriage, everything had been as she expected it should be. It was only in the last while that some sort of longing and regret had settled over her days. It was perhaps the fact of her inability to have a second child that had planted the seed of sadness. Samuel's birth had been difficult. He was the only one that God was going to allow her.

Now there was trouble, and although her husband refused to talk about it and said that it would pass, she saw in her boy's eyes that it would never leave him, or them. Trouble was here for good, and so the nature of her own small secret had changed. It was beginning to flex its muscles, and she didn't resist.

She sat perfectly still for a moment. It was just after nine o'clock in the morning. Although she knew that Sam was out hitting a raggedy baseball with his friends, and Nathan was at work, she checked that the bedroom door behind her was closed. Then she looked at the sidewalk outside the open window, making sure the street was empty, although she was on the second floor and not really visible. The air that came in over the sill was humid and guaranteed the day's heat. It would rain in the afternoon as sure as two came after one.

She wondered what the air in California felt like. Different than this air, she was sure, soft and warm and dry, scented with the ocean and desert flowers.

She set the bottle of perfume carefully in line with its companions, and then she pulled open the dressing table drawer and retrieved a small brown paper bag. The top of it was neatly folded. She set it in her lap and unfolded it, relishing the formality. The bottle that came out of the bag was dark green, and the liquid inside was more precious than any of her other salves and scents. She unscrewed the metal cap. The scraping sound it made as it was twisted free of the glass neck was part of the ritual, and her insides fluttered with excitement.

She never used a glass to drink from. To do so would separate this bottle from the others, and they were all of a kind. All the pretty bottles made her pretty too. The gin smelled feminine to her, and it always tasted like she imagined that her perfumes would taste if she sampled them.

She checked the level of liquid inside against the light. It was more than half full. Good. She tilted the bottle to her lips. The burn in her throat and then her stomach promised that everything would soon be just as it should always have been.

"Everything is fine," she murmured softly to herself. "It will all be fine."

She thought about orange groves, the wind from the sea, neon lights, movie theaters, restaurants with valets in front, and a highway winding its way down the sunny coast.

She was getting deliciously sleepy, and she checked the level again. The liquor was nearly gone, but she had another bottle in the drawer. Until Sam's trouble, a bottle of gin had sometimes lasted about a week, but now she finished one almost every day. She would have to go out soon for more, maybe tomorrow, and there was always a risk of embarrassment or discovery when she did, but that wasn't a worry for now. She had enough to last through the nap she would take until Nathan came home from work, and then the interminable hours of making dinner and washing up and listening to the radio until bedtime. She would slip in here from time to time, but her takings from the bottle would be harsh and hurried, not at all like the lovely ceremony of the morning.

There was enough left in the next bottle to start the next day, and anyway, tomorrow was another day and no concern of this one. She looked in the mirror, smiled slightly, and returned her thoughts to California.

ᘛᘚᘚ

Present Day:

We were ushered into a sitting area. The furniture was old. Everything in the room was tidy, comfortable, and cared for. Tall mullioned windows looked out into a shady garden. Roy left us there and headed for the kitchen. I had no doubt that it was bright and clean, and that all the cabinet doors hung slightly ajar. Molly sat on a sofa with me, her shoulder touching mine. The contact felt good.

"You saw her?" she asked.

I nodded. "She looked mad as hell."

"You think so? I thought she looked scared, not mad."

"Scared of us?"

"Scared of something. She absolutely doesn't want us here, though."

She broke off as Roy came back in, carrying a tray. He dealt out cups and plates and put a coffee pot and a tray of sandwiches on a sideboard. When we were served, he sat down with us.

"I have a question, Mike," he said. "Do you mind if I ask what your dad died of?"

"They just said natural causes, probably heart. I didn't ask for an autopsy. Do you think I should have?"

He sat back and crossed his legs. "Not necessarily, no. I just wondered if you knew."

"Do you know anything from his medical history? Any ideas?"

"Maybe," he said. "It's pretty non-specific, and it might be a little hard to explain. I never saw your dad as an alcoholic, but there was a history of heavy drinking there, and at seventy-four years old that'll start to catch up. He had a bout of pneumonia a month or two ago, and he didn't respond to antibiotics as fast as I would've liked, but it wasn't enough to hospitalize him. He was still fighting it a little bit."

"So not in great shape to start with?" Molly asked.

"Exactly. Not in great shape to start with. He had a history of urinary tract infections going back five years or so, and he had one the last time I saw him. If you're look-ing for a medical cause of death, that's my strong suspi-cion."

I was baffled. "He died of a urinary infection? How is that possible?"

"It's more common in the elderly than you think. It can creep up. Sepsis, infection crossing the blood-brain barrier, et cetera. You don't feel that well, and then you're gone. Bear in mind, I'm saying that if you're *just* looking for a medical cause to pin it on. I think it's more complicated than that."

"Complicated how?" I asked.

"Complicated or simpler, depending on how you look at it. I can tell you that death is still a mystery to medical science. I'm not talking the obvious, like when someone is decapitated in a car crash. I'm speaking in a general way. We don't fully understand the mechanism in our bodies, or in our brains, that triggers death. We don't know why it happens when it happens, what causes the brain to begin the shut-down procedure. It's all carefully orchestrated. The organs fail one by one as they're turned off, the lungs fill with fluid—the process is inexorable once it's started."

He stood up, walked to the window and looked out. "Sometimes a person's brain starts that process, and it doesn't matter much if we know why or not. Our clumsy attempts to save patients cause them more discomfort than anything else."

Looking out at the garden, he fell silent and seemed to have forgotten us.

"Cause discomfort?" Molly prompted.

"Oh—yes. Well, dying people get thirsty. They need fluids as much as they ever did. But the kidneys are the first things to quit, and that glass of water, or the intravenous fluid we know they need, cause bloating and misery when they can't void it. Lack of fluids accelerates the process as poisons build up, so it's damned if you do and damned if you don't. Sometimes the best that medicine can do is get out of the way. We try to make sure they stay comfortable, or unconscious."

"He didn't go that way, though," I said. "He was sudden."

He looked over at me, eyebrows raised. "Yes, I know that. The trigger, the process, can also be quick, but the principle is the same." He walked across the room and put his hand on my shoulder. "Truth is, Mike, I think he was just done. He didn't want to go back home, and he made up his mind not to. He died instead. Simple as that."

"Something was bothering him," I said. "Something terrible that happened to him when he was a kid."

He raised his eyebrows. "Really? I wouldn't mind hearing about it."

"You already know at least some of the story. It involved your brother. There are pieces I don't have."

"I was afraid of that," he said. "Poor Eli just can't rest."

"You and Wanda, the woman at the church, knew my father when he was young. It still seems funny to me, I don't remember either of you, or even hearing about you. Seems odd for life-long friends."

"We crossed paths as kids, but we've been more in touch with each other as we've gotten old. I never had kids, and that put me in a different circle than your dad. Wanda Sutton lived her life in a different circle too, mostly in the city. High school teachers don't socialize with prostitutes and keep their jobs. And she only came back with her son a few years ago, poor woman. Hard life."

"You seemed pretty definite she wouldn't come here for coffee," Molly said, and then glanced over at me. "I gave her your number, Mike, in case she changes her mind."

"Wanda Sutton is the most bigoted woman I know," Roy answered. "Without doubt. She would no more be seen in a Negro household than—"

"But her son?" Molly interrupted. "Her son? He's not white!"

"People punish themselves all kind of ways. Arthur is her punishment. She reminds herself of how much she hates herself every day with that poor man. Whatever he's turned out to be, he never had a chance in this world."

"His father—was he ever around? Were his parents together?"

The doctor looked at her blankly. "No. His last name

is Sutton. He took her name. I'd be shocked if she claimed to know who his father is." He shook his head sadly. "She was a prostitute for years and years, all over the place, but at least some of that time in downtown Atlanta. I'm not gossiping here. Most people know it, and Wanda could care less who knows. I've heard tell she never had a white customer. She catered to black men with a preference for white whores."

"And she's prejudiced?" Molly asked. "That's absolutely crazy."

"You think so?" He laughed. "The power of self-hatred—wallow in what you hate the most. Believe it or not, there aren't that many black families around here that want to associate with an old white street-walker, so it works out. And Arthur came back to live with her, even though he knows she hates what he is. Imagine living like that."

"He looks dangerous," I said.

"Oh, he's dangerous, all right, in a petty chicken-shit way. He's been a small time criminal his whole life, and I imagine he's hurt more than a few people. He's most dangerous to women, children, and old people, though. His kind don't mess with anyone that might mess back, as a rule."

"And he's never been married?" Molly asked. "Never had any kind of normal relationship?"

He thought about it. "He was married for a little while, come to think of it. Tell you a story. The police got called to their trailer one time for a disturbance. In the morning, mind you. Not even lunch time. They both got taken in."

"How long ago was this?" I interrupted.

"Oh, maybe ten years now," he said. "Anyway, Florence, her name was, got down to women's detention and got processed. They both would have been out by the end of the day, but there was a little problem. I guess what with smoking smokes, and smoking dope, and smoking crack, there wasn't a damn thing Florence wouldn't smoke and not a time in the day she wasn't smoking *something*. Her lighter was pretty important to her." He suppressed a smile, remembering. "So she had the presence of mind to hide it before they cuffed her. Just in case she ran across something she could smoke, you understand. Hide it where no one would look. Now if she was going into county jail, they would have found it, mind you, but not city lockup for a couple hours on a domestic cool-down. She got the lighter inside the jail. So then—"

"Wait," Molly blurted. "She hid it *where*?"

Almost immediately she blushed and waved her hands in a *never mind* gesture. The old man regarded her gravely.

"As a doctor," he said, "I would call it her hoo-hoo, but I don't want to throw a lot of medical terms at you either."

He held the solemn look a moment longer and then dissolved into laughter. His hilarity was so infectious that I couldn't help joining him, and in a minute we were both wiping away tears. When it subsided, we looked at a red-faced Molly, who gave us the brush-off. It was several minutes before he could go on.

"She was locked down with a few other women, and this next part isn't really funny. I guess after an hour or two she thought she'd been in there long enough and started hollering for someone to come let her out. No one did, so she set fire to someone else in her cell."

"My God. She set a person on fire?" Molly asked, aghast.

"You bet," he nodded. "The woman was asleep, or passed out, and she lit up her clothes. Luckily, I guess, she wasn't wearing anything very flammable, and when a whole bunch of women started screaming and yelling.

That got the guards in quick enough. Earned her a six-month stay in Metro State prison, though, and with bad behavior it was a year before she was back in her trailer."

I stood up and went to the sideboard. I offered the coffee pot, and he nodded.

"And they're not together anymore?" Molly asked.

"No, no, she's long gone. Probably somewhere in the city if she's still alive. She and Arthur got into another of their disagreements one day and she locked him out of the trailer. He pounded and was yelling at her to open the damn door or he was going to kill her. Finally, he grabbed up a baseball bat laying out in the yard and took a swing at the door. I don't know if he thought he was going to knock it right off its hinges…"

His voice trailed off, and he sat staring at his coffee. We saw his shoulders begin to shake and realized he was laughing again. Molly and I looked at each other and smiled and then laughed with him, although we didn't know what was coming. His joy was infectious.

"Oh, Lord, I shouldn't laugh—there but for the grace—anyhow, he swung at it as hard as he could, and the bat bounced right back off the door and popped him in the knee. Busted it. He fell backward off the steps and lay in the dirt, howling and rolling around grabbing himself. Florence ran outside, picked up the bat, and purely laid a beating on that man, nearly killed him. Good thing for him the police showed up. I don't think any of the people watching were inclined to take up for him."

"And that was the end of the marriage, I guess?" Molly asked.

"That was the end, yes." Roy chuckled. "Arthur went back to live with his mother, and he's there still."

"Poor man," she said. "He looked so tough, so scary, but he's almost pathetic when you hear about his life. He's like a…sad…um…a sad clown."

I nodded agreement. Knowing people's histories often softened first impressions.

"He is a sad clown," the doctor said, suddenly somber. "Funny thing. In the dark, everyone's afraid of a smiling clown. Everyone. No one ever worries about a sad clown, though. We don't look past the teardrops painted on their cheeks and the broken umbrellas they hold up against the rain, and we should. Sad clowns are the ones that'll sneak up behind you and kill you."

CHAPTER 16

Sam Latta,
Marietta, Georgia, Monday, October 7, 1946:

The sheriff stood with the boy at the front door. The boy's mother pulled it open and stood with her hand against the screen, as if she were braced for a strong wind.

The sheriff took his hat off. "I've brought you your son, ma'am," he said. "He's been telling me a story. I think I'd better come in."

The woman stood aside, and they filed in. The boy looked around, unsure, seeming more like a guest than someone who lived there. He was thinner than he had been, and there were dark smudges under his eyes.

"What is it?" the mother asked, her voice rising. "What's wrong?"

The boy's father appeared. Home from work, he had been washing for supper, and he stood in his shirtsleeves, drying his hands over and over with a small towel.

"Evening, Ben," he said.

"Nathan." The sheriff nodded. He looked down at the boy. "Go along in," he said. "I got to talk to your folks now."

The boy trailed up the staircase in front of them, pausing once to look back over his shoulder before he left their sight.

The sheriff turned his hat in his hands. "We have a problem," he said. "Your son came to see me, Nathan. You keep a pistol in the house. Do me a kindness and check on it?"

The father went to his office and checked his desk drawer. When he returned, he offered the gun, butt first.

"No, I don't want it," the sheriff said. "Lose it."

"Lose it?" the father asked. He feigned bewilderment, but he knew.

Ben talked for less than a minute. When he was done, he raised a hand to quiet the parents' protests. The mother had her hands to her mouth, holding her composure by the thinnest thread. The father looked at the gun in his hand, as though it had come to life and was showing teeth.

"I'm not going to do a thing," the sheriff said, "unless I'm forced to. Done is done, and I'll be damned if I see this mess stirred up again. You're going to do your duty as parents and citizens and make sure your boy doesn't tell any more tall tales to anyone else. Anyone. Ever. Do not make me deal with this. Are y'all understanding me?"

The mother said nothing, staring and unaware of her own hands, which were crawling across her bosom, touching collar and buttons. The father nodded once, his mouth a grim line. He was clearly frightened and glanced at the stairway where his son had disappeared.

"Yes, we understand," he said. "We'll make the boy understand too."

"You best do that. If you don't, or can't, I think you'd do better to load your car and leave the county."

So it happened. The boy was dismissed and hushed, and the secret of the kiss grew larger and larger. The possibility of its escape became its authority. It was passed along through blood and marriage, and grew powerful with the passing years, even as its origins faded like an old photograph.

ᥱᢀᥱᢀᥱ

Present Day:

Dad's lawyer had an office off of Marietta Square, on the third floor of an old red brick building. Molly was with me when I went to see about my father's will. The lobby was cool and dim and had green linoleum on the floor. It smelled old. There were a couple of dusty plants in large pots. I rubbed one of the leaves. It was cloth, and my fingers came away grimy.

"Why are you touching that?" Molly asked.

"I just wanted to see if it was real."

"How could it be real, Mike? There's no light in here. Anyway, does it look like anyone in this building would remember to water it?"

Smiling slightly, she headed for the elevator and pushed the button. It didn't light up, and the floor display above the double doors was dark, too. We look for the stairs.

"I have trouble imagining Dad having a lawyer in the first place," I said. "But if he needed one, trust him to find this place."

"Was he the typical absent-minded professor?" Molly asked from behind me on the stairs. "Head in the clouds?"

"No, not really. He was disdainful of customs, and a little bit cheap. Spending money on a lawyer would have seemed stupid to him." We stopped at the third floor landing, and I pulled open the door. "He didn't really fit in. High schools are like jails, or the military, or any other institution where the people in them don't much want to be there. They need rules to exist, and he didn't much care about rules. He didn't defy them. He just didn't care about them."

"His classes must have been chaos," she said.

"That's the thing. They weren't. He didn't put up with any bullshit. He didn't pay attention to rules for students, and you knew right away that he didn't care about rules for teachers either. If you didn't want to be in his class, if you weren't engaged, he threw you out and not let you back. He couldn't have cared less what your parents or the school administration had to say about it."

We reached the door we were looking for. It had a frosted glass insert, with gold and black letters, like something from an old movie.

"He treated kids like adults, and he never negotiated with them. It wasn't a pose. He didn't waste time with stupidity, and it was part of his reputation. Kids really liked him, mostly. The administration didn't, but they put up with him."

"Was he the same way with you at home?"

"I don't know, Molly. He didn't notice me, mostly."

"And your mother?" she asked. "She taught at the same school? Was she the same?"

"No, she was a lot younger than him. She taught languages. French, Spanish. Most of her training was music, so I don't really know why she didn't teach it. She didn't really have the patience for teaching, period. She was too...romantic. She liked living in Europe. Georgia and everything about it, including me, probably seemed temporary to her."

"I'm sure you weren't temporary to her, Mike. Do you have any more pictures of her? I didn't see many when we were looking through your dad's stuff."

"Sure, at the house, I guess. There should be more. Why?"

"I want to know what she looked like," she said, "without the veil."

Robert Crider's office was a throwback to the South of my childhood. The floor was dark linoleum, the furniture was chrome and vinyl. The secretary who looked up at us was middle-aged and overweight. Although sleeveless, her dress looked hot and uncomfortable. When I identified myself, she checked her own handwriting in a large appointment book and pursed her lips disapprovingly. She reluctantly gestured to a settee against the wall. Molly and I sat. There was a large ashtray in a metal stand at my end.

The woman had an old computer on her desk, but the monitor screen was dark. She tapped on an electric typewriter. A floor fan behind her desk swiveled back and forth. When it reached the end of its sweep, it buzzed and clicked before it started back the other way. It hardly seemed to stir the air. There were piles of paper on every surface around her. I wondered if the fan had a higher setting would it create a snowstorm of deeds and certificates and records that could never be sorted out.

When enough time had passed to suit her, she stood up, opened the door to the inner office, and went in, closing it behind her. She came back out and sat down. The telephone rang, and she answered it and consulted some kind of a large ledger while she spoke. Finally, she hung up and looked over at us.

"Mr. Crider will see you now."

Molly and I looked at each other. I shrugged, led the way to the inner office door, and opened it. Roger Crider sat inside, looking at us expectantly. His hands rested on top of his desk, which was completely empty. It was the only clean surface in the room. Like his secretary, he had files stacked everywhere, most full to overflowing and contained by elastic bands. Four chairs faced his desk. Two were unoccupied by paper records and we sat down.

He suddenly stood up and reached awkwardly across his desk to shake our hands. He was tall and slightly stork-like. His white collar was loose and his graying hair needed a trim.

"So what can I do for you folks?"

"Sam Latta," I said, and when he looked blank, I prompted him. "I have an appointment about his will."

He raised his eyebrows and regarded me. Then suddenly, he stood up, crossed quickly to a filing cabinet, and pulled open a drawer. When he didn't find what he was looking for, he threw open the door to the outer office and left. I wanted to laugh and glanced over at Molly. Her face was serene, and she studiously didn't return my look. After a minute, he came back in, sat down, and opened a very thin file.

"Samuel Latta," he said. "I am his executor, which you may or may not know. Beneficiaries are, equally, Michael Latta and Angela Trevethan. The two of you, I take it."

"No. Angela Trevethan is my ex-wife," I said. "She's in Canada. Does she need to be here?"

He looked up from the file at us. "In this case, no, not really," he said. "There isn't much to talk about. There will be little to disburse, if anything."

"Well, not much," I said. "The house, car, whatever he had in the bank. We won't be disputing anything, though. The money isn't that important to either of us. I just need to wrap up his affairs, and get home."

"It's not going to be entirely that simple, I'm afraid. I've taken a preliminary look at things, and Mr. Latta's situation has changed significantly since this will was drawn up. Let's see, he amended it, ah…six months ago,

give or take, to include Ms. Trevethan as equal benefi-
ciary."

That was about the time our divorce had been final-
ized. My father had loved her and blamed me, rightly
perhaps, for the divorce. If he had changed his will, I was
surprised that he had left me in it.

Still, I was glad that his relationship with Angela had
survived our split.

"The house is heavily mortgaged. He's also borrowed
heavily against it, secured line of credit." He turned a
page, and shook his head. "You need to understand that
my first duty is to satisfy the claims outstanding against
the estate. To simplify, you and Ms. Trevethan will divide what's left after those are paid."

"You need to back up. He hasn't owed anyone a penny
in years."

"I'm surprised, given current economic conditions,
and the real estate market right now, that any bank would
let him get in this deep. There's also credit card debt. His
bank accounts are virtually empty. There may, of course,
be things that I don't see right now, but to be honest, his
pension income wasn't enough to meet his obligations,
let alone provide money for him to live. I'm sorry to give
you such bad news. You must be very disappointed."

"That house was paid for years ago," I said. "When I
was a teenager. When my mother was killed, he used the
insurance money to pay the mortgage off completely. I
don't understand this."

"When I last went over things with him, he was comfortable, in a modest way. Whatever's happened, it was
recent. I just haven't discovered what he's done. If he's
made a major purchase, it will come to light. There might
be a significant asset we haven't seen yet. He didn't dis-
cuss anything like that with you?"

"That doesn't make sense," I said. "He was frugal to

the point of being cheap. A year ago his old car threw a connecting rod. It would have cost ten times what the thing was worth to put in a new engine. Angela had to read him the riot act to get him to buy a replacement. He was going to walk everywhere. As it was, I think he spent a thousand bucks on a ten-year-old beater to get around in."

"Well, he's disposed of a significant amount of capital somewhere, and relatively quickly," the lawyer said. "He's close to penniless. A pension check and his Social Security every month, but a mountain of new debt. I don't know what to say."

"His money's all gone," I said dully.

"It appears that way, yes."

I shook my head, thinking about the phone messages, and about Wanda Sutton's history of extortion. "He was being blackmailed. It all makes sense now."

Beside me, Molly nodded. She was thinking the same thing.

"Why do you say that?" the lawyer asked.

"He came up to stay with me in Canada. He was terribly upset, looking for help. He was getting around to telling me about it and died before he finished. He was frightened by something that was happening down here. He said people were angry and out to get him for something he did a long time ago. We found threatening phone messages on his machine." I was getting more and more angry. "He was being blackmailed. That's why his money is all gone."

The lawyer was shaking his head. "Blackmailed about what? A scandal? He was an old man!"

"Something happened when he was just a kid. He felt bad about it apparently and tried to make amends. It blew up in his face."

He looked out of the window, lost in thought. "It does

seem to fit the facts," he said. "Preposterous as the idea is, it explains some things."

"The woman who I think was threatening him has a history of blackmail. She went to prison for it once."

"This is dreadful," he said. "I'm not sure where to go with this."

"Can I even sell the house? Am I free to do that?"

"You might be better off to let the creditors take it, to be honest. If you assume any part of your inheritance, you'll assume the whole thing, including the debts, and unless the money turns up, it may end up being painful."

"Do I have time to think about it?"

"A little while, of course. You'll protect your own position if you don't remove anything from the property. A few photographs or mementos no one will mind, but anything of value should be left alone, I'd say. If you decide to walk away from the situation, it could be made out as theft later on."

"So I probably shouldn't even be in the house?"

He seemed to shake off the formality he had been trying for. "I think," he said, "that you'll end up wanting to get out of Dodge on this one. The more distance you put between yourself and this estate, the better for you. So, no, don't live in that house. If it means a lot to you, it'll probably be cheaper to buy it from the bank after they put it on the market than to protect your interest in it now."

"Time to go on home then, I guess," I said. "Let's lock the damn place up and go home."

"Do you yourself know why he was being...extorted?" he asked.

I shook my head.

"So taking this to the police could be ultimately embarrassing," he said.

"How so?"

"There was something he was willing to pay everything he had to keep secret, apparently. If you go to the police and they uncover it, it could be...regrettable. How can you know?"

"Good point," Molly murmured.

We sat quietly, thinking about it.

"I have a suggestion, if you like," the lawyer finally said carefully. "I employ an investigator from time to time. A young woman. She's awfully smart about things like this. A little bit...unorthodox, perhaps, but very, very good at what she does."

"An investigator?" I asked. "Like a private eye?"

"Exactly," he said. "Although these days, more of it's done on computers than standing in shadowy doorways. Employing her to see what became of—well, pretty much everything your father owned—may perhaps set you at ease, and it might preserve your father's memory."

"Go for it," I said.

"Unless things change dramatically, the estate won't bear the expense. She'll bill you directly, and that can add up significantly if it takes very long. I don't know if perhaps you want to approach your ex-wife about sharing the cost. It's her inheritance money that's missing, too."

"No, do it. Get her started. I'm not worried about the cost. I just need to know what happened. I kind of made a promise to my dad. I'll take whatever help she can give me. What's her name?"

This time he didn't have to consult any notes. "Cotton. Her name is Sydney Cotton."

"Tell her she can start by looking into the death of a boy named Elijah Tull. Eli. I think it happened in the summer of 1946. Everything that's going on is tied into it."

"Tull." He wrote it down. "Elijah Tull. 1946."

The lawyer stood up. He shook our hands again when we left.

CHAPTER 17

Nathan Latta,
Cobb County, Georgia, Friday, October 1, 1948:

Water moved, muddy and slow, beneath the bridge. A man got out of a maroon 1937 Ford coupe, walked to the edge, and dangled a pistol over the rail.

He wore business clothes and might have been taken for a police detective, but there was a furtiveness to him that belied that first impression. He was there to get rid of the gun. He stood, bouncing its weight gently in his palm, as if undecided if he should release it into the current below him or not. The pistol felt poisonous, and he wondered if it carried a memory with it, a cold inanimate realization of what it had done.

The man sold ball bearings, or at least he had. Bearings were his bread and butter, although his company carried other things, too. His territory extended south of Atlanta, as far away as Macon and Augusta. The war had to be fed, and it ate all of the new machinery that North America could produce. But the continent still had to struggle on with its daily economies, making do with what could be patched and repaired. The bearing business was good, and Nathan Latta had done reasonably well for himself.

His prosperity pained him, though. He had been old enough at the outbreak of the first war to understand the concept of honor, of duty, and of personal sacrifice and heroism. He watched the young men leave, dressed in olive, and waited anxiously for his turn. He was still too young to go. His oldest brother, ten years his senior, left and did not return, choked by gas and lost in the blackened mud in France. His mother did not recover from the loss of her first child, and Nathan imagined in some vague and childish way that he would put his family and his childhood right when he was called to wear a uniform of his own.

That call never happened. Hitler came too late for Nathan Latta. He applied at recruiting stations throughout Georgia, but he was too old. The nation threw an entire generation of young men at the monster overseas, but it didn't need him. He wore a tin helmet and carried a flashlight as a blackout warden. It was all the duty he could do, and it embarrassed him, for he didn't know the nature of duty, which required the least as much as it did the most.

When the war ended, it removed the acuity of his guilt but underlined that there would be no wars, no more chances for him.

The end of the war also put a dent in his income. America rushed to stores and showrooms to buy the first brand-new cars and electric iceboxes and radios it had seen in years. The country seemed to roll in post-war wealth. Stalin was fumbling the gate latch to let his dogs out, but he was not yet news, and from New York to Oregon it seemed that the horizon showed nothing but the promise of a new age. The war-tired nation had no more appetite for making do, for waste not, want not, and the bearing business suffered, as failed machines were scrapped rather than fixed.

Nathan, who felt like a failure for prospering during the war years, began to actually fail as the rest of the country was getting rich. By the time that Ben Early had pulled into the drive in his radio car, bringing Sam home, the sense of failure had begun to override almost everything else.

Nathan looked back at his car, parked at the other side of the bridge. He had brought it home when Sam was a toddler and had waxed it with his son's outgrown diapers, laundered to rags, every weekend. Now the car sagged on its springs and needed another valve job. He hoped that it would get him where he was going. He had a sense that he would be walking long before he decided that he had gone far enough.

He left no note for his wife and son. It was better if they didn't know exactly what had happened to him and, anyway, he had nothing to say. They were broke. His wife's sister would take her and the boy in.

His son had withdrawn. The woman had retreated into her bottle, though she brightly denied it when he brought up the matter of her drinking.

He had taken a mistress in the last two months, a plain young woman who worked in the dispatch pool for his company. She thought that they might marry. He didn't love her, and his coupling with her was so far outside of his notion of himself as a man that it had somehow freed him to do this unthinkable thing.

He was also leaving her behind without word or explanation.

At last he willed his fingers to open. The gun left him and dropped twenty feet to the brown water. The splash was tiny, and it was gone. Nathan shook his head once, walked back to his car, and got in. He sat still for a full minute before the door clunked closed and the engine ground to life. He drove away west.

Present Day:

Back at the house, Molly held a framed picture of my mother in her lap. Head bent, she studied it. The photo had been taken on a set of steps, and, in it, my mother leaned over me, holding both my hands. I remember being told that it was taken on an Easter Sunday. I appeared to be about a year old.

"That's her," I said.

"She's beautiful. I couldn't really see her face under the veil."

"It's called a mantilla," I said.

"What's a mantilla? Where do you get them?"

"It's a lacy drape that you wear like a shawl and can pull up over your head, too. Mexican women use them to cover their heads in church."

"Well, I want one. It's the sexiest look I've seen in a while. Like a nun—chaste, but chic, too, you know? It's going to be my resolution to start wearing hats. I like them and I only have baseball hats. A mantilla or two would be a good starting point."

"I like hats, too," I said. "On you, not on me."

"I saw her eyes. She looked over at me. Flat, no shine. Definitely a ghost. Startled the hell out of me. I don't think I've ever had one sit right in front of me and I've had no inkling, no premonition. She felt natural. She was younger than this picture, though. Younger than me. It would be nice to pick your age and stay that way." She passed the photograph over to me. "How old was she when she died?"

"She had just turned forty."

"I would have said she looked closer to thirty when I saw her. So now," she said, "you have to figure out what she's doing here."

"She probably came back to pay her respects to my father."

"That's silly," she said. "Why would a dead person go to a funeral? Presumably she can see your dad on the other side. She didn't come here to view his body. She sat right in front of us. She must have something to tell you."

"Maybe goodbye," I said.

"She already said her goodbyes," Molly said simply. "Think like a woman. Mothers take care of their children, always and forever. You're still her child. She came for a reason, probably to make sure you knew you hadn't been abandoned."

"Or maybe to warn me about something."

"Maybe so," she said. "If you think she's here to warn you, then you'd better start listening to her, Michael."

ぐつぐつ

I got a call from Sydney Cotton, the private investigator. Her voice on the telephone sounded very young.

"First of all, I'd like to get into the house," she said, without much preamble.

"No problem. We're staying here."

"I want to turn the place upside down, go through every scrap of your father's things."

"I don't have any problem with that. Crider's the executor; he should have given you the go-ahead without waiting for my permission."

"He did, Mr. Latta," she said quietly. "I'm trying to be decent about it. Mr. Latta was your father, not his, and I don't want to hunt through his drawers without it being okay with you."

"Call me Mike, please. I'm not saying that to be friendly. There are too many 'Mr. Lattas' in this conversation."

She had a nice laugh. "You got it. Mike. Sydney. Let me tell you what I have so far. You said I should look at Elijah Tull, and I did. It's quite a story. On the surface of it, you might think it would have been a legend, a civil rights rallying point. When you hear the whole thing, though, it doesn't serve anyone. It's a tragedy that ends up not really having a point. There's no real moral to the story. Just better forgotten. I grew up here and I don't remember it ever being mentioned."

"I grew up here too, and it's all news to me. I don't remember hearing a thing about it."

I could hear her shuffling paper.

"There are multiple sources on this. We have records and transcripts of a grand jury prelim trial, and a separate capital murder trial. All of this is on paper; I'm pulling out one file after another, which leads to more. I should tell you most of this all took place in Milton County, which didn't officially exist after 1931. In practical reality, it was still a functioning county government in the '40s. I mention this because I seem to be running back and forth between Cobb and Fulton county courthouses to get records. None of this is on computer. It's time and miles. I'm running into a lot of time on this. Time is money for you."

"I don't care about that," I said. "I'll get you paid to date and keep it current."

"I wasn't implying that I was worried about it, just keeping you informed. Instead of giving you chapter and verse, I've made up a timeline of whatever events seem to be related. I'll just tell you like a story, okay?"

"Shoot. I'm all ears."

"All right. July 2, 1946, a Tuesday, this came up in the

grand jury trial—okay, I'm not going to do this, I said I wouldn't—"

"Do what?" I asked.

"Cite sources, say what I found where. I'll just tell it. There was a general store on Barne's Ferry Road, semi-rural, outside of Marietta. There was an incident behind the store. There's an allegation that an eleven year-old girl, Wanda Sutton, had indecent congress with a boy the same age, Elijah Tull. The girl's father, Floyd Sutton, owner of the store, came upon the scene and the boy fled. Sutton was able to run down the boy's identity pretty quickly by questioning the store's Negro customers."

I rummaged in a drawer and found a pen and some old bills to write on. She went on.

"The next day, July third, late at night, the father and his wife's brother, a man named Will Davis, went to the Tull house and removed the boy from his home, in front of his family."

"Did you get a sense of exactly what the indecency was?" I asked. "Indecent congress?"

"Yes, he kissed her on the mouth."

"All of this over a kiss," I said.

"Mr. Latta, you're from the South. Things might be different now, but you must have enough tribal memory to understand how serious it was. If this had gotten out, the Sutton family was ruined. The daughter was sullied, dirty. The family was shamed. And if you think this was just a white thing, think again. There's an element of the local black community that would have been gleeful over it and their gossip potentially far more vicious. The whites would have whispered, the blacks would have been openly contemptuous. The Suttons were facing disgrace."

"I'm ashamed to say that I agree," I said. "They could never have lived it down."

"Important," she said, "because monstrous as what those two men did to an eleven year-old boy was, they may not have been monsters. The pressure of the situation was intolerable."

"Awful," I said.

"Yes. On July tenth a boy's body was found in a field. It had been badly flooded the previous month and the crop ruined. It was still a muddy swamp. The body was covered in mud. He was identified by his clothing, and by his father's watch. The boy was allowed to wear it from time to time, and he had it on when he was taken. His face was too mutilated to be recognizable. He had been beaten badly and shot in the head."

"Severe head injuries?" I asked.

"I saw the coroner's pictures, thankfully in black and white. I'm worried they'll give me nightmares for years. The cranial pressure from the head shot, the beating and a week of decay—oh my God. His head was like a big gray basketball. It looked like a screaming basketball, because his mouth was stretched open sideways, his jaw was broken so badly. Gray skin in tatters, and no eyes, just holes in the mess."

"Jesus," I said and meant it as a prayer.

"The Tull family, father, mother and a older brother were all present when the boy was taken. They knew the storekeeper well and identified him to police. The men claimed they took the kid for a drive and talked to him about proper respect for a white girl. They admitted to slapping him, but said they dropped him on the road to his house, basically unharmed, an hour or so later. It was a lie. He was never seen alive again."

"They were arrested?"

"Sutton and Davis were picked up and charged, yes. Testimony and deliberation was all over in one day, July twenty-second. The grand jury passed over charges and freed the two."

"How the hell does that happen?" I asked.

"Simple. The boy's body could never be positively identified. You can't bring a murder charge without conclusive evidence that there was a victim. This body was an unknown male child killed by persons unknown. For the purpose of a murder charge, there was no reliable ID of the victim. Remember, no DNA, no dental records, no fingerprints. Were patched overalls and a cheap wristwatch good enough ID?"

"It was enough for his family to claim him and bury him."

"For his mother, yes. For the jury, no. Couldn't prove it was Eli Tull, couldn't prove that Eli had been murdered. The defense lawyer suggested he was off picking crops in Mississippi, hiding out. Davis and Sutton walked."

As the story came clear, I was thinking about the boy that was my father, somehow caught up in the middle of this horror. It was breaking my heart.

"It gets worse. A reporter for *Look Magazine* interviewed the two men. The magazine was national. They paid six thousand dollars for the true story. It was a fortune, and the men were assured of immunity under double jeopardy. They agreed to tell the truth for the story."

"Disgusting," I said.

"For the record, I agree, Mike. I think you have to realize that the grand jury was reluctant to indict white men in the murder of a Negro—sets a bad precedent, even if it wasn't strictly unheard of. The whites in Milton County would have been mostly horrified by what had happened to a young child, even if they were quiet about it, but civil order had to be maintained. Still, the Sutton family was absolutely ruined. Few whites would speak to them on the street, let alone patronize their store. They were going to lose everything, and six thousand dollars was a real fortune, the only means they had to save themselves."

Molly came in with a cup of coffee and set it within my reach. I nodded my thanks.

"The article was published almost a year later. It was very subdued, for such an explosive subject. I've read it, and it's so vague and confusing. You can infer the truth, though. The two men took Eli to an unused tanning shed. They hung him by his wrists and beat him. They wanted him to admit his guilt and swear to keep quiet. Apparently, he was defiant, and the beating turned into murder.

"The boy insisted for the hundredth time that he hadn't been anywhere near the store that day. Sutton finally lost it. When he stopped, it was too late. They realized that the boy could never recover from his injuries, so Davis shot him in the head to 'end his misery.'"

Her voice shook. This young woman was crying for a boy who had been dead for over sixty years. I liked her for it.

"Eli's father got wind of some of this, although the article was months from publication. I guess the men must've talked. He finally snapped. On a Sunday morning, August fourth, a little over a month after the whole thing started, Jacob Tull took a gun to the general store. It was closed, but Sutton and Davis were inside. He shot Davis in the head, and gut-shot Sutton. The little girl found them. Her father was still alive, but he didn't tell her who did it. It was obvious though."

"Was it?" I murmured.

"Elijah's father, Jacob Tull, was found guilty in record time. He was hanged for the murders on a Saturday, October fifth, only a couple of months after he was arrested. The execution date was moved forward, because there were fears that prison security was being threatened by mob violence, and a petition to move him to a different prison was denied, deemed too dangerous. I can't find anything that supports that. What I do find shows the white community was quite sympathetic to him. Black or white, he was a father who lost a child in a horrible way."

"They didn't usually execute people on the week-ends?"

"I have no idea," she said. "What's weird is that the state of Georgia didn't hang people in 1946. They had been using the electric chair at Reidsville for at least twenty years. Until 1924, hanging was done in every county, and the execution was the responsibility of the county sheriff. Then it all got changed to one location, Reidsville, and they used the chair. It's like they turned back the clock in this one case. I can't see how this was even legal. Hanging him was irregular at best. I don't know if I'll be able to get to the bottom of this."

"The reason for blackmailing my father is somewhere in here, but I don't see it," I said. "I know it was Wanda Sutton, but I don't know why."

"I gather from what Crider told me you're worried that this could embarrass the family?"

"I could care less about that," I said. "I just want an-swers, and you may be a lot faster than the cops."

"So we'll start with Wanda Sutton," she said. "See if we can get her to open up."

"We need to look at *all* the children, Sydney. We have to follow the children that were there for this kiss that started everything. What happened to those kids that day? What was so bad it scared my father to death over sixty years later?"

"Same difference," she said. "It's down to Wanda. The others are dead. They can't tell us anything anymore."

I doubted that was true, but I kept my mouth shut.

That night, I dreamed that I came upon a huge golden

bier, covered with carved figures. Someone stood behind me, out of sight, and told me that it belonged to my father. He had left a gift for me, they said. I walked around to the front of it and saw his dead body stretched out at the base, lying on its side. He looked younger than he had when I had last seen him.

A small package rested next to his midsection. It was a rectangular box, wrapped with purple paper and finished with a thin bow. I came close and reached for it. He opened his black eyes and looked at me. I pulled my hand back.

He stared at me without speaking. I had the vague realization that his mouth had been sewn closed and he couldn't speak. We gazed at each other for a few seconds, and then he stirred and slightly changed his position. His eyes lost their dark focus and closed. He settled and was again still.

"He's asleep," the voice behind me said. "He can't wake up."

"He isn't dead," I answered. "At least he isn't dead. I don't know what to do with him, though."

"He can't wake up," the voice repeated. "He can't wake up anymore."

I was flooded with grief and woke up in my childhood bedroom, my face wet with tears. I had lain in this room, in this bed for thousands of nights. He had always been somewhere outside this door, first with my mother, and then by himself. Now he was gone. If he was anywhere, he was somewhere else. He had left me here, all alone in the house that he had abandoned. He couldn't wake up anymore.

I stared up at the dark ceiling. The shadows there were absolutely still.

Downstairs in the front hall, my mother's piano sounded. Two soft notes floated up to me, and then there was a pause. I held my breath and waited. Finally there was one more, a tiny echo that filled the rooms and lingered on and on. At last, the house was quiet again. I turned onto my side and cried myself to sleep.

CHAPTER 18

Wanda Sutton,
Milton County, Georgia, Friday, October 1, 1948:

The girl sat on a hard wooden chair. Her feet didn't reach the floor. She slid her bottom forward on the varnished seat until she could touch the tiles with her toe.

"Sit up straight!"

The woman behind the desk glared at her and then turned back to her typing. She tapped a steady staccato, punctuated by a bell, and then she slammed the carriage back to start it over again.

The building echoed and smelled faintly of old cigarette smoke and floor wax. The walls were aqua, the ceilings were high, and all the doors had pebbled glass. The door to the inner office behind the row of chairs was open, and Wanda Sutton could hear conversation. It was about her, and she listened hard.

"...must warn you...incorrigible. This may not be like other wards you've taken."

"There's nothing that good, healthy food, and plenty of exercise won't cure. A sound mind in a sound body is how we look at it."

"A firm hand…boundaries…respect."

"…children of suicides, especially…"

Eventually, they came for her. The man who decided what happened to her wore a shiny gray suit with dandruff flakes on the shoulders. He carried a miasma of body odor with him, morning or afternoon, and he punctuated incomprehensible questions to her with long, absent silences. She was glad if she never had to see him again.

The couple who was taking her away was younger than she expected, much younger than her own mother and father had been. The woman wore a tailored skirt and blouse, and the man had a tie held to his shirt front with a gold clip. They looked like children playing dress-up, and they crouched in front of her.

The woman had a large gap between her front teeth, and her tongue poked into the space when she spoke. She sounded like a baby when she talked. "Hello, sweetie," she lisped. "Aren't you pretty? You're coming home with us. Isn't that wonderful? We're so happy to have you."

Her face came close. Her eyes and nose and lips became huge, blocking out everything else. Wanda couldn't breathe. Panic bloomed, and she tried to squirm out of the chair. She was caught painfully under the arm. The young man had her. She twisted her body and began to scream.

"We know what to do from here…"

"…fine once she's settled…"

"…case meeting every quarter…conference in a month."

They went down a broad flight of steps to the glass front doors. Outside was another broad set of stone steps. The woman's grasp was hot, and sweat formed between their palms. Wanda's feet barely touched on the way down. At the bottom, there was a glass light globe on a post, which was supported by a metal lion. She thought that the lion could eat these people and save her, but its snarl was frozen and indifferent. The iron eyes stared at her and seemed to say goodbye, goodbye, and goodbye.

For the rest of her life, whenever she felt that she wasn't alone, and that she might possibly be loved, the image of the lion appeared to her. She was desolate, although she didn't remember where or when she had seen it, or what it meant.

"I never thought we'd get out of there," the man said. "She's certainly a *bad girl*."

"That's just what we wanted," the woman answered. "Isn't it?"

They crossed gravel, headed toward a black car. Wanda knew it was an older car because it had an old-time radiator and spoked wheels. The man opened a rear door and put her in, giving her a push at the last moment. She sat up on the back seat. The horse hair stuffing smelled musty.

The man and woman got into the front. The man took off his hat and put it on the seat between them. The woman sat sideways so she could look back at Wanda. "She is pretty, isn't she? She really, really is."

"You bet," he answered. "Like you said, just what we wanted."

"Don't forget, we have to come back in a month. We have to talk about her progress."

They laughed together, leaned toward each other, and kissed. Wanda felt her bladder loosen, and hot urine soaked the seat beneath her. She was immediately cold as the flow eased.

The woman had broken the kiss and was staring at her, her nose wrinkled. She reached back, snatched up her skirt, and poked at her.

"A bad girl, and a dirty girl," she said. "A very dirty girl."

"Just what we wanted," the man said, and started the car.

ↄ/ↄↄ/ↄ

Present Day:

I tapped on the door of the guest room. "You up?"

Molly opened her door and kissed me a good morning. We were still in separate rooms, but she was markedly warmer. I was hopeful that the specter of Angela would leave us soon.

"That investigator's coming by in a little while," I said.

"That seems so funny. A private investigator. Marlowe, Spade, Spenser. Pistols and trench coats."

"Milhone, Warshawski, and Plum in this case," I said. "Nancy Drew. Sunny Randall. I guess private eyes are still out there, not just in books. Insurance companies and lawyers use them a lot."

On cue, the doorbell rang. I looked out at Sydney Cotton. She didn't look like what I thought a private eye ought to look like.

"Mr. Latta?"

I'm not a big man, and people rarely strike me as small, but she was five-foot-one-on-her-tiptoes little. Red-haired. She set some files on the step and fished in her purse.

"Give me a minute," she said. She lit a cigarette and talked to me through the screen. "I have some more info for you."

"You can come in. Bring your smoke. The house is going to have to be cleaned and sold. It doesn't bother me."

"No. It's repulsive. I actually quit, sort of. I chew spe-

cial gum and wear a patch and try to smoke less. My nic-
otine consumption has at least doubled since I sort of
stopped smoking."

Behind me, Molly laughed and reached around me to
open the door.

"So what do we do first?" I asked.

Sydney took a long pull on her smoke. The coal
looked as long as my little finger. Molly went to find an
ashtray.

"It depends," she said. "What are you trying to do
here? I know you're trying to find out what happened to
your dad, but then what?"

"I hadn't thought that far."

"Well, how we approach this depends on what you
want in the end. If we get some kind of evidence that
Wanda Sutton blackmailed your dad, what then? Are you
looking to recover the money? Do you want her arrested
and prosecuted? What?"

"I don't need the money," I said. "I guess I don't want
her to have what she stole, but that's about all. I want the
truth about my dad."

"Even if you prove this and involve the police, it could
be a long time before you ever see a cent, so it's if that
isn't a big motivation. A couple hundred thousand isn't
nothing, but you can also spend it in a few hours. It may
be gone."

"I just want to know what happened to my father," I
repeated. "I can walk away from the money if I know."

"Well, then, let's go talk to her. I told you I needed to
go through your father's things, but she might have all
the answers we need. We'll do it now. This isn't something we call ahead for; surprise is good."

"You think she'll talk to us?"

"A big part of what I do," she said, "is talking to people who don't want to talk to me. Sooner or later some-

body always says something." She stubbed out her cigarette.

We waited for Molly to finish dressing, and then we
went out to a green minivan parked at the curb. I got in
the back, leaving the front to the women. Sydney removed the key from the ignition and reached across to
unlock the glove box. She pulled out a handgun in a fabric holster and dropped it into her handbag, which was
resting between the seats.

"You think you'll need that?" I asked.

"I've never needed it yet, but I've always had it with
me," she said. "Goes with the job."

"How did you get into this kind of work?" Molly
smiled. "It's really cool."

"I was married to a guy who did it for a living. I
helped out. When we split, I realized that I'd been better
at it than him, so there was no reason to stop."

She drove quickly and well, comfortable behind the
wheel of the van. We entered the freeway that circled the
city.

"You said you're from here, right?" Sydney asked me.

"I grew up here, yes. Haven't lived here in a long
time."

"I know it might seem like that's obvious, your dad
living here and all, but you don't have much of an accent,
so I figured he could have come here later in life."

"I've been gone for more than twenty years, so I kind
of lost it. My ex-wife always said the accent came back
when I was stressed."

"And you?" she asked Molly.

"I'm Canadian," she answered. "Far from home."

"You two are a couple, I gather?"

I cringed at the question. Molly glanced over at me
and smiled.

"We're together," she answered. "You grew up here?"

"I did. Wasn't born here, though. Gulfport, Mississippi. I was born the day Hurricane Camille came through and flattened the place. My father used to say the storm brought me—about three foot tall and nothing but attitude."

I realized that she was older than she looked.

We got off of the freeway after only a couple of exits. When we were stopped at a red light, Sydney pulled a battered street guide from the dash and flipped pages. As the light turned green, she nodded once and tossed it back.

"She lives in Smyrna now," Sydney said. "I hate driving here. Smyrna cops'll stop you for two miles over the speed limit, and with a gun in the car, getting stopped means my day is shot. They check my permit for an hour, like they've never seen one before. I think they'd drive by a rape in progress to stop a speeder."

"The rapist doesn't have to pay a ticket. No profit in it."

"Exactly." She laughed. "Not that I mind stopping speeders—but everywhere else in Atlanta people drive like it's a Nascar qualifier. You go to the grocery store and the person in front of you dawdles for an hour getting through the checkout. They're so slow it makes me crazy. They chat for ten minutes with the cashier who they don't even know, wander out, and say hello to all the people they don't know in the parking lot, and then they get behind the wheel and lay about a city block of rubber leaving. It's just nuts."

She wheeled us into a side street. The homes were mostly small and older, a mix of immaculate and run-down. The street was heavily treed, but like much of the area, there were no flowers, even on the well-tended properties. The red clay was so acidic that people tended to just lay pine straw over anything that wasn't grass.

Sydney pulled over and shut off the engine.

The street sat baking in the heat, quiet except for the drowsy buzz of insects. Wanda Sutton's house was an unkempt bungalow, partially obscured by bushes. A narrow driveway ran up the left side. The laneway between it and the house next door was filled by a new-looking boat on a trailer. The rig was canted slightly over because of a soft tire on one side. A shiny black motorcycle leaned on its kickstand near the street.

"That's a new boat, just about," I said. "Way more than anyone needs for the lakes around here, and it looks like shit already."

She looked across the street at it. "Looks pretty nice to me. You know boats?"

"I live on an island."

"Guess you do, then," she said, and got out. "Hang on a sec."

She was lighting a cigarette as I came around the front of the vehicle. I waited as she took a few drags and then stepped on the butt.

"New Harley too," I said as we crossed the street. "Must be Junior's. What's his name? Arthur? That and the boat have to be his."

"I can't see Wanda riding it, no."

"Guess my dad probably bought it for him."

She looked at me sharply. "If this is about you jumping to angry conclusions," she said, "you won't help me here. This is about trying to get information, not starting a fight."

I raised both hands in a placating gesture. In behind the screen of bushes, the bungalow was dark and worn out. Small air conditioners hummed in both windows. The front porch was screened in, but there was no doorbell button.

Sydney tried the screen door and found it unlatched.

She shrugged and we went in. She rapped her knuckles on the inner door.

It was immediately pulled open, as though the woman on the other side had been waiting for the knock. Wanda Sutton stood there and stared at us without speaking. She wore wide blue shorts and a sleeveless blouse. A dingy bra strap slid down on her upper arm, as though it had surrendered to her pendulous breasts. She had an elastic bandage wrapped around one ankle and bare foot. The bottom of it was filthy.

I stepped forward. "Ms. Sutton, my name is Mike Latta. You knew my father Sam. I saw you at the funeral. I appreciate your being there. I wanted to talk to you about him."

She was still. One hand rested on the door frame. Her chin was up and her eyes were slightly narrowed. There was a curious dignity in her defiance.

"I figured you'd be around sooner or later," she finally said. "You better come in."

CHAPTER 19

Wanda Sutton,
Marian, Georgia Saturday, January 7, 1950

"Wake up!"

A hand grabbed Wanda's shoulder, pinching the skin. She sat up and squirmed away. Another girl's face loomed over her, lit only by the moon in the dormitory window. Her eyes were dark holes. She grinned blackly, and a missing front tooth turned her head into a jack-o-lantern.

"It's time to go," she hissed.

Everyone in the long room was awake. The littlest girls stood silently on their bunks, too frightened to cry, as the group went by. Wanda found herself drawn in behind the last of them, out the door and down the staircase. The first of the twenty or so was racing down the ground floor hallway before the last of them had started down the stairs. They ran, thin cotton nightgowns billowing out behind them, like a posse of ghosts.

Bare feet slapped on the linoleum floor as they passed classrooms, offices, and staff quarters. The tall space was illuminated dimly by occasional night lights set into the high ceiling. Portraits of dead state officials watched them from the walls as they went by. Midway down the hall, a door opened.

"Stop right there! All of you!"

A middle-aged house monitor stood in her door, hair in curlers. The tone of command was impossible to ignore. The wild flight slowed and came to a stop. Tattered night dresses fell limp and came to rest against pale calves and ankles.

The matron's body was thick and strong under her robe. She stepped into the hall and stood there, legs spread and fists on hips. She was used to girls and showed no mercy in her dealings with them. Some of the most recalcitrant had been broken and bent to her will in the privacy of her quarters.

"Stand where you are," she commanded. "All of you. When I've identified each of you, you'll go back to your beds and wait."

The leaders were well up the hall. They turned and started back toward her. The lesser girls retreated a step as the two oldest and strongest approached. The one in front was a sixteen-year-old, her hair blown around her face like a mad corona. Her eyes rolled and snapped.

"What did you say, cunny?" she asked. She came up the hall a slow step at a time. "You'll identify me, will you? Do y'not know me? Bring it here, you old bitch, and I'll introduce myself. You don't know us because to you we're animals. We all look alike."

There was nervous laughter. The matron stood her ground. She was unflinching and took a step forward. Her breathing deepened and her rage settled on the group like a damp blanket. A few of the girls looked suddenly uncertain, blinking in the dim light.

"How dare you, missy?" she choked. "How dare you defy me?"

The younger woman advanced on the older with her

fists clenched. "And how dare you treat us worse than cows in a barn?"

The chief girl's punch flew and connected with a wet smacking sound. The woman raised her hands to her bloody nose.

As soon as she bent, the girls were on her. She fell to the ground. Night dresses whirled and spun above her. She grunted loudly when the first bare feet stomped down.

Up the hall, a door opened and there was a shout. Another staff member was awake. Half the girls broke free and ran toward the voice. Before they had taken a dozen steps, the door slammed closed again and there was a loud clack as the lock was engaged. Bodies slammed, but the barrier held. They finally gave up and returned to the group.

The woman on the floor no longer moved. The blood that her bathrobe didn't soak up began to spread on the linoleum floor.

Wanda stood and stared down at her, mesmerized.

Her reverie was broken by the sound of running feet. She looked up the hall at the departing girls. After one last look at the bleeding body at her feet, she ran after them.

Flying down the long, wide hallway, her heart grew dark and she was filled with black, blind joy. She jumped in the air as she ran, full of the hateful bliss of it. Ahead, she heard glass smash as the art room was breached. They poured inside, intent on the shelves that held tins of turpentine and flammable oils.

Within minutes, the first fires were lit, orange and yellow and blue flowers that blossomed and began to grow in the warm night.

ՇՋՇՋ

Present Day:

We sat in Wanda Sutton's living room. The air conditioner vibrated the window frame and blocked much of the light coming into the room. The space was reasonably tidy, but cramped. A huge flat screen television dominated the wall opposite the window. It was turned on with the sound muted—a make-believe judge silently admonished a defendant. The cabbage smell of old marijuana permeated the house.

Wanda pointed us toward a couch and then disappeared. When she came back, she had made up her face so heavily that I didn't recognize her as the person who had answered the door. She wore a pink and white nylon shift and walked by us uncertainly on her heels. As she went toward the kitchen, I saw that she had removed the bandage from her ankle.

"I wasn't ready for company," she simpered, addressing only me. "I knew I'd see you, but maybe not so soon. I'm just about fixing to have a cold beer, if you want to have one with me."

"No, thank you," I said. "We just need to talk to you."

She stared at me, and her face, reddening in patches, showed how haphazard her makeup was. "You look like your daddy," she spat and turned away. "Suit yourself."

When she came back into the room, she sat down heavily in an armchair across from us. She popped a can of Milwaukee's Best, sucked off the foam, and sat it on the table next to her.

"So what do you want?" she asked. "You have about ten minutes until my son gets home. He don't like people in the house."

"You knew Mr. Sam Latta, obviously," Sydney started.

"Why don't we skip the shit?" She was looking at me.

"You have something to ask me? Speak for yourself. Don't hide behind your women."

I wanted to know why my father had spoken to her at the end of his life. I wanted to know why he told me it had opened a Pandora's Box, and what it was that she had blackmailed him with. I wanted to know why she had destroyed my dad.

I surprised myself with what I said. "I want to know about the kiss."

"Why?" she asked.

She peered at me intently. She didn't pretend ignorance, or ask me what kiss I was talking about.

"I want to understand. Maybe it's time someone did. You're the only one left alive who was there that day." I looked down at my hands. "Maybe I want to know my father, a little bit."

"What did he tell you?"

"Not all of it," I said. "He never got the chance."

She took a long pull of her beer and put it back down. She seemed to reconsider and picked it up for another drink. She gestured to the can. "You sure?"

I shook my head, and Molly spoke up beside me. "I'll take one, thanks."

Wanda hoisted herself up. Molly followed her out and turned in the door. "Glass of water for you, Mike?" she asked and nodded vigorously at me. *Accept the hospitality.*

When they came back, I took a polite sniff of my tap water and set the glass on the coffee table. Wanda sat across from me again and engaged in her beer.

"The kiss?" I prompted. "What do you remember?"

"Oh, I remember everything," she said. "Summer of '46. We just moved here from Mobile. My daddy's daddy had a half-brother, owned the store and was getting out of it—too old. He sold it to us. It was something for my daddy to do. He was just back from the war. He was in the Pacific. When he came back, I didn't really remember him. My mama said it was on account of he came back so different."

"How old were you?" I asked.

"That summer? I was eleven. We was in back of the store, your daddy and I. He was sweet on me, if you must know. So we was sitting around, just talking about this and that, the way kids do. There was a little nigger, been hanging around all day, and he came up and kissed me. I have no doubt at all he had more than that in mind, neither. There was no one back there, and of course I screamed, scared to death. Your daddy just stood there staring, chicken-shit little bastard that he was."

This was already different from the story that I had heard, but I kept quiet.

"Good thing my own daddy heard me scream," she said, "and ran outside to chase him off."

"He did more than chase him off, didn't he?"

She looked at me slyly. Her drawl intensified, a parody of Southern sweetness. "Yes, and that's a fact, isn't it? That's history, as they say. You don't have to be clever to know about that."

She was fat and old, but she had once been a little girl. I tried to summon some pity for her.

"That boy brought it on hisself," she went on. "My daddy was just fixin' to scare some sense into him, and that boy kept denying he was even there. My daddy needed him to see what he done was wrong and own up to it. The rougher it got, the more that little bastard kept denying it. Said he wasn't going to own up to what he didn't do. Said he was home the whole day, was never at the store. Little fucking liar. Even after he couldn't talk no more, he kept shaking his head *no*."

I felt a mounting horror as I realized what she was telling us. Molly spoke for all of us. "Oh, my God," she said. "You were *there* when your father killed him?"

Wanda took another swig, and smacked her lips. "Course, I was. How do you think my daddy identified him? All he saw behind the store was a little nigger running away. I went with them to pick him up."

Them.

"Your uncle was there, too." Sydney said. "He was your mother's brother. Did he live in the same house with the rest of your family?"

"He did live with us. Came to help out with the store. Stands to reason he'd be there, don't it? I was his sweet girl." She smacked her lips at me again. "Anyway, the court said they didn't do nothing wrong. There was a trial and they was free to go, weren't they now? The judge and jury didn't disagree with what my daddy and my uncle did, and they said so as official as you'd ever ask for."

"I think the case was dismissed on a technicality," Sydney said. "They couldn't establish proof that the body belonged to Eli Tull."

The detective had warned me against getting emotional, but it was her own face that was red.

"He was just a little boy," Molly said. "A baby. How could they? How *could* they?" Her hand shook as she put the beer can on the table. She didn't want Wanda's hospitality any more. Her voice shook when she spoke. "The court certainly didn't say that what they did was all right."

"So you say, missy. So you say."

I decided to interject. "Where does my father come into the story? He was there that day at the store, but was he your friend afterward? Did you talk to him about what happened?"

"I didn't have any friends afterward, nor did my mama. We were the shit in this town, until finally she hung herself and I got sent away. All my people gone. As for your daddy, he came to me only a few months ago, didn't he?"

At last. I had sensed as much. This is what we had come for.

"He sat right there, with his crocodile tears, and said he was sorry. Drunk old bastard. Asked me to forgive him for shooting my daddy and uncle like a couple of stray dogs, the nigger-loving son of a bitch."

"Shooting your—" I felt shock run through my entire body. "What the hell are you talking about?"

Molly was staring at me, open-mouthed. The distress in her eyes mirrored mine.

Wanda Sutton slammed her beer can on the table and struggled to get up from her chair. Molly crossed to her and gently pushed her back, taking both of her hands in her own.

The old woman's face was red, and her voice deepened and got rougher. I realized that she was crying.

"He came to confess, but I already knew! *I knew what he did!* I was on the porch of the store when he did it and saw through the window. He ran by me on his way out! I watched him shoot my daddy like a dog! Like a fucking dog! My mama hung herself, because of him! *It was all because of him!*" She had made it to her feet, struggled across the room, and slapped my water glass from the table. "Now get the hell out of my house you bastard, and remember that. I knew what he did. I knew it all along and never told a soul because I was gonna kill him myself. For sixty years, I waited for that day, and the nigger-loving bastard up and died on me before I could do it."

She was screaming. Her cheeks were wet. We all stood up and backed away.

"What the hell?" I repeated, again and again, to myself.

"He killed my daddy! I hope he likes it in hell. Now get out! Get out of my house!"

We got out. A two-tone cream and copper station wagon pulled into the driveway and parked behind the motorcycle as we went down the walk. It was antique, from the '50s or '60s, and looked immaculate. I recognized Arthur Sutton from the funeral. He got out of the driver's seat and glared at us over the roof. His hair was done in cornrows. I was startled at how oddly pale his eyes were. Another man was slumped in the passenger seat. He looked at us impassively through the open window, but did not get out.

"What the fuck?" Arthur asked.

I didn't answer.

"No, thanks," Sydney answered.

In the van, she fumbled her keys out and into the ignition. I saw that her hand was shaking. Molly sat beside her, in tears. I was stunned. My ten-year old father had shot two men to death, and I simply wasn't able to process what was going on around me anymore.

"Well, at least," Sydney said, "we came to the right place."

CHAPTER 20

Sam Latta
Marietta, Georgia, Sunday, August 4, 1946

The boy carried his guilt like a knapsack. He had refused the kiss and the other boy had been forced to take his place. He knew that the girl's father was a murderer. He knew that he himself was partly to blame for the little boy's death.

His own parents were inaccessible. He had been gently shushed and told that the matter was not his concern, nor was it the concern of any folks like them. The black child's murder had taken place across a great divide, in a place he should never go. That grown people had caused the death of a child destroyed something fundamentally childlike inside of him, and his waking world took on the strange and heavy cast of a nightmare.

He took his burden back to the general store, because he had nowhere else to take it.

"Well, well, well," the uncle said. He looked down from atop a shaky wooden ladder that leaned against a rafter, a dead light bulb in his hand. The girl's father stood at the bottom, holding it steady. He stared at the boy with no expression.

"I thought we told you to stay out of here, boy. You don't listen too good, do you?"

"I know what you did," the boy said. "I'm going to tell the police."

The father spoke up. "You're a regular goddamned broken record, aren't you?"

He looked up at the man on the ladder, and the two of them laughed.

"You ever hear about double jeopardy?" the uncle asked. "Double jeopardy. The law says we didn't do nothing at all, and that's true forever even if we say different."

"I'm going to make you tell what you did," the boy said.

"Oh, we'll tell everyone, don't you worry. There's *Look Magazine* people going to pay us to tell the world. We're going to be rich and famous from this deal, so get on out of here before I lose my patience with you."

The boy reached into the pocket of his corduroy pants and pulled out the pistol that had been resting heavily against his leg. He had removed it from his father's desk drawer. It was a revolver, smaller than the Colt the men had used on Eli. The uncle whistled, long and low.

"Lookee here, Floyd," he said. "Look what this boy brung us. What you gonna do with that, son? Shoot us?"

"I'm going to make you tell the sheriff what you did," the boy said.

Now that the gun was out, it felt heavy and useless. The men were unimpressed. This was not what he had imagined, and he felt the tears start.

"You don't listen, do you?" the uncle taunted. "We can tell anyone we like. The sheriff won't do nothing. Now if you don't want to end up like that little nigger, you turn around and get your ass out of here."

"Give me that," the girl's father said.

He let go of the ladder he had been holding and took a step toward the boy, who was badly startled and pulled the trigger. The gun kicked and hurt his thumb. The sound and smell made him think of red paper rolls of caps.

The father was sitting on the floor, looking at him stupidly.

"You son of a bitch!" the uncle screamed and started down the ladder, which swayed dangerously.

Terrified, the boy swung the gun toward him and fired twice. The first shot went wild, into the roof of the store. The second caught the uncle in the crown of his head, and he fell backward off the ladder, knocking cans off a shelf as he came down. He hit the floor hard and bounced once on the wooden boards. He lay on his back and kicked his feet. The boy was reminded of a dog that dreams about running. There was an overpowering smell of shit, and then he was still.

The father had fallen back on one elbow, and he looked up at the boy, his eyes wild with fear. He clutched at his chest. "Help me."

His voice gargled horribly. It sounded like a monster. Terrified, the boy turned and rushed out. His feet thumped across the porch boards, and then flew over the packed clay in front of the store. He ran for his life. The blonde girl came around the corner and stood on the veranda, watching him get smaller and smaller on the dirt road until he was gone.

એન્

Present Day:

"It's nice being here, where it's warm all the time, but I guess I belong up north," Molly said. "I'm ready to go home."

A warm Southern twilight was coming down, covering us like a lavender blanket. We walked along quietly for a little while, past the old homes and churches. An occasional person nodded at us while strolling the other way, or waved from a front porch.

"Do you miss your dad?" she asked.

I nodded.

"I'm starting to. The more I find out, the more I wish I had known him better. I never had a clue."

She held my hand while we walked. The air was soft and sweet. "Maybe he was scared of you, Mike."

I looked over at her, surprised. "Scared of me? Why would he be scared of me?"

"Scared that something terrible might happen to you, and he wouldn't be able to stop it. Scared that he'd fail you, the way he'd been failed."

Lights were coming on in the houses we passed. We were wandering the streets and roads of Marietta, and I had only a general sense of where we were. We matched steps. Molly was wearing bright aqua running shoes that made me smile.

"Maybe," she went on, "all the times you thought he didn't care, he was watching you. Watching from a safe distance. It was the only way he knew how to be."

She stopped and turned me to her.

"You do have a way of seeing right through things," I said.

"I do, yes," she agreed.

"A Southern woman wouldn't be caught dead in those shoes, though."

She pulled me into a long kiss. Her hair was soft under my hand, and she smelled and tasted like everything good. It was a long time before she spoke again.

"Too bad," she said, "for Southern women. They don't know half the things that I do."

CHAPTER 21

Country Mart,
Marietta, Georgia, Thursday, August 23, 1979:

Boo Bixby sat behind the register and alternated glances between the magazine on the counter, the clock on the wall, and the beer cooler at the rear of the store. He'd take a case of cold ones with him when he closed for the night, and deciding on the brand broke the monotony of the endless last hour of his shift. Working here was like being the kid in the candy store. He had the keys to the kingdom.

This was the best summer of his life, although he didn't know it. High school was behind him and college was on hold, although not out of the question. He had a pretty blonde girlfriend, a light blue Pinto, a rented room, and an alcohol problem that was still a couple years away from really being a problem. None of his disappointments had landed yet.

He also had this job. The store's owner pretty much avoided the place, stopping by every morning to sign purchase orders and collect receipts, but otherwise leaving the place to Boo and a ditch pig named Marsha, who called herself the manager. Boo couldn't stand her. She was a few years older than he was, fat and unpleasant and probably destined to work here for the next twenty years. She did the early shift, passing the store to Boo at three in the afternoon. By that time the milk, bread, and slushie rush was over, and he only had to deal with the occasional case of beer or pack of smokes.

Late evening was also when the robbery risk was highest, but it wasn't a huge worry. The Qwik-Mart up the road was a much tastier target. This place was isolated on a secondary highway and mostly catered to foot traffic from the nearby trailer park. If he was held up, the cops would swoop down on the mobile homes. Most of the pot-heads and hookers who lived there would go to jail for one thing or another and they all knew it, so there were seldom problems.

He had heard that the place had been the site of a couple murders years and years ago. The owners had been killed inside the store. It was probably a robbery, but it was before he was born, so he really didn't give a shit. Some kids had told him the locals thought the place was haunted. Thankfully, he wasn't from around here and hadn't been raised on voodoo shit like these people.

The building was ancient, although there had been a few pathetic attempts to modernize it. A couple of crappy self-serve gas pumps had been added to the front, but gas was always a nickel a gallon less just a mile up the highway, so the pump lanes were usually empty. The glass doors opened under the overhang of the original front porch, and the aisles of metal shelves and refrigerated coolers ran underneath the unfinished wood rafters that had always been there. The name on the sign, Country Mart, tried to play up the rustic theme. *Country, my ass*, he thought. *Shit-Hole Nowhere Mart*.

He dished out a soft pack of Marlboro 100s to a middle-aged woman with hair the same color gold as the package. She counted coins onto the counter. He swept them into the till and watched her leave the parking lot on foot. The Electric Light Orchestra was shining a little love on the radio, so he turned it up and went back to his magazine.

He heard a voice from the back and thought a customer had come in unnoticed. He lowered the volume.

"I know what you did," the voice said.

It was a female, sounding neither old nor young. He leaned over on the counter and peered up the beer aisle. Empty. There was a convex spot mirror mounted near the ceiling in the back corner. He thought that maybe he saw movement in its reflective surface, but he could never see anything clearly in it anyway. Stupid thing. He definitely hadn't noticed anyone come in, and he decided he'd better go look at the back. He came out from behind the counter, snapping off the radio as he went by.

"I know what you did," the voice said again into the silence. Whoever it was, she sounded upset, although that might have been his imagination.

He went to the rear of the store. It was bright and empty. He stared blankly. The woman's voice had been quite audible. Suddenly his face cleared, and he headed for the door in the back wall. There was an open space that ran the length of the cooler case, behind the racks of beer and wine fizzies. The cases and bottles were loaded in from behind the display, and someone likely slipped in and was sitting on the floor in there having a secret party. It didn't occur to him that it was something he might someday try, if he were broke and desperate.

He pulled open the access door. There were a few cases of fast movers, Bud and the silver bullets, Coors Light. Why anyone would pay the same money for this new watered-down beer was beyond him, but so far people did. Light beer was one fad he figured would go away before long. Other than that, the narrow space was empty.

There was a single toilet off the back hallway. It wasn't really for customers, but the regulars all knew about it. The door was normally ajar when it wasn't being used. He saw that it was closed, and he relaxed. The owner of the voice was in the can. She had put a scare into him, and if he thought of it when she left the store, he was going to mention that it was an employee-only restroom. Serve her right to embarrass her.

Returning to the front, he looked out the glass doors at the parking lot. Definitely empty. He sat back down, reached for the radio, and froze.

"I know what you did, you little bitch. I know what you did!"

The woman's voice came faster, pitching upward at the end. "I know…"

The last was softer, almost a croak. It was followed by a muffled thump as something fell. Boo hurried down the aisle to the back hall. The door was still closed.

"Are you okay in there?" he called.

He reached out and grabbed the bathroom doorknob, expecting it to be locked. It turned easily. "Hey! Are you all right?" he hollered and eased it open.

The toilet and sink looked back at him. The room was empty.

Boo Bixby suddenly knew that something was behind him. Behind and up above, near the ceiling. He knew he mustn't look up. All at once, he felt very, very cold.

Very, very slowly, he turned himself around, keeping his eyes on the floor. He didn't pick his feet up, but shuffled and slid them. He made his way up the center aisle under the bright fluorescent light, his eyes glued to the linoleum under his shoes. He slid his left foot forward, then his right. The store was deadly quiet. The silence was so complete that he imagined he could hear the blood rushing around his body. Cans and boxes on the very bottom shelves rolled by in the periphery of his vision in agonizing slow motion.

It was so cold that he could see his breath.

At the halfway point, there was a creaking noise above him, and then another and another, as if something heavy—her—was swinging back and forth, suspended from one of the exposed rafters. Boo fought the urge—command—to look up. He finally made it to the front and unglued his feet from the floor. He went through the door and cleared the steps to the parking lot in a single motion. The night air was incredibly warm.

He stood beside the driver's door of his Pinto and gasped. He looked up at the lighted building for several minutes, and then he climbed the steps to the door. He locked it, and then peeled the key off of his ring and dropped it through the mail slot.

A woman's voice came from inside of the store. It had a strange quality, almost as if a crow were talking. "You're a *bad girl!*" it said. "I know what you did, you bad girl!"

The voice went on and on, but the Pinto's tail lights had already receded up the highway until they were out of sight, and there was no one there to hear it.

ᑯᔕᑯ

Present Day:

We walked slowly through the old cemetery. Roy moved between the stones, bent slightly at the waist. He was using a cane today, feeling his age. He stopped here and there, stooping to read an inscription or to pick up a piece of trash. The grass was high and brushy outside the burial ground, but the inside was surprisingly well-tended.

The lot was enclosed by a black wrought-iron fence that appeared to be freshly painted. The area farthest from us was dotted with mature trees, and the headstones there were varied and ornate, red and black and white marble. The section we were in was populated by simpler markers, mostly concrete. The lettering on some of these was nearly gone.

"I've never been by here, that I remember," I said.

"No reason you should have. Not really a white part of the world out here, and the highway doesn't really go anywhere." He gestured at the church. The white paint was peeling from the clapboard in places, but it didn't really look abandoned.

"This started out as a Catholic church," he said, "once upon a time. Catholics don't stand a whole lot higher than black folks do down here, you know, but by the 1920s this part of the county was mostly black, and they left. That's their section over there."

He gestured toward the elaborate monuments at the far end. "I give them credit for leaving their dead behind when they moved the parish. Everyone all together now. All equal."

"Like Heaven," I said.

He looked at me appraisingly. "Something like that, yes. Here's my little brother, Eli."

I looked at the worn cement marker. The weathered inscription read:

Elijah Tull
February 11, 1936 - July 4, 1946
Love Lives On.

"My mother always hated this stone. She tried to change the dates, but they wouldn't let her."

"Change the dates?" I asked. "Why?"

"He was taken from us late on a Wednesday night, July third. He got pulled out of the house and we never saw him again. July third is the last of him for us. They killed him sometime in the early morning of July fourth, and when she saw that date she was reminded of the missing hours. July fourth was a reminder of the time he was lost to us, off being tortured. She wanted the date of death to read July third so she didn't have to remember what really happened."

He pointed at the adjoining headstones. "There's my mama, and my daddy next to her."

"When did they stop using this place?" I asked.

Roy looked up at the old church building. "I couldn't say for sure. Twenty years ago, maybe? The congregation got bigger, and folks started to have a little money. It was a big deal, building the new church. I still have feelings for this one. Survived the Catholics and the Baptists both."

"I'm surprised your mother's here. I thought she died fairly recently," I said.

"She did, yes, she did. The graveyard's still a going concern, for those that want to use it. My father and my mother and my brother are all here, and it's where I'll be, too. There's no cemetery at the new church. The congregation still owns this property. We do basic maintenance on the building, enough it doesn't get to be too much of an eyesore."

He moved off a few feet, and I followed. "Here's my daddy."

We looked another cement marker. This one was harder to read.

"I don't mean any disrespect," I said. "I thought they buried executed men in some corner of the prison yard."

"Maybe they do. Remember this was a hurry-up execution. They hung him here in Milton, when Georgia executed people in the chair down in Reidsville. There was something not right, and I don't think they cared who took the body away as long as someone did it quick. I think the sheriff at the time fixed it so we could take him home."

He pulled a pair of sunglasses from his breast pocket and put them on. His voice was suddenly cold, almost hostile. "Not really fair he died for something he didn't do," he added.

I was startled. "I guess they executed him for something my dad did, didn't they? I'm sorry."

"Guess they did," he said. "My daddy was the only blameless one in the whole mess, and he died for it, anyway. No sense in sorry now. Done has been done for more'n sixty years. Do you mind if I ask you something?"

"Not at all."

"Where did you inter your daddy?"

I felt a stab of guilt. I hadn't even given it a thought. It was something I still needed to take care of.

"I have to pick up his ashes from the funeral home. I flew his body down here to bury him, but I found out my mother was cremated, so I had the same thing done for him. She wasn't interred. He kept the ashes. I'll put them in the same place."

His voice warmed and sounded normal again. "You can leave them here if you like, in this cemetery. I'm on the church board that administers it."

I was touched, and said so.

"And, Mike," he said, "It does matter what you do with a body. When we die, we leave it behind. There's no more use for it, that's true, and it's wrong to attach too much significance to it." He stopped and touched my arm. "But—and it's a big but—it's the same as any other favorite possession the dead person had. They don't use their favorite wrist watch any more, or look at their favorite painting. Still, we honor those keepsakes and treat them respectfully. Same with their body. It was the most important thing to them on earth, and there can sometimes be a sentimental connection. It's best to handle earthly remains with some care, some respect. I think the dead know."

This place was worth thinking about. This graveyard might appeal to them, being so eclectic and forgotten. Additionally, maybe resting near the Tull family, central to the story my dad had tried to tell me before he died, might be healing.

"I can give you a little piece of ground over in the corner there. And don't worry about the cost. We don't charge for plots here. We have a fund at the church for families that need help with funeral expenses. You can make a donation to that if you want to. I won't hold you to it, though."

A yellow dog nosed its way among the grave markers in the far end. I watched him as he found a shady spot to his liking under one of the trees and lay down. After a minute, he stretched out on his side and went to sleep. The breeze gently rustled the leaves and grass, and insects hummed softly. I thought that I'd like to join the dog under his tree and drowse the afternoon away.

"This would be a good place for them," I said. "Thank you."

We started heading slowly back to the car.

"The store is near here, right?" I asked.

"The old general store? Scene of the crime? Yes, just up the road. Empty now. Like to see it?"

"I would, yes."

"No problem. I could use some lunch. We can stop on the way."

"Do you remember your brother?" I asked.

He stopped and turned to face me. "Remember Eli? Sure, I do. The sad thing is that I can mostly remember the night they took him, terrified and crying. My mama begging and him being dragged out of the house. I don't remember much about him during happy times. That's always the way, isn't it?"

I agreed.

"Sometimes," he said. "I remember him more clear when I come here. I even remember his voice. Guess that's why I come here as often as I do." He leaned up against a marker. "She never forgave me. My mother. Eli was the favorite, the good child. She always thought that if one had to be taken, it should have been me."

"That's awful," I said. "You were how old when it happened?"

"Eleven. Eli and me were less'n a year apart. We even looked alike. That may have been part of the problem. My mama looked at me and saw him. I don't know how awful it is. It's the way of families. She did her best by me for a few months after we lost my father, and then she sent me away to live with her sister. She couldn't look at me anymore."

He drew a figure eight in the dirt with his cane, looking down as he thought. "For a long time after that, I lay in my bed at night and prayed that I could go back in time. I'd make those men take me instead, and none of the bad stuff that came after would ever happen. I was the older brother, stronger and smarter. They should have taken me, and it would all have turned out all right."

"It would have made no difference, Roy. It isn't what was in the cards. They would have killed you."

"I know that now. I didn't know that when I was eleven."

"So many victims," I said. "So many victims of one moment. So much guilt. All of this over a couple of kids kissing behind a store. And my dad dies sixty-five years later being threatened about it. Dies terrified and broke."

"Sins of the fathers," he said heavily. "Echoing down."

"Oh, come on, Roy. These were children. There was no sin. It was just a tragedy. Tell me something if you know. I got my father's story second-hand, but I understood that young Wanda kissed your brother. She was being precocious because my dad didn't want to play whatever kissing game she proposed. Yesterday, Wanda contradicted that. She said that your brother was the instigator. Do you know which is true, or have a guess?"

"She kissed my brother," he said. "He did *not* kiss her. I guarantee it."

"Why? Did he tell you about it when he came home that day?"

"No. He never said anything to me. I don't have any memory of that day, just that night. It was a normal day. I would have remembered if he told me about kissing a white girl, though. Anyway, he couldn't have. It isn't possible."

"How can you be so sure?" I asked. "He was too shy?"

He laughed. "No, not generally shy. My brother loved his fun. That's why everyone loved him. He didn't so much as talk to white folks, though. Never a word. He would never have gotten fresh. Never."

He pointed back in the direction we had come from, back at his family's graves. "My father," he said. "His own father and mother were lynched in the '20s, and he saw it. He lived with the absolute conviction that it was going to happen to him, too. In the end, if you think about it—it did. He was lynched by a group of white men in uniforms. His voice shook if he had to speak to a white person."

"And the kiss?" I prompted.

"My father was terrified of white folks, beyond any reason. My brother and I grew up with that. I don't think it ever really affected me, but my brother was scared sick of white people, too. He wouldn't have willingly spoken to a white girl, let alone kiss her. Let's go."

He levered himself up from the headstone he had propped himself on and began to walk slowly. "That, to me, is the worst thing of all. He was dragged out of the house by a couple of white men. To him, it must have been like the worst monsters or bogey men came to life and took him away. Poor baby. Poor, poor child."

CHAPTER 22

Sam and Jenny Latta,
Marietta, Georgia, Tuesday, February 23, 1982:

She came out to the driveway and stopped at the front bumper of her blue bug. Dismay crossed her face as she realized that she had left her glasses behind. They were sitting on the kitchen counter.

"Shit," she said. "Forties. Spare me."

Since her last birthday, she had needed glasses for some things, and she hated them. Carting them around and keeping track of them was a nearly constant irritation. She usually wore them to drive now, but she was late. She had managed without them for years. She shifted the heavy briefcase onto her hip, set her coffee mug carefully on the car's curved front hood, and pulled out her keys. She saw the pebbles glittering on her seat at the same time that Sam came out of the front door. Although they taught at the same school, they never rode together. He gave her a small wave as he headed across the front lawn to his yellow Volvo, parked out at the curb.

"Sam, c'mere a sec," she called.

He glanced at his wrist watch and then changed course over to her.

"Look at this," she said, pointing.

A chunk of cement lay on the passenger seat of the VW. Small pieces of green safety glass littered the interior. Sam leaned in and grabbed the rock, and then straightened and tossed it out into the road.

"Weird they'd come up in the driveway to smash a window when mine was out on the street," he said. "Piss anyone off lately? Student maybe?"

The question irritated her, and she looked up to retort. She saw that he was smiling at her, the first smile in a long time, and her anger died. She felt a tiny flood of warmth.

He saw her smile, the first one in a long time, and he wondered how it was that her beauty escaped him for such long stretches of time. They hardly talked anymore.

He was surprised by depth of his missing her. "Ride in with me," he said.

"I can't just leave it here all day with the window wide open," she said. "Someone might steal it."

"They'd be doing you a favor. It's past time you junked this thing."

"I love my bug," she said absently and wrinkled her brow. "Wait—I have conferences tonight. I can't go in with you. You'd have to hang around for an hour or two after school. Don't we have something you can put over it? It might rain this afternoon."

He almost told her that he would wait for her at the end of the day, but instead he turned and walked to the garage. She watched him go, and almost called after him to suggest that they both skip school today. She bit her lip. She was surprised at the depth of her missing him.

He came back with a translucent roll of plastic and some tape and set about covering the broken window. When he was done, he opened the door and swept the loose bits and pieces of glass onto the floor.

"I'll see about getting this fixed tomorrow," he said.

"My hero."

She started to get in and hesitated. Abruptly, she turned and kissed him. She could see the surprise in his eyes. They both wanted to linger, but didn't. He heard the anemic rattle of her little engine start up behind him as he walked to his car.

Six miles away from them, a man named Ennis Dougherty looked at a clipboard. He sat high above the massive radiator grille of his Mack Super-Liner, travelling at a steady sixty miles an hour along the two-lane state highway.

His last stop was a warehouse near downtown, and the waybill said he'd be leaving three pallets there. Problem was, he only remembered seeing two pallets in the trailer at the last stop. Was it possible? A paperwork screw-up, or was a whole goddamned pallet missing off the truck? He glanced up at the highway from time to time. The two-laner was nearly empty, and he sped up. He needed to make time before he hit the morning freeway into Atlanta.

The small blue car clattered its way out of the neighborhood. She realized she should have used the delay in the driveway to go back inside for her glasses. At last she came to the stop sign where the road crossed the highway. She always felt a pleasurable tingle of risk when she stomped on the gas to take the underpowered bug across the two lanes to the other side. Sometimes, if traffic was heavy, she had no choice but to pick a gap and go. There had been some close calls.

This morning, the northbound lane was clear approaching from her side. She looked to the right. It was hard to see through the plastic taped to the window frame, and she squinted, wishing again for her glasses. The road seemed clear, and she stepped on the gas.

Her neck broke at the first touch of the truck's front bumper.

Ennis Dougherty looked up at the road at the very moment the VW crossed in front of him and vanished from sight under the flat plane of his front hood. He had the smallest fraction of a second to hope that he had been seeing things, and then there was a series of thumps, as though his trailer had crossed a set of train tracks.

The huge truck slewed to the right, and, as the front end nosed softly down into the ditch and came to rest, time caught up with him and he blew the horn. He began to cry, sitting high up in his cab. Tears rolled down his cheeks as he blasted the air horn again and again.

Jenny felt none of the violent impact. There was only a curious, gentle tearing as she came free of her body. She got out of her car and stood beside the truck. Looking up, she was overcome with pity for the man behind the wheel. She wanted badly to comfort him, but she had torn loose from the road, too. A veil was falling over the scene, and she could see the things here less clearly with every passing moment.

All at once, she understood that she had been dreaming, and that her time on earth was illusive. No dreamer could touch a dream once they were awake. Reluctantly, she turned away. She had a long way to go today, and the body left behind under the front of the truck never crossed her mind as she started walking.

Far, far away, in a city that looked very much like the Berlin of our world, twilight fell. It was a ruined city, but by design rather than history, and it held no sense of desolation. Every building was warm, romantic, and mysterious. Every hall and every room waited for her, hushed. It was completely dark.

As she approached, windows began to glow with light, one by one. As the glow spread across her horizon, she was reminded of fireflies, and she laughed with the absolute joy of it.

She began to hear snatches of laughter and conversation from open windows and doors as she wound her way through the streets. She had never been here before, but she knew the place better than she knew her own heart. She turned corners and climbed stone steps without hesitation. Finally, she saw the sign for the Blue Moon, and she went in through the door.

Her staff was gathered in the kitchen. They stood silently, looking at her. Finally she threw up her hands, smiling, and they broke ranks and gathered around her.

"Welcome home, welcome home, welcome home..."

"Let's get ready to open, people," she said. "A big night at the Blue Moon."

"The Blue Moon...the Moon is open again...she's come home, she's finally here...she's home..."

The gray days were finally over. She marveled at how real it all was. The loveliness ran through everything like the vibrations in music.

From time to time, she glanced up from what she was doing. Her eyes lingered on the door, watching for Sam to walk through it. Time would bring him, and the waiting would make the advent sweeter.

⌒⌒⌒

Present Day:

The old Pontiac station wagon was parked on the shoulder near the entrance to the church yard. From fifty yards away, I recognized Arthur Sutton leaning on a front fender and studying us.

"Arthur Sutton. Wonder what he's doing," the doctor said. "He doesn't have people in here."

"I think he's letting me know he doesn't like me visiting his mother."

"Bullshit. C'mon, get in."

He drove to the gate, slowed, and lowered his window when we came abreast of the station wagon.

"Hello, Arthur," Roy said. "That's quite the ride, '59? '60? Safari wagon. I had a Chevy Nomad, kissing cousin to that, years ago. Sold it for about five hundred bucks. The things we do when we don't have a crystal ball, right?"

Sutton didn't reply. He stared in at me, sitting on the other side of the car.

"How's your mother, Arthur?" Roy persisted. "Doing all right?"

"If there weren't motherfuckers like this one coming to my house to bother her, she'd be good," he finally said. "She's freaking out, and I ain't happy a bit about it."

His voice was surprisingly soft and breathy. He tilted his chin at me. "Got that, motherfucker? I don't want to catch you even on my street anymore. Leave my mama alone."

I started to answer, but the doctor put his hand on my arm and I subsided.

"Your mama is an old friend," he said. "Mr. Latta went to pay his respects to her. There's no cause to be upset about it. He won't have a reason to go back, I'm sure of it."

He raised the window, gave a small wave to the younger man, and drove on.

"If he keeps spending my dad's money on old cars, I'll be him visiting again," I said. "Bet on it."

"Now, now, Mike. Arthur works hard selling dope. No reason he can't buy a nice thing or two for himself."

I smiled, in spite of myself.

"Now, lunch first, or go see the old store?" he asked.

"If it's not that far, let's stop at the store first."

"You got it."

We passed a small, half-finished housing development. Huge semi-mansions sometimes seemed to be the only housing that was built anymore in the south. This street had two or three completed houses and several poured basements. Survey flags stirred in the wind, faded to pink. There was no construction equipment and no sign of activity.

"That project looks like it's coming along slowly," I said.

"Shit," the doctor snorted. "They throw those big houses up anywhere they can find cheap land. No sense of neighborhood, no sense of community. Then strangers from somewhere else buy new homes here, right in the middle of a black area, and they think they have a manor in the woods." He looked over at me. "I'm not talking about segregation, you know. I'm talking about history, tradition. The things that make a place your home. A barn with shutters on the windows and central air conditioning on a plastic street full of other big barns isn't home, far as I can tell."

The pines began to crowd close to the road. I looked into the trees as they rolled past. They were getting denser and the forest was growing darker.

"As for that place back there, they started building about the time half the other palaces around here were going into foreclosure. Serves 'em right. You have to feel for the poor folks who took on a huge mortgage for the couple houses that got finished. They have a bunch of half-framed houses and basement holes for neighbors."

He slapped the steering wheel and laughed. "Now *that's* creepy. Forget graveyards. It's a street like *that* I'd hate to walk down at night."

The two lanes of blacktop went straight through the

trees for several miles, the blur of trees on either side only occasionally broken by a house.

"This road probably hasn't changed much over the years, has it?" I asked.

"It looks just the same as it did fifty years ago, except of course when your dad and I were youngsters it was dirt, with gravel on the good parts. Here we are."

"Imagine—my dad walked along here more than sixty years ago."

"Sure, he did. Me too."

We turned onto a weedy lot. The paving was broken and heaved. The old store sat and glowered at me, somehow black. The sight of it made me hurt physically. Shingles on the sloping roof were missing, and the windows were boarded up. It had clearly been derelict for a long time. It sat in the daylight, but it gave off an overwhelming impression of darkness, a sense of cloudy nights.

This was the place that must have haunted my father's dreams. This was where he had pulled a trigger as a child and watched two grown men die. I wondered if he had come back here from time to time over the years, or if he had completely avoided the place.

"We can walk around," Roy said, "but I won't go in. It's all closed up anyway, or supposed to be. No way to look inside."

There was a sign mounted on the covered front porch above the door. It said "Country Mart" in faded letters. There was a drawing of an old-fashioned spinning wheel beside the letters.

"Country Mart," I said. "Nice."

"It was always Bradford's Store," Roy said, "even when the Suttons owned it. There was never a sign, it was just Bradford's."

There was almost no paint on the building. The wood had weathered dark. Most old wooden buildings turn silvery when the paint has been gone for long enough, but moss and mildew had turned this one rotten, almost greasy.

"I don't much like it here anymore, not that I ever did," the doctor said. "Too many bad memories. I don't even like to drive by. This place has been closed more than it's been open since the Sutton family had it. The county has sold it for a song to someone every few years, someone who thought the low price guaranteed they could make a go of it. They all went under, and the county took it back for taxes every time, 'til the next sucker came along. It was even an art gallery for a little while, if you can believe that."

From underneath the cheap facade of modern convenience store that the previous owners had tried to paste on, the original general store seemed to be reasserting itself. The long porch only needed a couple of old men in rockers, a sleeping cat and some tin signs to roll the years away. Under the eaves, the plate glass windows that had been added were boarded up.

"It's been empty a long time this time, by the looks of it," I said.

"Yes, a long time," he agreed. "The last people had a couple gas pumps out front here. One of the underground fuel tanks started leaking. They had to dig it out and clean it up. That closed them. Since then, no one's been tempted to try again."

We walked around to the back. Behind the walls, I sensed movement from inside the building.

"Here's where it happened," Roy said.

The woods came up to the edge of a large area of packed dirt. Generations of sharecroppers had worn a path to the back door to pick up what they needed, and often stayed for a time to smoke, play dice, and listen to gossip. This had been a social center for a lot of years. I tried to picture my father being here as a young boy. There was an old water pump standing by itself. Its handle was gone.

"Looks like this was a popular spot," I said.

"It was. We came here to shop, or just to pass the time."

"Only blacks?"

"Sure. No reason for a white person to come back here. They went in by the front door."

"The day Wanda kissed your brother there was no one else around?"

"No. It was an afternoon, mid-week in July. Tobacco would have finished planting, and it was time to start getting in peaches. Folks were busy. You'd mostly see people hanging around here after the first week in December, when the last of the cotton is in. Your dad, Eli, and Wanda had the place to themselves that day."

"Do people still hang around back here?" I asked.

"No, not really. Don't think so. The store's been shut, and the population's different. A few people probably come here to do dope, that kind of thing."

"It's just a bit strange that it's not all overgrown back here. It's still clear, like it sees a lot of traffic."

"I don't know if anything *will* grow here," he said. "This place has a terrible reputation. There are places that have seen too much shame, I guess."

I thought about it and nodded. "Places remember," I said. "There are old houses that are full of memories—children and birthday parties, Sunday dinners, engagements, and grandchildren. They're haunted with what life is, and that makes them a little bit alive. You can wake up in a house like that, hear a creaking on the stairs, feel comforted, and go right back to sleep."

"Not this place," Roy said. "Nothing happy here."

"No," I said. "Fill a building with enough hate and violence, and it gets sick. It starts to turn in on itself and obsess. It can't forget what it's seen."

I heard what sounded like a sigh. I couldn't tell where it came from.

"What's worse, it doesn't *want* to forget. It replays things over and over to keep whatever negative power it has as fresh as it can."

I looked at Tull. He didn't look back. He was staring at the structure, his face slack and thoughtful.

"People still live in those buildings sometimes," I said. "Live or do business, go to school, whatever. I think the chances of getting sick, of getting divorced, of doing something crazy that lands you in jail are higher if you stay in them. Most people don't believe, though. Even if there are dishes flying from the cabinets by themselves, they don't believe there's any haunting."

He nodded. "Buildings like this one are so haunted," he said, "that it leaches out and poisons the ground underneath them. You can tear the damn thing down and build something brand new, and it'll be just as sick as what was there before. The ground's no good anymore."

"People are afraid of this place?" I asked. "Is it because of the shootings? The men my father shot?"

"No. Not many people remember about that anymore. They just say it's haunted. Sixty years of local legend. People claim to have seen and heard things."

"Do you think it is?" I asked.

"Yes, maybe I do. Wanda's mother...Florence, her name was. I remember her—not that old, but a bitter woman all the same. Disappointed with her life. She hung herself inside there. I always thought she had more to do with Eli's killing than people realized. I wouldn't be surprised if she drove those men to do what they did."

"Why do you think it's her?"

"I saw something myself, years ago. I never knew

what it was for sure." He looked away. I waited and, finally, he spoke. "In the early '70s I drove by here on my way to a house call, early one morning. The place was between owners again. Closed. I was passing, and I saw a woman with a ladder going up the front steps. Looked like she was going to do some work, and I wondered if someone bought the place and was fixing it up. I slowed down a bit, interested. She stopped at the top and turned around and looked at me."

He stopped, clearly debating whether to go on.

"And..." I prompted.

"And I recognized her. It was Florence Sutton. I hadn't seen her since I was a child, but I recognized her. I stepped on the gas, but I saw—I saw—she was carrying the ladder, and she was also carrying a rope, so help me God. I'm sure you think I'm crazy."

"Not at all," I said. "You have no idea. I absolutely believe you."

He was obviously stricken by his admission, and I changed the subject.

"Are you ever afraid of dying?" I asked.

"Am I ever not afraid of dying? I'm a doctor. I can't kid myself about it the way most people can. I know better than anyone that it comes to us all."

We stood there in silence. The old store was still, almost as if the building were listening to us.

"I think," he said, "maybe I'm expressing myself wrong. I made my peace with Mr. Death when I was still a young man. I think what I'm afraid of is dying wrong. I see the people who die without leaving behind anything good. Being the world champion of anything doesn't matter. Getting rich, being good-looking—none of it. What matters is decency, and doing the right thing, and raising your kids up right. You *do* take those things with you. They last forever. They spread like ripples in all the lives that follow you."

"Do you think we go on from here?" I asked.

"I know we do, and from what your Molly has told me, you do too."

I was surprised. Molly didn't confide very often. My measure of Roy Tull went up. "I see things sometimes, yeah. So does she. She told you about that?"

"Some of it," he said. "I think the world of that young lady. I don't think I'd be inclined to doubt much of anything she told me."

"It's not like I walk around seeing dead people every day," I said. "Once in a while I see a person who's...out of place. Someone who seems out of kilter, somehow. I realize that whoever I'm seeing has moved on, but for some reason, they're still here."

"How do they look? Are they transparent or something?"

"Not at all," I said. "They seem perfectly real, because they are real. They aren't here in the same way that they used to be, but they're very much still here. As real as you or me, you know? But with a different physicality than they used to have."

"Believe it or not, more than forty years as a physician doesn't make me doubt you. When you've been present at as many deaths as I have been, you start to notice that there's a remarkable similarity to being present at a birth. There's a physical change at death. I can't describe it."

I was starting to feel like I wanted to get away from the store. Things were stirring, and I wanted no part of them.

"Tell me," he said. "If you've seen what seems to confirm that life goes on afterward, are you still afraid of dying?"

"I've seen some incredible beauty. I think I've seen

angels. I've also seen some crazy, scary shit, enough to make me believe that you're not automatically flooded with wisdom and light and grace just because you die."

I turned to go.

"I guess that makes me the same as you. I'm not so much afraid of dying as I am afraid of dying wrong. I don't want to die wrong."

CHAPTER 23

Roy Tull,
Halifax County, North Carolina, Saturday, July 23, 1949:

He was fishing with a cane pole held out over the muddy water when the car hit the bridge railing above him. There had been occasional cars and trucks passing overhead, and their tires on the boards made a brief sound like a musical riff as they drove over the small bridge. When they left the other side he could look up and see them briefly on the road before they were swallowed by the greenery, and it was mildly interesting to guess what kind of vehicle had played the short wooden song before it appeared at the other end.

This one played only a few staccato notes before there was a loud crack and its headlights appeared at the edge of the bridge, looking surprised. It was a big touring car, creamy yellow with red wire wheels, and it paused and then followed the broken railing down into the water. The people in the car screamed as though they were on an amusement park ride. It was less than a half dozen feet from the roadway down to the water, but the car broke the surface with an impressive splash, which drenched the boy. He set his fishing pole down beside him.

The car had landed on its wheels. The creek was neither deep nor fast-moving, and the water just broke over the window sills of the vehicle. He could see heads. There were at least four people inside. A woman continued to shriek, sounds of alarm rather than pain. The boy knew the difference. The driver's door was pushed open against the slow current, and a man waded toward him. He was a handsome man. His pale suit and red suspenders matched the car. A woman's voice followed him.

"Get some help, Francis! Send that boy for the police!"

He turned and looked back at the car in the middle of the stream. Only the top of the hood and the tall roof were visible above the gentle stream.

"For what?" he called back. "Are you nuts? I can't have the cops here! We'll be all over the papers."

Another man had levered himself out of the vehicle, and he waded chest-deep to the front passenger door. He slowly forced it open and helped a woman emerge. She was very pale and had dark hair plastered to her cheeks. Even from the river bank, the boy could tell that she was beautiful. Another woman continued to scream from the back seat.

"OhmyGodohmyGod I'm stuck. I'm gonna die here. Somebody. Get me out, don't leave me. Pleeeease!"

The wet man on shore looked at the boy and jerked his head toward the car.

"See if you can help out, wouldya? Six bits in it for your trouble."

The boy stood up and waded into the water. He automatically scanned for snakes. In Georgia, they would have been a concern in water like this, but North Carolina was altogether more civilized, even with its snakes. Still, the habit was ingrained. The water was cool and felt good. He made his way to the car. The second man and the dark-haired woman were by the rear door, and they looked at him as he came near.

"My leg. Owwww—Larry, get me out," the woman in the car wailed.

The second man, Larry, looked at the boy through water-spotted spectacles which had miraculously stayed on his face during the crash.

"Hush a minute, Bappie. You're in no danger. What's your name, son?"

"Roy, sir. Roy Tull."

"Can you swim, Roy? Her leg is stuck fast somehow. Let him by, Ava."

"I can swim, sir."

The man said there was no danger, but Roy had seen the big car shift in the current. He knew that the bottom of the small river was uneven and that the car was resting close to the hole he had been fishing. If it dropped even six inches, the woman in the back seat would drown. The woman named Ava looked at him. Her dark eyes were apprehensive. She knew.

He took a breath and plunged. There was almost no visibility under the water. He could make out the edge of the car door and nothing else. He felt his way down the woman's leg, and sensed her trying to pull away from him. He felt the problem—the seat cushion she sat on had dislodged and slid forward in the crash, trapping her ankle on the floor. He pushed at it hard. It only had to give up an inch before her leg came free.

The group of them thrashed their way across the soft bottom to shore. The first man, Francis, was standing up on the bridge with another man who had stopped his car to offer help.

"This fellow's going into town," he called. "He'll have them send a wrecker for us."

"Have a taxi sent, too," the woman called Ava said.

"Unless you want a parade. Ask him if he has a cigarette. Mine are wet, and I want one awful bad."

Francis scrambled down the embankment and held out a red-and-white package of Luckies. He lit one and handed it to her

"You can scram, kid," he said, doling out smokes to the others. "Give him a buck, Larry."

"Wait," Ava said to him. "Don't leave. I need to talk to you. Get your dollar, though, before they forget all about you."

Bappie sat on a rock and rubbed her ankle. "This would be a party if we had a bottle," she said.

"We do," Francis said. "Hey, kid. Be a sport and get wet again. It's a good cause. There's a bottle in the map box."

Roy did as he was asked. The water seemed colder the second time in, and the car waiting in the middle of the creek seemed like a dead animal. He wasn't quite sure what the map box was, and he submerged himself several times before he located the bottle.

"I had a full one in there, and a half-full one," Francis said when he handed it to him. "He brought the full one. You're all right, kid. You're a real lucky charm."

"What's your name?" Ava asked.

"Roy Tull, ma'am."

"Thank you, Roy Tull. That could have ended badly for my sister. I want to repay your goodness."

"Awwww, leave the kid alone," Francis said. "He has places to be."

She ignored him and kept her dark eyes on Roy's. She was very beautiful for a white woman. "I came from here," she said. "I lived here as a girl. Do you live nearby, Roy? Are you a dark son of Carolina?"

"I stay with my aunt, ma'am. I come here from Georgia."

"What do you want most?" she asked. "What can I do for you?"

The question confused him, but he thought he'd better answer. "I want to be a doctor, ma'am. A doctor."

She looked steadily at him for a moment and then looked over her shoulder at the second man. "Can he do that, Larry? Be a doctor? Is there a school?"

"I don't know. There are Negro doctors, I suppose. Winston-Salem, maybe."

"See about it," she said. "Look after it. I want this boy to become a doctor, if that's what he wants to be." Her eyes returned to his. "Good luck, Roy Tull."

✄ↄ∾ↄ

Present Day:

When things went bad, they went bad fast.

I met Sydney for breakfast in Atlanta, at a place called the OK Cafe. I had never liked to eat in the morning. I pushed away my fried potatoes, nearly untouched, and concentrated on my coffee. Across the table, she ate pancakes, eggs, and sausage with complete concentration.

"How's yours?"

"Good," she said between mouthfuls. "I'm an absolute pig for breakfast. I probably won't eat again 'til tomorrow."

I looked out the window. Two Atlanta police cruisers pulled in and parked away from the other cars in the lot. Four officers met between them, walked across to the front door, and out of sight. In a minute, a hostess led them back and past our table. They were all large and creaked with the weight of the equipment they carried. The last one caught my glance and held it until they were past our table.

"So what do we know?" she said. "Enough to make a decision?"

"How do you mean? Decide on what?"

"Primarily, whether to chase this any further. Is Wanda Sutton your blackmailer, and if so, what are you gonna do about it?" She waved happily to our server and indicated her empty cup. "Bottom line—do you think she's guilty of extortion? If you do, what have you seen supports that?"

"Run-down house with a brand new Harley in the drive," I said, ticking off a finger. "Restored antique station wagon, with what sounded like a hot rod engine under the hood. Recent purchases, and not cheap either."

"Huge big-screen television on the wall," she countered. "I'd like one of those myself. My TV's so old it has dials on the front." She looked up at the waitress and nodded her thanks for the refill.

I asked for the check.

"Also remember," she said, "that if these people got a windfall, they aren't likely to redecorate their house. They won't invest, or tour Europe. They'll buy some toys, but a lot of any windfall is going to partying. Mother and son both."

I remembered something. "The boat. New, and looked like he used it once and lost interest."

"Right," she said. "Lots of recent money, and no one's working at a legit job. Wanda gets a small monthly check, and Arthur probably sells a little dope—no apparent reason for sudden wealth. Without trying to prove anything, does your gut tell you it's your dad's money?"

"I think so, yes."

"And talking to them? Impressions?"

"Guilty as hell. She's insanely angry, and he's ready to blow just at the sight of me."

"Agreed. By rights, you should take your suspicions to

the cops. You could get someone to listen. Blackmail's a serious crime, and Crider probably has a contact in the system that he could push a bit to investigate. But it'll be tough to prove the money was your dad's—my God, he's dead. Your biggest and only witness is gone. It would drag out for years. Legal fees, whatnot—a couple hundred thousand would be long gone before you ever saw a cent of it."

The check came. I waved Sydney off and counted out some bills. "I don't need the money," I said. "I told you that. Forget that part of it."

"You could probably tip off the tax people if you wanted to cause them some trouble. Let them show the IRS where the income to buy all the stuff in the driveway came from. These aren't sophisticated people, and they have a long history of trouble. They'd feel like the roof had fallen in." She fished in her purse. "I need a cigarette. Let's go outside."

"I think," I said when we were on the front steps, "that I don't have a whole lot of stomach for destroying these people. My dad's gone. I've been trying to imagine what he'd want. I think he'd tell me that enough is enough. Terrifying these poor, ignorant people might feel like sweet revenge, but maybe it's bad karma."

It was just getting light, and the air was already warm and humid. It was going to be a scorcher. I loved the air in the South. On the island, summer mornings were often cool enough to need a jacket. Sydney was taking deep drags on her cigarette.

"So what do you want, at the end of all this?" she asked. "What's the best outcome in this shitty situation? Your dad killed her dad, and she got her revenge years and years later. What's the ending?"

"I'd settle for confronting Wanda," I said slowly. "I don't care about her son. What happened behind that store has taken out so many lives. I just want some end to it. It's a cliché, but I want my dad at peace."

I nodded to myself and thought about it. That felt right. We had stopped walking, and Sydney stood still and looked at me.

"I can't quite put my finger on it," I continued, "but I think my dad wants me to break the cycle. I don't know what he would have told me if he had lived long enough to tell me the whole story, but he was haunted. I want all of this to stop."

"Then let's talk to Wanda again. You can tell her what you think she did, and see what develops."

"I know what you did," I said softly.

Sydney raised an eyebrow in question.

"*I know what you did*. That's the message she left my dad on his machine, and that's the message she left me. Time to turn it back on her."

"Done," she said. "I'm gone for the rest of the day. How does tomorrow morning work for a trip to see her then?"

I agreed, and she dropped me off at my father's house.

"We need to confront her," I told Molly. "We need to tell her that we know about the blackmail."

"Will that do any good, Mike? I mean, she's an old woman. She's been bad her whole life. Do you expect to change her? Do you think she'll just see the light?"

"I'm not sure. I can feel my dad's hand here, some-how. She needs to know she didn't get away with it."

We sat in silence for at least a minute. Finally she spoke. "In a very real way, she killed him. She at least precipitated his death."

"It seems like that," I agreed, "but is that what my dad would tell me? He was also tired of the whole thing. Maybe he wanted it to stop."

"Yes. You know what's missing? In that whole story

about your dad, and what happened when he was a little boy—from the very first, do you know what's missing? What could have changed all of it?"

"What's that, Molly?" I asked.

"Forgiveness. No one ever got forgiven for any of this, at any point. That's what's kept this alive."

I thought about it. "You think my dad wanted me to forgive her?"

"I didn't know your dad," she said. "You have to decide if he did and then do it for him."

"I really do love you, you know that?"

"Yes. I know that. I'll go with you when you go see her."

The phone rang. It was Roy Tull. "You busy?" he asked. "You and Molly feel like getting a line wet?"

"I don't fish," I said, "but I'd like to get outside."

I covered the phone and asked Molly. She shook her head no.

"I want a nap," she said. "Go ahead. It's nice that he's reaching out to you this way. Have fun."

"Molly's pretty tired, but I'll be over in a few minutes."

The doctor met me at his front door. "Come on in, Mike. I'm going to carry a jacket, I think. At my age, it can feel cool down at the water. Be right back."

He went up the wide main staircase and disappeared. The expansive front hall gleamed with lemon polish. Just off of the front entrance, the glassed French door that led to the doctor's office area stood ajar. I saw a figure standing behind the sheer curtains.

The old house was silent, except for the gentle tick of a brass clock that sat on a table at the bottom of the stairs. Everything was tinted yellow by the late-afternoon sun. As I watched, the office door swung gently closed and latched.

"Don't worry, Mrs. Tull," I said. "I won't ever show up without an appointment."

For the second time in her presence, I felt a purple-white *pop* behind my eyes and saw the image of a tree, like a photographic negative. It had bare branches. *It's a hanging tree,* I thought.

Roy came back downstairs. I glanced over at the office doors. The figure behind the curtains was gone.

Outside, the doctor went into the garage. He emerged with a red plastic toolbox and well-used rods and put them into the trunk of his car.

"Where do you fish?" I asked him as we drove off.

"Oh, hell, it's just the river for me. I fished my whole life, sometimes for my dinner, and I never had benefit of a boat. Put me on any river bank and I feel right at home."

He parked on a dirt shoulder and led us down a scrubby, wooded path to the water. "If you grew up here, you know what a copperhead looks like, don't you?" he asked over his shoulder.

"I know what they look like."

"Good. My eyes are shit. Pull me out the way if you see one. You have snakes in Canada?"

"Snakes, yes. Nothing on the island, though, and nothing poisonous at all."

"Not like here, then, where you step all over them. It's worse, of course, as you head south. Funny, the nicer the weather, the more nasty, venomous shit you have to deal with." After a pause, he laughed. "In your case, seems like that holds true for people, too. Bet you'll be glad to get back up north."

"Actually, I'm close to wrapping up and getting a flight."

"Good. Better you get on out of here. You sent Wanda Sutton around the bend, I think."

"Why do you say that?" I asked.

"I've talked to her on the phone since you went to her house," he said. "She's damn near beside herself."

"She's been calling you? Really?"

He ignored my question and reeled his line in. He was quiet and pensive. "Is that what you were after? To drive that old woman crazy?"

I felt my face get hot. "Do you feel sorry for her, Roy?" I asked. "After what she did to my dad, you think I should have taken her age into account and left her alone?"

"I didn't say that, not at all. I'm just curious what you think you'll get from her."

I thought about it. "I want an admission of guilt, Roy. I want her to say she's sorry, even if she's not. I want an apology to my father, even if it's too late."

"You think she'll give you that?"

"Maybe. And you know what I think my dad would say?"

He looked up from the water and held my eyes.

"I think," I went on, "my father would say that the apology was enough, and that she needed his money more than anyone else, including me, and to leave it alone from there."

He nodded. "Maybe so."

"But I *will* see her again," I said. "Before I go home I'm going to see her again. I want that confession, and I want that apology."

I felt some clarity and resolution for the first time in days, and it was like a weight being lifted off me. We looked at the muddy water for an hour more without a nibble and then headed back.

CHAPTER 24

Dorothy Tull,
Marietta, Georgia, Saturday, September 6, 1947

The Book said, "What a person desires is unfailing love. Better to be poor than a liar." She knew the reference: Proverbs 19:22.

She lay in her empty bed, staring up at the ceiling and trying to pray. Unconsciously, she whispered the words. "Better to be poor than a liar," and "unfailing love." She had never imagined her life like this. Her husband and her son were a year in their graves, and there was no comfort for her, not even in the son she had left.

Dottie Tull had been faithful to her husband for a decade. Jacob was a good man and she had gracefully accepted her duty to him. Their lives had been good. The two boys looked as though they would follow in their daddy's footsteps and grow into kind, decent men. They were as alike as peas in a pod, with only their intimate mannerisms to distinguish the one from the other. Roy had his father's gravity. Eli was more imaginative.

She'd strayed from her connubial promise for the first time during the previous summer. She had been cajoled and charmed for three months prior. She had been firm and proper in her refusal of the man's attentions, but secretly she was delighted when he did not move on to easier pickings.

She had gone in early July to begin late replanting of several failed tobacco fields. There had been far too much rain in June, and many of the planter's holdings were nothing but mud. They were going to attempt a second planting that might or might not yield a poor September crop. It had rained yet again early in the morning, reducing the field to a soupy mess. The workers had been sent home, and when everyone was gone, Dottie allowed herself to be seduced in an empty drying shed.

The sex had been rough and expert, in a way that had opened her to possibilities she had never imagined. She had come home rubbed raw and aching for more of the same. She had gone to bed that night and pulled the night dress over her head before she got between the sheets. Jacob had been shocked, and she shushed him with her mouth. She mounted him, and thinking about the drying shed, she had climaxed almost immediately. At almost that very moment, the hammering started on the door.

She had screamed her voice away as Eli was dragged to the waiting car. Six days later, his little body was found in the muddy tobacco field she had been sent to work in, and it was quickly revealed that he had been tortured and killed in the same shed she had fornicated in. A weaker mind than hers would have snapped like a twig.

The men who killed Eli were themselves killed, and poor Jacob was taken in chains to have his neck broken by a rope.

Her remaining son, Roy, was a liar.

She was sending him to her sister in North Carolina. She refused to live every day of her life with the reminder of her sin talking to her, eating from her table, and sleeping under her roof. Roy had to go.

"Unfailing love," she whispered again, and closed her eyes.

ↄ∕ↄↄ∕ↄ

Present Day:

Sydney, Molly, and I drove by the Sutton's house, and looked at an empty driveway. The motorcycle was gone, and the station wagon was nowhere in sight.

"Well, we know Arthur's not here, anyway," I said. "Perfect."

Sydney parked across the street from the house, grabbed her purse, and opened the driver's door.

"Got your gun?" I said, smiling.

"Bet on it," she said. "You think these people are funny?"

"Kinda," I muttered.

Molly and I exchanged a look, then got out and followed her across the street.

As we came up the weedy front walk, we could see a piece of paper taped inside the screen door. We stood on the top step and read it.

I am at the store. Youre car is with me. Sorry about this.

"Should we wait?" Molly asked.

"Might as well. We're here now," I said. "If she's just shopping, she'll probably be back soon."

"At least until Junior gets home. If he shows up, we're getting the hell out of here.

"No," I said. "If he gets here first, I'm going to talk to him instead. He knows what's going on. I have a message to deliver, and then we're going home."

We sat in the van and waited. The first fat raindrops spattered on the windshield.

"Shit," Sydney said. "It's going to pour all day. Every time I have to wait in the car for someone, I do it in the rain."

The drops turned into a staccato tapping and then a roar. The street was blurred by the downpour. I sat and thought and became increasingly uneasy.

"That note bothers me," I said. "She's at the store with his car. Why does she say *Sorry about this?*"

"Guess she's not supposed to use it."

"It's the word choice that bothers me," I said. "Not *sorry*, but *sorry about this*. It seems funny somehow."

Sydney didn't answer. She turned the key on and the wipers swept the glass. The rain was too heavy for them to improve things much. The inside of the glass was beginning to fog. There was a young boy on the street, walking away from us. He was little more than a blurred silhouette in the deluge. I felt sorry for him.

He looked back at us over his shoulder. Molly sat up in the seat beside me, staring at him. She gripped my hand.

"That's Eli," I said. "Drive, Sydney. I know what store she's at."

The copper-colored wagon was parked on the muddy asphalt in front of the boarded-up general store. There was no one visible inside it. The rain was coming down harder than ever, and the afternoon was getting dark.

"Stay here," I said. "Both of you. No sense in all of us getting wet."

"What the fuck is she doing here?" Sydney breathed.

"Don't know. Can't think of anything good."

I had a baseball cap with me, and I put it on. I opened my door, and took a deep breath before I dove into the rain. I went to the Pontiac. It was empty. The keys hung from the switch on the dashboard. I left it, ran to the building, and up the front steps. On the porch, I wiped the water from my face and looked back at the van. It was a blur, and I couldn't make out the faces behind the windshield.

The front door was boarded up tight with screwed-in plywood sheets. I tested the edges. The wood had swollen and was probably tighter than when it was installed. There was an expanse of plate glass running the length of the porch. It would have been added when the old building was modernized. Each large pane was also covered with wooden sheeting, except for the top three or four inches. None of the glass behind the wood appeared to have been broken.

Someone still owned the place. Whether it was the bank or the county, there would be some provision for entering the building to inspect or do emergency maintenance. I sketched a wave in the women's direction, snugged my wet hat down, and ran to the back of the building. My heart jumped into my throat as I turned the last corner. I tried to stop, dug in my heels, slipped and fell. Someone was standing behind the building. Looking up from the ground, I realized it was only the old iron water pump, standing lonely vigil in the mud.

I picked myself up and went to the back entrance. The rain was warm, and so heavy I felt in danger of drowning. The door was metal, faded green with rust streaks. I pushed on it and it opened. I didn't go in.

"Wanda?" I shouted. "Ms. Sutton?"

There was no response. I took a couple of steps inside. The short hallway was barely illuminated by the murky day behind me. A padlock lay at my feet. It was still snapped closed. I turned and saw that the hasp had been ripped loose from the door jamb. There was no water on the filthy linoleum ahead of me. Whoever was here had come in before the rain started. I looked behind me and debated returning for the women. I wanted the security of another person as much as I wanted the gun in Sydney's purse.

The most dreadful often turns to adventure when we have company. I had seen more ghosts than I cared to, and when I was by myself it turned my guts to water. When I had someone beside me, the terror was delicious, exhilarating. In point of fact, we weren't designed to be alone. We are social to our bones, little pieces of a great whole, and I desperately didn't want to be alone right now.

However, I also had a strong sense that this place, and what was unfolding here, was my inheritance, and I wasn't supposed to share this legacy with anyone else. Instead of going back to get Sydney and her gun, I started slowly forward.

The hallway was perhaps a dozen feet long, with a single door opening midway up on the right, and another farther up on the other side. The light from the open door at my back disappeared where the passage opened into the gloom of the main space beyond it. I nudged open the first door, and, as my eyes adjusted, I could make out a filthy toilet. The ends of pipe protruded from the wall where a sink had been ripped out. The mirror on the wall was covered with what looked like writing. I couldn't make sense of it.

A shadow seemed to coalesce and move in the dim glass. I squinted, desperately wishing for more light.

A few steps farther, the door on the left opened into a pitch black space that was long and narrow. I got my cell phone from my pocket, opened it, and held it out. The feeble illumination from the display did nothing to help me see, and I closed the door again. I would have to come back to this area later if Wanda didn't turn up.

I moved into the store itself. There was a band of gray light coming in at the top of the windows that lined the front. The sheets of wood screwed over them didn't quite reach the tops of the frames. The illumination was minimal, and my eyes adjusted by degrees. Some of the metal shelving had been left behind, and the cashier counter was intact. Old cigarette and snack food advertisements still adorned the walls. The rustic, open ceiling soared high overhead, the edges of wooden beams and trusses visible before they disappeared into the dark overhead.

I knew that Wanda wasn't all right. I didn't know what form not all right would take, though. She could be dead, or hurt, lying in a corner. She could have lost whatever sanity she possessed and be sitting on the floor drooling. Worst of all, she might have taken a violent turn and be waiting somewhere in the dark, holding a knife or a gun. I had known where to find her when I had seen the note. I had no doubt that she also knew I was coming.

I found her where I least expected to. In the near-dark, at first my eyes rejected the sight of her and passed on in their search, but eventually they returned to her. She was right in front of me. She stood, unmoving, in mid-air. I jumped backward, my heart feeling like it was going to explode. I saw spots, and it was several moments before they cleared and I could make out the rope that held her up.

She hung almost in the exact center of the store, her back to me. Her hands were by her sides. She was twisting very slightly back and forth on her line, as if nudged by the smallest breeze, although I couldn't feel any air movement. I stood very still, hardly breathing. There was something grave, reverent, holy, or maybe unholy, about the moment. It was time to go, but I felt a need to be sure that it was Wanda before I ran out. I felt like she deserved to have me find her, and she would not be really found until I had seen her face.

I moved in a wide circle around the body, always

keeping my eyes upward on her, moving my feet with a sweeping motion to avoid tripping over debris in the half-light.

When I had made my way to the front of her, a dim gray wash illuminated her face. It was Wanda Sutton. She wore a flowered shift and one bedroom slipper. I didn't see the other one. The blood-darkened face had a look of distaste; her tongue protruded slightly from her lips, as though she were repulsed by the situation she found herself in. Her blonde hair was tousled, and her eyes were slitted.

"I'm sorry," I said.

A step ladder lay on its side beneath her feet. Up close she smelled terrible. I felt badly for her. It was a hard life that hung ended in front of me, and I found myself reaching for a prayer.

As I turned to go, she opened her eyes. In the dim light, they looked filmy and the whites were dark, perhaps bloodshot. She looked around the room, moving nothing but her eyes. Her gaze settled on me. I felt the pulse in my ears, and the sudden weakness in my arms and legs.

"I know what you did," she croaked.

"Not real," I whispered.

"I—know—what you did." Her vocal chords were ruined. The speech sounded painful.

"Not real," I said a bit louder and started to move away.

Her hair became darker, and her stocky body slimmed. The flowered shift looked white and seemed longer.

"Get up here, you bad girl."

I found my legs, and moved quickly toward the door. Back in the hallway, I turned and looked back. Her legs were kicking violently, and her hands were over her head, grabbing wildly at the rope in a paroxysm of regret.

She swung back and forth, and the beam she hung from creaked.

"Not real!" I shouted.

"I know what you did!" she screamed.

I turned and ran directly into Molly, who had been standing behind me.

"Oh my God, Mike," she breathed, staring up transfixed. "Look at her! Look at her—"

"Go!" I screamed. "Go!"

We ran. I slammed into the door at the end of the hall and we were back outside in the rain. I skidded around the corner of the building and sprinted for the van, hustling Molly ahead of me. We pulled open the passenger door and scrambled in. Sydney looked at us, her eyes wide.

"Pull out to the road," I yelled at her. "Park on the shoulder."

"What happened?" she asked, her voice stretched thin.

"Don't talk, Sydney! Get us off the property, right now!"

She put the van in gear, and I heard whining as the tires spun on the wet blacktop. We left the parking lot and slewed onto the highway.

"Pull over and stop!" I shouted.

From the shoulder of the road, I looked back at the store. There was no movement except for the shimmer of the rain.

"Sorry," I said. "Didn't mean to yell. We had to get off the property. This is safe enough."

I sat forward and pulled out my cell phone. I was worried about the wet, but it seemed to be working. I called the police.

Six hours later, Molly and I stood on Lemon Street in front of the police station. The dispatcher had called us a taxi. The rain had stopped, but the street was wet, and absolutely empty. There was a traffic light at each end of the short block. Unsynchronized, they ignored each other, changing color from red to green to yellow with complete disregard for what the other was doing. The place had gone to bed without me, and even with a mostly silent Molly beside me, the loneliness was crushing.

"I've never felt so rotten about anything in my life," I said.

"Hush, Mike."

"I feel like I caused this."

"Hush."

Sydney was long since gone home, and I didn't remember the city well enough to try walking back to the doctor's house. Even though I had grown up in the area, the place felt alien to me, like something I had once dreamed. I saw the cab's headlights turn into the street, and I stepped out and waved.

Wanda's death was apparently a suicide, but it was still under cursory investigation. Sydney, Molly and I had watched from the backs of separate police cruisers as emergency crews attended the general store. The circumstances of my finding the body were confused and uncomfortable. Sydney had quietly advised me to stick with the truth and refer any questions I was unsure of to Crider the lawyer. The police officers who had spoken with me had progressed during the evening from vague excitement and suspicion to bored disinterest. They finally let us go.

The old doctor met us at his front door, wearing a plaid bathrobe. "I would have picked you up," he said. "Hungry? Coffee? Tea?"

I thought about it, and Molly answered for both of us. "Tea would be all right, thanks."

We sat at his kitchen table and watched him boil water and make toast. When it was ready, he sat with us.

"I'll be glad to get home, Roy," I sighed.

"I bet. You're okay to go? They didn't tell you not to leave town or anything?"

"No. At first they were a little bit pushy with me. I think Wanda and her son are known to them, though. I hate to say it, but they're—"

"Trailer trash," he finished drily. "No tears shed for her loss. I'm familiar with the phenomenon. Did young Arthur show up?"

"I never saw him, no. They kept us at the store for about an hour before they drove us to the station to talk to us. They still hadn't taken her out at that point, and I never saw Arthur."

He stood up, walked to the counter, and dropped more bread into the toaster. He spoke with his back to me. "So you think that's it? You think she was your blackmailer?"

"I think so, yes. Her son probably was involved to some degree, but I don't care. It's over."

"Do you feel like you slew your dad's dragon, so to speak?"

"I would never have wished this on anyone," I said sharply. "I didn't want her to get away with torturing my father, but I didn't want anyone dead either."

He came back to the table and set a plate of toast in front of me. "Not what I meant. I'm asking if you feel more at peace about things."

"I'm not sure, Roy." I sighed. "It's been a hell of a day. I'd like to say that I righted a wrong, but I didn't. To be honest, I don't know why my dad gave her any money, or gave in to blackmail. She couldn't have seemed like much of a threat."

"That may be where her son came in," he said. "There may have been physical intimidation. Arthur's kind of a pathetic creep, but he's no stranger to physical threats on folks who are weaker than him. I can tell you from experience, age is a humbling process." He sipped at his tea, lost in his own thoughts for a moment.

I sat quietly.

"For a strong man like your father, realizing that he was no match any more for a cowardly punk like Arthur could have been devastating. If he was drinking, and already prone to depression, who knows what kind of obsessive thinking could have developed. If he was feeding them money to leave him alone, and it finally ran out, that might have been the end of him."

"It all fits," I said. "I guess the question is whether I leave Arthur alone, knowing what I do."

"Yes," Molly said. "Enough. Your dad never wanted this. It's time for us to get home."

"I can tell you, he's going to be lost without his mama, more than you think. Without her around, he's going to dry up and blow away. I can bet you he'll be dead of one thing or another inside a year. I guess you'll have to follow your heart."

"Right now I'm too tired to feel anything, Roy. I'm grateful for your kindness. It's nice seeing you, but right now I wish I was home."

"Molly tells me you have a big reason to get yourself home," he smiled. "Nice surprise."

"What is it? She won't tell me."

"And you think I will? You think I got this old by being foolish?"

Molly laughed. She wagged a finger at Roy. "Hush, you," she warned. "Not a word."

"Not a word," he repeated, smiling broadly. "Sorry, Mike. I think too much of this girl to get on her bad side."

I felt good about that. A bit of the day's dread eased itself off of me.

"Do you want to take care of your parent's ashes before you go? We can do it in the morning."

I did. It was time to send them on their way.

"Yes, please," I said. "We'll do it in the morning."

CHAPTER 25

Roy Tull,
Chapel Hill, North Carolina, Tuesday, June 5, 1956

T he hand-painted sign over the front door read *Domus Corvi in Solem*, which was someone's attempt at Latin. Crows in the Sun House was neither a fraternity nor a sorority. It was a large, comfortable off-campus dwelling for Negro students at the university. In a student body of just over seven thousand souls, seventeen were black, and eleven of those lived at Crows in the Sun. The neighborhood had been wealthy before the century's turn, and the house was enormous. It was white with red shutters and needed paint.

Four young women occupied the ground floor, while the second and third stories belonged to the men. A fifty-year-old widow owned the place and ruled the students under her roof with an iron hand. They accepted her laws and edicts with mostly good humor. As student housing went, it was remarkably clean and quiet.

Roy was at the back of the third floor. It was warm, but an electric fan sat by the window blowing air across the room. It rattled at the end of each sweep before it started back the other way. There was a pitcher of ice water on the dresser. The curtains were green plaid and moved gently. The room was drowsy and pleasant. Roy stretched on the bed and considered a nap.

Far below him, he heard the screen door slam and then the sound of voices in the front hall. Steps, more than one person, climbed the carpeted stairs to the second floor, and then continued up the wooden ones to the third. Voices murmured their way down the hall to him.

"Here you are, ma'am. You have a visitor, Roy."

"Thank you," the woman said.

He rolled his legs off of the bed and sat up. It was the dark-haired woman, Ava, who had been in the car that went off the bridge a decade before. For a white woman to enter the bedroom of a Negro man in the Chapel Hill of the day was outside of any possible propriety, but this one was a sort of royalty, and beyond such things. She swept in by herself.

"Should I leave the door open?" she asked.

"Open is fine, ma'am," he answered.

"Oh, for heaven's sake, don't call me 'ma'am.' We've discussed that, Roy. I'm thirty-four, not old enough to be your mother or even your Sunday school teacher." She pulled the straight chair out from the small desk. "May I?"

Roy was embarrassed that he hadn't offered. He didn't know how to act around her. It wasn't that she was white, or even that she was beautiful. He could have adjusted to those things. She was ethereal, not quite real. She always seemed to be intensely present, absorbed and interested in him and in the moment, with a completeness that was unique. At the same time she had an air of indifference, a disregard for whatever was outside of her focus. The risk that she took visiting him didn't merit her passing consideration.

She came to see him once a year. Her bond to him was

permanent. He had possibly saved her sister from drowning when she was trapped in the rear seat of the big sedan, but Roy felt it was more than that. There had been recognition, a connection, the moment that they saw each other. It was familial. She had asked him what he wanted most, and he had said he wanted to be a doctor. She had stayed the course to get him there, opening doors and providing money for tuition and his living expenses. A local lawyer was liaison, but she came to him every summer.

Today she wore a pale green sleeveless dress that had a full skirt. When she sat down, he caught the scent of gardenias and the tiniest trace of her musk from the day's heat. Her nose was straight and her eyes were still and dark.

She sat and looked at him, perhaps to note if he had changed since last summer. "You did well this year," she said.

"I work hard. Held down a job nights, too. I can give you some money to help pay my way."

"You already paid your way, Roy. I don't need your money, and I don't want you jeopardizing your marks clearing tables."

"I won't," he said. "The job hasn't gotten in the way of my books."

"You're working six nights a week. That's nearly as many hours as a grown man not in school. I want you to stop."

He was surprised. "How do you know? Are you checking on me?"

"Roy, this isn't just about you. You've brought me into your dream now. And quite honestly, there are enough busboys in the South, and not even a fraction of the colored doctors that are needed. At least promise me that you'll cut your work hours in half."

He thought about it. "I believe I could cut back a couple of shifts a week," he said.

She smiled at him full force. "In half," she said. "And no girls! No kissing when you should be studying!"

He felt the blood drain from his face.

"There will be time for girls and kisses later." She laughed. "But not now."

He paused a beat, stared at her, and then stood up and headed for the door. "Excuse me, ma'am," he stammered. "Don't feel so good. I need to splash some cold water on my face."

He bolted up the hall. Her voice followed him.

"I'll know if you do," she called, teasing. "I'll see it on your face! I'll always know what you did, Roy Tull. One look at your face, and I'll always know what you did!"

 споро

Present Day:

"I guess I go on alone from here," I said. "Both of them gone. It didn't really hit me 'til now. I guess you enjoy the connections while you have them, because in the end you're alone."

We were in the old graveyard. The sun was hot. We had dressed with respect to the occasion, but when Roy and I began to take turns digging the shallow hole, our jackets and ties had come off. Molly had wanted to take a turn, worried about his age. Roy declined her offer, feigning outrage. It was just the three of us, in among the headstones, along with whatever ethereal company we had drawn.

"I think the opposite is true," Roy said. "We're all alone when we step through that door, but only briefly. You can't take anything along, and no one can go with you. You're alone for that split second you step over that big gulf, and I think you decide in that moment what's going to be on the other side. You're not alone, you're never going to be again, and you understand that you never were."

"My dad always said life was a long series of good-byes."

"No goodbyes where they've gone," Molly said. "No more ever."

She turned me to her and enfolded me. She was citrusy and floral and soft in my arms. I knew that however strange the place, she was my home. I looked over her shoulder.

There was a tree twenty or thirty yards away. A young boy sat on the lowest branch, swinging his legs. His dog was lying on the ground beneath him, head on paws. The boy saw me looking at him. His face split in a smile that was brilliant even at a distance, and he waved enthusiastically at me. I winked back at him.

"I'll arrange for a marker for them later, if you leave me their particulars."

"Nice. Thank you."

I looked at the boy in the tree. His head had swollen to the size of a pumpkin. One eye was gone, and his flesh hung in tatters. I smiled at him, ever so slightly.

"I know who you are, Eli," I murmured.

As if satisfied that he had identified himself, he reverted to his normal appearance. His sunny smile was back. Between us, the old man leaned on the shovel, resting, and looked at the road.

"I hate good-byes," Molly said.

An elderly red pickup slowed a little as it came abreast and then accelerated noisily past. It disappeared around the bend a half-mile away, leaving behind heat shimmer that made the road look wet.

"It never really ends, you know," Roy answered. "We mark the ends of things, but it all goes on and on. You're a part of something that never stops, not even after you're gone, and you live better when you remember that. They're on their way, and I guess now you're on your way too."

"We're on our way home," I agreed. "Let's go."

We walked out of the cemetery. As I passed through the gate, I turned back to wave to Eli, but the tree was empty.

I found myself once again in Robert Crider's office. The lawyer's secretary wasn't at her desk, so I sat down to wait for someone to appear. The inner door was ajar, and after only a few seconds the man peered out. I re-introduced myself, and he looked confused. Just as quickly, his brow cleared as he placed me. He waved me in.

"I won't keep you," I said. "I have a plane out of here this afternoon. We won't be recovering any of my father's missing money."

"I'm sorry to hear that," he said. "The market isn't going to yield much equity in the house. There's certainly going to be a shortfall, and that likely makes your position as heir untenable. We'll proceed as best we can without you."

"No," I said, smiling. "Settle the estate. I'm his son. If he owes money, I'll take care of it. He didn't raise me to do anything different. He doesn't deserve to leave here in debt to anybody at all, and he won't."

He looked across his desk at me, surprised. He stood up and shook my hand, and I left him. I felt like I was losing a heavy burden, little by little, scattering my father's ashes in the wind.

We said an emotional farewell to Roy Tull on the front steps of his lovely, crooked house. Sydney Cotton's green van waited for us at the curb.

Roy promised a visit. I promised to take care of Molly.

"All right," Molly said. "I've said it before. I hate good-byes. I'm going. Come see us. Her eyes suddenly brimmed, and she hugged him. "This has been a lot, hasn't it, Roy? It's been a lot. Come see us where it's happier."

"I will. Love you, young lady," the old man said. "See you soon."

I picked up our bags and went to the street. I got in, put my seatbelt on, and waved. The old man waved back, turned, and went into his sinking, doomed home.

Behind the wheel, Sydney looked tense.

"What's wrong?" I asked.

"Arthur Sutton's car was parked here when I drove up. He moved when he saw me. I'm pretty sure he's sitting around the corner. He has another man with him."

"Well, let's just go," I said. "He can play whatever game he's playing. He's only interested in me, and I'm leaving."

"Ever heard of drive-by shootings?" she asked. "Who knows what frame of mind this man is in."

I saw that she had her pistol wedged on the seat beside her.

"Don't you worry about shooting yourself in the leg if you go over a bump?"

"Screw you. I don't like this a bit."

"C'mon Sydney, he's been following us around for days."

"Let's go, Mike," Molly urged. "I don't like this."

We turned the corner and saw that the old Pontiac wagon was parked at the side of the road. I leaned forward to look in the rear view mirror on my side. The car pulled out to follow us.

"Wait until we're away from the houses," I said. "I don't need someone calling the cops. At the top of the street there's a place you can stop. There's a small parking lot you can pull into."

"What are you going to do?" she asked.

"I'm going to see what he wants. I have a plane to catch. I don't want to be screwing around with him at the airport."

"You're not paying me to do this, you know."

"I have news for you," I smiled. "I paid your bill yesterday, remember? This is all out of the goodness of your heart."

The parking area at the end of the road was empty. Sydney pulled in and stopped, leaving the engine running. As I got out, I saw that she held the gun in her lap. I walked to the rear of the van. The old wagon was parked twenty or thirty yards away. The front doors opened, and Arthur and the dreadlocked man I had seen him with before got out. He was carrying a pistol down by his side.

"Put the fucking gun away, asshole!" Sydney called.

Molly walked past both of us and went directly to Arthur. My heart was in my throat. She took his hand.

"He's just lost his mother, for God's sake," she called back to us. "Put the guns away."

I joined them.

"What do you want?" she asked him gently.

"Gotta talk to you."

"So talk to me," she said. "You don't need the gun to talk to us."

Up close, I was aware of how unhealthy he seemed under the muscles and tattoos. His skin had a yellow cast that was mirrored in the whites of his eyes and his teeth. His henna-colored hair and light irises enhanced the effect. He smelled of dope and looked as though he hadn't slept in days.

"I'm sorry about your mother, Arthur," I said. "It's a hell of a thing."

My sympathy was genuine, and for a moment he was taken aback. He sagged, and looked lost for a moment before visibly struggling to recover his anger. "They told me you found her. Was it you put her there?"

"I found her," I said gently. "No one put her there. She put herself there."

"You might as well have," he stormed. "Harassing her. Phoning her at all hours like you did."

"I talked to her once, Arthur," I said, "about my own father. I wanted to talk to her again, but I was too late. I never called her. What do you know about my father?"

"I don't know nothing about your fucking father," he said. "What are you talking about?"

"You're driving a nice car, a new motorcycle, a boat. Lots of new toys. Where'd you get the money for all that?"

"I'm a businessman. Where I get my money's not your business, bitch."

"It is, if it belonged to my father," I said. "Is that where you got it?"

"Only if he's my customer."

He turned to the man behind him. "Do you know his daddy, Leon? Is he our customer?"

The man didn't answer. He stared at us impassively, arms crossed, gun dangling.

"Did you get money from your mother?" I asked.

"My mother had a check for six hundred and seventy-eight motherfucking dollars once a month, motherfucker. Anything else she got from me."

"There's nothing else to talk about, Arthur," I said, and started to turn away. "Leave me alone. I'm sorry for your loss."

"She didn't kill herself, you know," he said. "I know she didn't."

I turned back and stared at him.

"They found her with one slipper on her foot. I found the other one in the hall by the door. You think she went out to do a suicide wearing one shoe?"

"She wasn't herself," I said. "I'm sure she wasn't thinking clearly."

"Well, she wasn't in her right mind to take my car," he said. "She knew better'n that. She had no fucking license either. But you know why else she didn't kill herself?"

I waited.

"She was too fucking mean, that's why. She might've killed someone else, but not herself."

I turned and started for the van. We were done.

"Which leaves you, turkey," he called after me. "The midnight caller. Unless you scared her into it, saying you know what she done, over and over. You wait, fucker. We'll be talking again."

I stopped in my tracks. "What did you say, Arthur?"

He was already in the wagon, and the hot rod engine turned over and rumbled. The rear tires shrieked and then grabbed when he turned out onto the street.

"Did you hear that?" I asked Molly. "She was getting phone calls. Like my dad. The caller knows what she did."

She shrugged, and got in the van. Sydney heard what we said and shook her head.

"Fuck it," she said, and rolled her window down and lit a cigarette. "Who knows if someone was calling her. Sounds like bullshit, to cover up the fact that he was the one making phone calls."

"Could that be true, though? That she was being called too? '*I know what you did*'?"

"He's blowing smoke up your ass, Mike. He has guilty knowledge, and he's playing you. He doesn't know what you're going to do, so he's laying down a bunch of crap. He knew about the calls—so what? He probably made them on his mom's behalf. He has kind of a high, husky voice."

"Maybe," I said.

"Anyway, he's out of your life. You're done with this, off to a different country. This whole sorry mess is finished." She threw her cigarette out of the window. "Let's go get your plane."

ⲉⳉⲉⳉ

The departure board told me it was seventeen minutes until boarding. I rested, beyond dozing, beyond moving, at peace. Molly had her head on my shoulder. I needed to think about my father, but at some point in the future, not now. Wanda's death had put him to rest.

I was startled when the phone in my hand vibrated. "Hello?"

"I know what you did."

I was stunned. The force of the caller was appalling, something old and sick and twisted. I felt sick to my stomach. It felt like Wanda on the other end, though that was impossible.

"I know what you did?" My voice seemed loud. "Is that your only line, fucker? I know what you did?"

I heard a tiny click as we were disconnected. "Fuck," I breathed to myself.

"What is it, Mike?" Molly asked, alarmed. "Who was that?"

It was ridiculous to think that Wanda was calling me. *Calling me from the store.* It had to be her son. Maybe we needed to go back and get the police involved, after all.

I looked at the exit, over at the security gate. I heard our flight announced, and the airline person opened the door to the jet way. I shook it off. I had had enough. I stood up, shouldered my bag, and led Molly onto the plane.

"Are you okay?" *Molly* asked. She looked over at me from her window seat and touched my hand. We were at cruising altitude, and people were moving in the aisles.

"I'm fine," I said. "I'm not sure that I'll ever be relaxed on an airplane again."

Her eyes were sympathetic. "I know. You never really told me. How do you feel about your dad killing those men?"

"I don't know. The story fits him."

"Fits how?" she asked. "He was a school teacher. He never showed you anything violent, did he?"

"No, not at all. He seemed...impervious? He didn't care about violence, somehow. I'm not sure how brave he was. He just wasn't impressed by violence or threats."

The drinks cart reached us. The cabin attendants chocked the wheels and began to lean across seats in bright inquiry, anxious to pour. I waved them off.

"I'm going to have a beer," Molly said. "I hate beer, but I'm in the mood. What's a good beer, Mike?"

"They're all good. No reason to be picky about beer." When she had been served and taken a sip, she settled into her seat and I went on. "I think that was part of his strange popularity as a teacher," I said. "Strange because Mr. Tibbs he definitely wasn't. He didn't take any shit from any of his students, but he wasn't trying to be tough either. Tough kids didn't impress him, and I think he actually got through to a few of them because of it. They respected it. It was genuine in the sense that he wasn't capable of being intimidated."

The cabin was jarred as we passed through turbulence, and the seat belt light illuminated. I gripped my armrests tightly. Molly peeled the fingers on the hand nearest her loose and held them in her lap.

"Oh, boy," I said, and let my breath out. "One time when I lived in California, he took it into his head to visit me. It was weird. I have no idea why. He took the bus instead of flying because it was cheaper. Three days and nights of sitting in the same seat to save a buck. Imagine. His bus got into downtown LA just after midnight. I didn't even live in LA but that didn't matter to him. He knew I lived in Southern California, so Los Angeles was where he was getting off."

The plane lurched, and the plastic panels in the cabin rattled. It didn't seem so bad with my hand captured on Molly's lap.

"So there I am in the very worst part of downtown, and in the '80s the downtown bus terminal wasn't a place you wanted to be even in the daytime. They had security guards prowling around who looked like they belonged on death row, and at night the sidewalks out front looked like a war zone with all of the homeless people sleeping on the ground."

"I thought you guys were completely out of touch after you left home," she said.

"Mostly we were. There was just that one visit. He spent three days on a bus, stayed with me for two, got bored, and got back on for the three day ride home."

"He must have cared a lot about you to do that, Mike. I don't imagine you were entirely pleasant at that point in your life."

I thought about it and shook my head. "He wanted to eat at this twenty-four-hour cafeteria that was a downtown LA landmark. It had been there for about seventy years or so, and I remember the food on the menu was like stuff you would have seen in the 1930s. Tapioca pudding for dessert, like that. Bizarre. He absolutely had to go there to eat. It was the only thing he showed the slightest interest in the whole time he was there."

"So you took him?"

"I did. The place was close enough to the terminal that

we decided to walk. At one o'clock in the morning, there we were, walking down the meanest streets in California. There were scary people staring at us everywhere I looked. I was twenty or twenty-one, and I'll tell you a secret. Most twenty-year-old guys have the delusion that they're tough. I did too, but I was scared to death. Scared to death."

I paused, remembering, and trying to think of the words for what I was trying to say. "I looked over at him. He was probably close to fifty years old, and not very big. A school teacher. He was getting the evil eye from all these potential muggers, and he *didn't care*. He refused to even notice them. He wasn't afraid because he just didn't care, and it made him one of the scariest guys on the street that night."

"Maybe it was an act for your benefit," she said. "Or maybe he really was brave. Or some of both."

"I don't think it was an act, Molly. It's really the way he was. He wasn't a bad guy, but he saw something so awful when he was a kid that it scarred him. He wasn't tough. He just wasn't able to really care what happened to him anymore."

"Maybe it's something else, Mike. Maybe he never cared much what happened to him, because he cared so much about what happened to everyone else. Maybe when you kill a dragon when you're only ten years old, you never get to be the same as other people again."

PART III

ECHO ISLAND
ONTARIO, CANADA

CHAPTER 26

Elijah Tull,
Milton County, Georgia, Saturday, August 12, 1967:

E li sat in the choir loft and watched dust motes float in the colored light. He was bored in the way of young children, which is vastly different than the boredom of adults. Grown-up ennui was a defeat, selfishness, a deadening of the senses to wonder. A child's boredom was an explosive charge of curiosity and interest that was restless. It simply hadn't yet locked onto a target.

He understood that he was dead, but he didn't know yet quite what it meant, or what he was supposed to do about it. He did know that he had to wait. He had somewhere to go, but not yet. There was something not revealed, and, as a child, he accepted the reality of that, however impatiently. He had a feeling that it had something to do with his older brother, who he loved with the usual adoration that was the way of younger brothers.

He had already waited twenty-one years in this place, and there were decades of waiting still to come, but time meant nothing to him. A year and a minute were the same.

The church had been built for a white congregation, but a Roman Catholic one that was in retreat in the state, and so it had been abandoned to the black Baptist worshipers who used it now. Consequently, it had a choir loft stretching across the back wall, although the current choir sang on Sundays at the front of the church. There was a piano up there that was kept in tune and used by the locals for lessons and practice.

The original tenants had left behind the glorious windows, rich with images of blood and martyrdom. In very late afternoon, just before sunset, the western-exposed glass made the air heavy with glowing blues and reds. It was then that Eli liked to come and play in the choir loft. He thought that the colored atmosphere gave him substance. Today, however, the soft warm light didn't hold its usual fascination for him. He fidgeted.

He sat up, interested, as the church door banged open beneath him. Footsteps scuffed the boards below and then noisily mounted the stairs to where he sat. He watched as first the head and then the shoulders of a boy about his own age came into view. The youngster was carrying a thin book of sheet music. It was borrowed, old and delicate, and the boy had been cautioned again and again to treat it with reverence. He set it on the piano and wandered over to the rail. He stood looking down at the pews for several minutes, but nothing happened. He eventually sighed and turned to the piano, settled on the bench, and began to play.

There was an old hymnal in the rack on the seat back in front of Eli. He stared at it and steadied his breathing. He closed his eyes and concentrated and then launched his shoe at the book, a mighty kick. It shifted a fraction of an inch. When it rocked back, it made a tiny click, the barest tapping sound.

The boy at the piano stopped playing and looked over

his shoulder at the noise. Seeing nothing behind him, he resumed his playing.

Eli shifted his hips for more leverage and closed his eyes again. He felt the energy inside him as it built. When it climaxed, his foot shot out and connected with the pew in front of him. This time there was a satisfying knock from the varnished wood. He sat up and looked at the other boy. He had turned himself around on the bench and sat, wide-eyed, piano forgotten. Eli sat facing him, smothering giggles, until the boy turned back around and began to play, much softer than he had been. His shoulders were hunched, as if he expected a blow from behind.

It was time to change tactics. Eli stood up and walked carefully around to the other side of the piano, where there was a grouping of items that had been placed upstairs for storage. There were several stands made of filigreed metal for holding flowers, and assorted other items that were seldom used. He spotted what he was looking for. It was a tall candle holder, a relic of the Roman ritual, with a circular base made of polished wood. It still held the half of a desiccated candles. The smell of ancient beeswax from it was faint and pleasant.

The slender holder was as tall as his chest. He braced his legs, grasped the carved wood, and pushed. It didn't budge. He looked at the other boy, who was concentrating again on the sheet music in front of him. Eli swung his arms back and forth in a wide arc, limbering them until he felt ready. On his toes, he leaned himself against the candle holder and began to push. There was no movement. He closed his eyes and concentrated all of his essence, all of his will. There was an imperceptible shift under his hands and then, in a rush, he felt his balance change as gravity took the job away from him.

The candle holder toppled and hit the floor with a clatter. The boy at the piano sat bolt upright, eyes wide and rolling. In dreadful slow motion, he stood up and turned toward the stairs, trapped in a frozen, sluggish body that hardly moved. Then all at once the spell broke. He yelled out loud and pelted down the steps in a tangle of arms and legs, with Eli trailing behind. He crashed into the door. It flew open with a bang and he was flying across the packed dirt of the dooryard, windmilling out to the road, running until he disappeared up the dirt lane.

Eli came behind him, laughing with the sheer happiness of the moment. He jumped and whooped. It would be impossible to watch the small boy, dancing alone in the churchyard, leaping and spinning with the purest joy, and not to smile along with him.

Shadows were lengthening across the churchyard as Eli, still giddy and reeling with the hilarity of it all, skipped back toward the tiny cemetery behind the church. He bent and scooped a handful of tiny pebbles, then reared back and threw them as far as he could, a final burst of gladness.

It had been a good day after all.

の

Present Day:

I was glad to get back to the lake and my island, back to the melody of pine and rock and water that had become essential to me. I wanted to feel the sun and wind and cold spray that had become home, get back to the beaches and barbeques of a Canadian summer, back to the place where past and present, light and dark, seemed to overlap like no other place that I knew.

On the marina docks, Molly stood and waited for me to finish fueling my boat. The breeze off of the water blew away the gasoline fumes and brought me the odor of warming water, trees, and wood fires. Over all of it, the subtle coconut-oil fragrance of summer lingered.

From the corner of my eye, I saw Molly fish in her shoulder bag and then put her cell phone to her ear. "It's the doctor," she said, handing it to me.

"I've been thinking about that visit," he said. "Do you think I still can do it? Impose on you as a guest?"

"We'd love it."

"I've never been to Canada, and always wanted to. At my age, you start to think as much about what you haven't done as what you have, and it starts to seem like the first list is a lot longer than the second." He laughed. "If I flew up there, just say for an afternoon, you'd be able to get me to a hotel? I could fly out the next day. Kill two birds with one stone; talk to you and cross Canada off my list. Am I being rude? Inviting myself?"

"You aren't being rude. Hang on a sec."

I conferred briefly with Molly. She took the phone.

"You're staying with me," she said. "There are no hotels nearby. There's a small town near us, but no hotel for about thirty miles. I live on shore and my house is a bit less rustic than Mike's cabin. I have lots of room."

I glanced at her gratefully. After my father's death, I felt less than secure about an elderly person staying on the island, so far from help in an emergency.

"Absolutely," she went on. "We're about a three hour drive north from the city, so a short visit would be silly. Long way to the airport. If you can manage the time, why not come for a few days or even a week or two? It's beautiful in the summer. Actually, it's beautiful all year. We'll see you soon...I can't wait."

She gave me back the phone.

"I think I'm too old to try Canada in the winter," he said, "but summer sounds good. Real good. I'll call you in a few days maybe, does that sound okay?"

"I need to give you Molly's home number. I have really spotty cell service on the island. There aren't many towers around. I usually have to go out to the very end of my dock to get a signal. If I'm at home, you'll mostly get a 'customer not available' message if you call me."

"You don't have a regular phone?"

"I have an underwater cable out to the island for electricity, and they could run a phone line the same way, but the expense is unbelievable. More cell towers will come our way one of these years, and I've just gotten used to it."

"I've been at the beck and call of telephones and pagers for the last fifty years or so," he said. "That sounds just about perfect to me. Sign me up, and I'll be in no hurry to get back here. We'll do this soon."

We swapped some information and hung up. Molly and I walked over the lawns up to the marina building. Bill was coming down the steps. He spotted us and smiled broadly. Molly ran to hug him. She turned to me when I caught up.

"Okay, you have to wait here. I'm so excited, I really am." She turned back to Bill. "Is Diane here?"

"She's upstairs, waiting for you," he said. "You gonna get Mike's surprise?"

"You bet!" she called over her shoulder.

The marina owner looked at me from the corner of his eye as Molly ran inside. He seemed to be suppressing a smile.

"How was your trip?" he asked. "Considering the sad occasion, of course."

"Glad to be back, Bill. Why are you looking at me funny?"

His smile widened. "I'm not," he said. "I've been taking care of your surprise for the last week. I'm so happy you're here to take it home with you."

"Oh, shit. What is it? Tell me."

"Nope. That would spoil the surprise." He grinned. "Wouldn't dream of it, spoiling what Molly's got all planned for you. I will say, it couldn't be happening to a nicer guy."

We stood together and watched the door, waiting for Molly to reappear. The marina was in full summer swing, and people went in and out constantly. The main building had been converted from a large old frame house. The white clapboard and black shuttered building set in the pines lent the operation a country club feel. Green grass sloped down to the docks and covered slips on the water. The whole thing was nestled into the forest, and the outbuildings and parking areas were hidden in the trees.

The marina had a gas pump at the docks, and a small store and snack bar in the main building. For city people who came to live on the water during the summer months, it was a place to gather when the isolation of their properties became oppressive. It was a civilization fix, and people did their errands, real or invented, and then lingered to socialize or simply to sit on the grass and watch other people.

"Little bit of bad news, while we wait," Bill said. "Her husband's back. He's staying at her house."

I was flooded with anger. "Again?" I asked. "What the fuck is with this guy? Is he ever going to leave her alone?"

"I don't know if she wants him to leave her alone, Mike," he said softly.

"Meaning what, Bill? That she's an idiot? The guy's a piece of shit, a coke head. He feeds off her, that's all he's good for. He doesn't love her."

"We don't know that," Bill said mildly. "Anyway, you and I don't have to like him even if she does. Don't tell me you've never made a fool of yourself over love."

I was doing that now, I thought bitterly, but didn't say it.

"Do us all a favor," he continued, "ask her to marry you. Quit messing around. You know you want to, and you know you should."

"Should I? She's never shown me the first clue about what she thinks about me."

"I think everyone else in the world sees what you two don't see about yourselves. It's a damn shame you aren't together. Listen, do me a favor. Diane's not going to tell her that he's back until after she gives you this thing she got—doesn't want to wreck the moment. This girl's been over the moon about what she's giving you. Don't you spoil it for her neither."

On cue, the marina door banged open. People using the walkway stood aside and then stayed to watch as Molly was pulled out by a very large white animal on a leash. It took me a moment to identify it as a dog. It appeared to be several hundred pounds of hair led by a huge black nose. They bounded down the wooden steps until they reached us, and I watched the muscles in Molly's legs flex and tighten as she hauled them to a stop.

"Isn't he beautiful?" she beamed.

"Yours, Molly?" I asked stupidly.

"No, he's yours." She laughed. "You need a dog, on that island by yourself. He's going to be perfect for you."

My last dog was buried in the blueberry patch at the eastern end of my island. I still missed the tough, muscular, boxer every day.

This dog seemed, in contrast, to be a complete buffoon. His eyes were obscured by long hair, and I bent and brushed it back to look at him. He extended one large front paw, and when I took it, he put the other one up. I found myself bent at the waist, both front paws in my hands, while the dog balanced on his hindquarters.

"Isn't that cute?" Molly asked. "I've never seen a dog give both paws at once, have you?"

I released him, and he promptly fell over onto his side. He lay on the ground, one eye visible from under a wing of hair, and looked at me, betrayed. Molly crouched over him and made soothing noises, and the dog stretched himself out across the sidewalk. I glanced at Bill from the corner of my eye. He raised an eyebrow and gave me a sardonic thumbs-up.

"He's beautiful, Molly. He really is. Does he have a name?"

"The guy who sold him to me called him Fabian. I hate it. I named him Blue, if that's okay with you."

"Fine. Why Blue?"

"I always wanted a dog named Blue," she said. "He's the first one that came along that I got to name, so there you have it. The guy said he's crazy about cooked carrots. He won't eat them for me, though."

"He eats about damn anything else," Bill said. "I never saw a dog eat like this one."

"What kind of dog is this?" I asked.

"Old English Sheepdog," she said to me and then turned to Bill. "I can't tell if he's fat under all the hair. Do you think he is?"

"That's like asking me if an elephant's fat," he said. "Maybe it is, but I couldn't tell you without comparing it to another elephant, and we don't have any more of these dogs for me to look at. No point in comparing it to another dog, I don't think."

We laughed.

"You hush. You'll hurt his feelings," Molly said, and looked at me. "They're usually gray with white heads and feet. All white is really unusual. Since our last baby was a white boxer, I knew it was meant to be. Another white dog."

"Where did you find him?"

"In an ad. I picked him up in Kingston. He was losing his home in a divorce, weren't you, baby? But you're home now."

The dog hadn't moved. He stretched out on his side, content to block the sidewalk, oblivious to the people stepping over him. Bill gazed at him and shook his head.

"Better you than me," he murmured. "Much better."

Bill's wife, Diane, appeared at the top of the steps, holding out a phone. She brought it down to Molly, who took it, answered, and then turned her back to us.

"I'm sorry. I was on the phone..." I heard her say as she moved away.

"Hi, Diane," I said. "You've been babysitting this mutt?"

She pushed her glasses up her nose. In contrast to Bill's wry humor and general calm, Diane was perpetually harried.

A snowstorm of paperwork always enveloped her desk at the marina. She was an extraordinarily bad cook who was always ready to serve me seconds. She and Bill had been together for a long time. I loved them both.

"Yes, it was like old times, having a dog of yours in the house, although I guess you didn't know he was your dog—or did she tell you?"

"No, she kept it a surprise 'til now."

"Are you surprised?" Bill asked, laughing.

"Oh, for sure," I said. "Really surprised. I hope I can get him in the boat. He doesn't seem to move."

"Wave some food at him. He'll move faster than you can believe."

Bill spoke to Diane. His voice was low. "Does she know?" he asked.

"She does now." Diane nodded in Molly's direction. "That's him now, hot under the collar, looking for her here because she doesn't pick up her cell phone. Arrogant man."

Molly came back and returned the phone to Diane.

"I have to go, sorry. I'm getting picked up. Ride should be here in a minute," she told me.

I felt my face fall and struggled not to reveal it. Molly's house was a short distance up the shore road from the marina. A quick pick up was definitely going to be Joseph.

She smiled at me. "Are you okay with this? Maybe I should have asked you first?"

"Okay with...the dog? No, it's a terrific gift," I said. "I'm glad to have the company."

I reached down and scratched him behind his ear. He didn't respond. Molly waved to Bill and Diane and I walked her toward the road and her ride. I could never compete with Joseph's looks or his charm, but maybe Bill was right. Maybe it was time to move on from my past and gamble on my future.

"Can I ask you something?" I blurted. "What gives with this guy? Are you punishing yourself? You're punishing me with it...this is hard to watch. You know how I feel about you."

"Joseph?" she asked, surprised. "He's my husband, Mike. You forget that. What am I supposed to do?"

"Ex-husband," I corrected.

"He's having a problem. He needs me. What am I supposed to do? Turn my back on him?"

"It isn't normal to drop your whole life when an ex-partner calls."

She stopped walking and turned toward me. She was clearly shocked. "Really? Really, Mike?" Her face flushed, and her hands were clenched by her sides. Her voice was savage, and rising. "It isn't, Mike? Really? Why don't you *fuck* your ex-wife and tell me about it?

Why don't you do that, and expect me to understand?"
She was breathing heavily, almost hyperventilating.
"Why don't you just *wallow in* what you fucking *need*,
and when you finish fucking Angela, you and I can have
a nice girl-to-girl talk about how *bad* it makes you feel?
Who fucking does that, Mike?"

Behind her, a silver convertible nosed into the lot and
stopped fifty yards from us. I saw Joseph behind the
wheel, in sunglasses, his hair artfully tousled. He looked
good. When I was tousled, I looked like I needed a shower.

"What kind of a man does that? Tells a woman something like that? Did you think I'd admire your fucking
honesty?"

Joseph tapped on the horn, and she turned slightly to
wave at him. When she turned back, I could see she was
crying.

"Molly—"

"Shut up. And I see you and Bill talking. I know what
you're talking about. You know what? Maybe Joseph
didn't drop in. Maybe I called *him*. Maybe I called him
after I had flown thousands of miles to have my best
friend tell me who he fucked and how it made him *feel*."

She turned and started to walk away, looking at me
over her shoulder. "Maybe with this one, at least I know
what I get. Maybe that's as good as I'm going to do." Her
voice broke. "Take your ghosts, and your feelings, your
ego, and your fucking...*tragedy* and bother someone else
with them."

"Molly, wait. My ego?"

"Stay away from me," she called. "I'll sell my house
and move away if you don't, if that's what I have to do.
Leave me alone."

She crossed in front of the car and got in.

"Nice car, Joe!" I hollered. "Life is good when someone else pays your way!"

The silver car reversed and then sprayed gravel as it left. I looked after them for a minute then turned back to the marina. Bill was waiting for me. Diane had gone back inside. My face was burning. I cut across the grass to avoid him.

"I pulled your boat out and filled it," he called. "It's down by the pumps, save you a step."

I kept walking and didn't answer.

"You're forgetting your dog," he yelled after me.

I stopped, shook my head, and started back. The dog was still sprawled across the sidewalk.

"Man's best friend," Bill said. "Good to have at times like these."

CHAPTER 27

Sam and Jenny Latta,
West Berlin, Germany, Saturday, May 25, 1957

An orchestra played "Les Fueilles mortes." She smelled like flowers really did smell, of earth and sun and water with the barest sweet overlay. Her neck and shoulders were delicate, but when she leaned into him she was as heavy and warm as the world's foundation. They felt eternal, moving through the dark and the music, floating here and there on the drafts of burning candles.

The music changed. She took his hand and led him to the balcony. The ruined city spread beneath them in pools of light as far as they could see. He pulled out his package of cigarettes and offered it to her.

"I have my own," she said. She took one out and he lit it. She looked into his eyes over the flame.

"I won't leave without you," he said. "You know that."

"I was never going to let you," she answered.

The light from inside caught her hair and her eyes. He couldn't read her expression. As she turned away from him, he caught her fragrance again.

"Are we forever?' he asked.

She didn't answer. Below them a car pulled up and stopped at the porte-cochere. The driver came around and opened the door for a woman. She was dressed to the ankles in black and sparkled as she walked. Before she entered the building she stopped to check her clutch and then looked up at them on the balcony, as if in some feral way she was aware of their beauty. She shook them off and went inside.

"Are you going to answer me?"

Her elbows were on the marble balustrade. She thumbed her hair behind her ear and smiled coolly to herself before she glanced at him. She held the smile. Her blue eyes were purpled by the night-time. She was perfectly contained.

"Do you know what makes me sad?" she asked. "Being at the beach and seeing a wave come in. It rolls and breaks, and then it slides back and it's gone. It comes and goes so fast, and it'll never happen just exactly like that ever again. It was unique, and it won't come back. Ever again." She finished her cigarette and flicked it over the railing. It sparked on the drive beneath them and winked out. "Then I think—I'm wrong. Years and years from now, someone else will look at them and be sad, someone who will never know that I was even here."

Her bracelets glinted when she put her hand over his and turned it over to hold onto it. He was surprised by the vulnerability of her gesture.

Her voice softened. "The waves aren't brief at all. I am."

She looked back at the city. He thought he saw her brush away a tear, but the movement was so casual that he couldn't be sure.

"I'm not going to be here forever," she said, "so don't ever ask me that again."

He turned her to him and kissed her, and it had to be enough.

ひらひ

Present Day:

That evening, I stood on my front veranda as the night came. I hesitated, then flipped the switch to turn my dock light on. Molly's house was on shore a mile and a half away from the island, across open water. As long as we had both lived on the lake, our dock lights were always left on, visible to each other in the dark. *I'm home, and everything's okay. I'm here.* Tonight there was no light on her side.

I went in. The dog had settled willingly enough in the main room, and I looked in on him. He was asleep on the couch. His day had probably been nearly as long as mine. He worried me. The boxer had jumped easily from the boat to shore, or to the dock. She had flung herself where she needed to. If she missed, she had enjoyed the swim. She had been able to neatly jump to and from the high seat in my elderly Jeep. She had gone nearly everywhere with me. This dog was different.

Huge and awkward, he had been coaxed into my boat with great difficulty. Once underway, he cowered on the deck and lost his footing several times on the trip across the lake.

I figured getting him into and out of my truck was going to be a nightmare. I looked down at him and ruffled the long hair on his neck.

"Poor guy," I said. "We'll figure it out, I guess."

I lay on my bed and thought about Molly, just a mile away. I didn't suppose she was sleeping alone. Eventually, the windows began to fill up with gray light. I could hear a couple of crows fighting over their breakfast as I closed my eyes and slept.

೮ೞೞ

May was creeping toward June beautifully. The morning air coming through the screen was cool, and I could smell the lake. I saw Blue in the clearing in front of the cabin. He was sitting quietly, head up, observing his new territory. It was a sheepdog thing. He needed to be at the top of a meadow, sitting still and observing a flock of sheep. Maybe I should get him some.

There was a five-gallon white plastic garbage pail in the corner by the sink, with a snap-on lid. I was slouched in my chair, watching the dog outside and thinking about getting more coffee when a slight movement from that corner caught my eye. I watched idly. In a minute, the movement happened again. It was the trash can. It rocked slightly, and shifted just a tiny bit on the floor. Something was inside the can.

I didn't have a small animal problem inside the cabin, simply because there weren't any animals on the island, except a couple of squirrels on the far side that appeared geriatric and stayed away from me. The land wasn't big enough to support anything else.

Whatever had found its way into my trash must have gotten trapped when I put something in and snapped the lid closed. I had just about made up my mind to carry the whole thing outside to release whatever it was, when first one catch, and then the other, popped free with an audible click. I sat back in my chair. What I was seeing didn't make sense. Nothing could release the catches from inside the can.

The lid tipped and slid off onto the floor. It rolled toward me and fell over. The container was nearly empty. It had a clean white plastic liner, and whatever was in the can was caught up in it. I heard it rustling around in the bottom. I stood up and took a step forward, when a dark-skinned hand appeared and grasped the edge of the can. I sat back down.

The black boy pulled himself out in a single fluid motion, emerging from the small plastic pail as though he were climbing out of a man-hole. He stood in my clean kitchen wearing twill overalls shortened to the knee, and a battered pair of men's black shoes. They were too big for him, were laced tightly, and worn without socks.

I knew that this was Eli Tull, and I knew that he was dead. Whatever was left of his skeleton was moldering away under six feet of moist dirt in a Georgia graveyard, and it had been there for over sixty years. I was looking at something from the past. The problem was, he didn't exist, but he was standing as large as life in the middle of my clean kitchen floor. Whatever he was, he wasn't dead, not quite.

He stood and looked around the room, not making a sound. I felt his look settle on me. I kept my own gaze around his midsection as his appearance began to change, to grow and bloat. His clothes became filthy and the skin on his legs turned gray. He was covered with reddish dust. Against my will, my eyes were drawn upward to the horror of his face. His head seemed to have expanded to the size of a watermelon. His features were smashed, his jaw was broken and askew, and his eye sockets were swollen and empty. The smell of mud and rot filled the room, and I felt my gorge rise.

I held his eyeless gaze for long seconds, and then he was as suddenly just a small boy again. He smiled at me sweetly and went out through the screen door into the yard. I saw Blue on his feet, barking, but not at the boy. There was a yellow dog in the yard with him. The boy held his arms wide, and the dog leapt onto my porch. There appeared to be a joyous reunion, and then the two of them moved soundlessly out of sight.

I stood up to follow them. My legs felt arthritic as I hobbled outside. I was having trouble catching my breath. I could hear myself gasping, but I didn't seem to be getting any air. Blue was standing at the far end of the porch, still barking toward the trees behind the cabin. I joined him and looked, but the path was empty. I hushed him and listened, but heard nothing moving through the trees.

"Eli!" I called. "Eli! What is it? What do you want?"

A bird chattered, and leaves rustled in the breeze far above me, but there was no other answer. The sunny summer day was suddenly icy cold. I was desperately afraid, not of the small boy, but of his reason for coming to find me on my island.

ℰℐℰℐ

I pulled my jeep into the parking lot of Robertson's Market. Molly's purple truck was parked near the front door. I didn't want to run into her.

Inside, the store was warm and smelled of the cedar logs it was built of. It was still early, and full of the quiet murmuring of staff getting ready for the onslaught of the day. In another hour the place would be busy, and by mid-morning there would be a crush of cottagers that wouldn't abate until late at night.

I grabbed a plastic carry basket from a stack and waded in to find milk and dog food. The rest of my shopping was haphazard. I never used a list. The aisles were nearly empty.

I turned a corner to find Molly three feet away from me. She was examining green peppers with the absolute concentration she gave to nearly everything she did. Every time that I saw her was a revelation to me. Some un-known lost thing inside of me came back. Something broken was fitted back into place. I could have looked at her for the rest of the day, but given our last conversation I wondered if it would be better to turn the corner and leave her alone.

She looked up at me briefly and then back at the vege-table in her hand. She had seen me, and I had no choice but to approach her. She didn't look up when she spoke.

"Hi, Mike."

"Morning. Listen, Molly, I was an idiot. I'm sorry."

She put peppers in her basket and moved on. I fol-lowed. Her voice was even and without expression. "I don't think," she said, "that this is the right time to talk about it. How's Blue doing?"

"He's going to be fine. There's going to be some ad-justment. He has a little trouble with getting into the boat, so I don't think he's going to be a dog that goes every-where with me."

"He's a pain in the ass."

"I didn't mean that."

"Look, Mike. It's been pointed out to me that dumping a dog on you was pretty presumptuous of me. If you don't want him, I'll be glad to take him."

"Pointed out by—let me guess, Joseph?"

She looked up and held my gaze. Her eyes showed nothing, no emotion at all, and the loss of her flooded me. She started to move away. "Bye, Mike."

I stood helplessly in the aisle, holding my empty bas-ket, for a long time after she was gone. I had never felt so lost.

CHAPTER 28

Sam, Jenny, and Michael Latta,
Lake Alatoona, Georgia, Sunday, June 16, 1974:

The boy sat on a rock, shivering from the cold. He dripped water onto the stone beneath him; the drops collected in tiny pools on the warm granite and then formed black rivulets that ran back into the lake they had come from. He was trying not to cry. He didn't cry often, and he tried to hold onto his outrage at his mother, as a way of fighting the fright he felt.

His father sat beside him, not saying anything. After a minute, the man stood and walked a short distance to the picnic table where the mother sat. She didn't look at the man when he approached. He got a towel from a beach bag that was sitting on the ground at her feet and returned to the rock.

"I hate her," the boy said.

"I know you're mad, Michael, but there are some things you can't say in front of me. That's one of them. It's not allowed."

He tucked the towel around the boy's shoulders. Over at the picnic table, the woman stood up and went down to the water's edge. She was careful to not glance in their direction. She bent, pulled off her sandals, and walked down the shoreline, away from them.

"She hit me."

Michael was a quiet, contained boy, not given to sharing more than he had to, and he was humiliated by his own tears. Sam felt helpless. He had only vague memories of his own father, and he often felt that growing up without one gave him an essential disadvantage. He saw himself as an imposter, fundamentally unfit for the job.

"She hit you because she loves you," Sam said.

Michael gave his father a sideways glance, incredulous.

They had come to the lake for a lunch and a swim. Mike went into the water and had been twice admonished, by Jenny from shore, that he was getting himself dangerously deep. He treated this with seven-year-old disdain, until all at once there was no rocky bottom beneath his feet. He bobbed up, squawking, and then went under again, swallowing water. Sam had gone into the water with his pants and shoes on.

When Michael was underwater and Sam's splashing progress to him seemed to be in slow motion, there was a terrible moment when Jenny felt her sanity slip. She wondered if it were possible for fear to stop a healthy heart. Then her Sam had emerged with her Michael under his arm, waded in, and set him on the shore. Wild, she had run down and slapped the boy across the face.

Mother and son had looked at each other, speechless with grief, until the spell broke and time started again. He had shrieked. She had turned away, and each of them had taken a broken heart to an opposite side, leaving Sam helpless between them.

"She hit you because she loves you," Sam repeated. "She was terrified of losing you, and when she didn't, she was mad at you for scaring her. You scared me, too."

"That's stupid," Michael sobbed.

"Maybe so, but it's something you should know. When someone's really mad, they're scared underneath. Remember that. Someday, knowing it might help you."

Far up the lake's shore, the small figure of Jenny stopped walking and turned to look back at them. They sat and watched her as she started back in their direction.

എസ്എ

Present Day:

"Sorry about your dad," Kate said. "Come sit in the back."

She brought me coffee and a piece of pie and sat down across from me. "Something new. Saskatoon berry," she said. "I'm not convinced."

I tasted it. "I'm not either."

"They're expensive," she said. "I have no doubt they're good for you. I feel foolish, because I got talked into buying them because they're Canadian. They don't grow around here, and there's nothing more Canadian than the billions of blueberries and raspberries that do. I'm a fool."

"I think it's probably rare that anyone talks you into anything." I smiled. "Mark it on your calendar."

"My niece called me last night. She's pretty angry with you."

"I'm not exactly happy with her either, Kate. She's playing house with Joseph again. It's so far out of character for her that it makes me wonder if I even know her at all."

"You've known each other for a year now, Michael. You're obviously wanting more than friendship." She stirred her coffee and set the spoon in the saucer, clearly weighing her words. "She hasn't told me how her feelings run," she said, "or I'd put you out of your misery. I don't make any secret of it that I'd like to see you two together. At some point, things are going to move forward, or they'll move backward. I think it's been long enough that you'd best make yourself plain to her. You have your own issues, or you would have done so a long time ago."

"Maybe you're right," I sighed. "I have other problems I want to talk to you about, though. On the island."

I told her about my visitor the day before, the boy who crawled out of my kitchen trash can. Eli Tull. "It scared me to death, and if I scared easy I wouldn't be back on that island in the first place."

"No chance it was a kid playing around then?" she asked. "Got into your house, playing tricks?"

"No, Kate. This is a small trash can. A bucket. An infant couldn't hide in it, let alone a boy. Even so, it wouldn't account for horrible injuries on him appearing and disappearing. And the smell. Like the worst kind of swamp while he was there, and no trace of any kind of odor after he left. It was Eli."

"Sometimes ghosts are trying to frighten us," she said. "They're angry and bitter at where they find themselves, and they lash out at the living."

"I don't think so, Kate. He changed into something awful, but it wasn't for long, and when he changed back he gave me this nice, shy smile, like he was apologizing. I think he was making sure I knew who he was." I struggled for the real sense of what I had seen. "It sounds weird, but I think he was partly…playing."

"Like children do."

"Yes. Not entirely playing, though. He came for a reason."

"I wish Molly had been with you," she said. "She has

a knack for actually talking to them, not just seeing them."

"I wish someone had been with me. The dog's useless."

"Where is your new friend?" Kate laughed. "Out in the truck?"

"No, he's at home. He doesn't like getting in and out of the boat, or the truck for that matter. Too big and clumsy. Happy to stay and sleep on the porch."

"My Molly loves him, though, so she does. Thinks he's a fine animal."

A group of older men at a front table gathered themselves to go. They waved back to Kate on their way out.

"So…you think the whole thing was keyed on you," she said, "not the place. Not the island or the cabin or the kitchen. An active apparition, not a memory. Aware of you, and trying to interact."

"Yes, definitely active," I said, "and one that has come here, all the way from Georgia."

"Can you tell me about Georgia?" she asked. "Your father's story? Molly told me a lot of it, but she said you found out something awful about him—didn't say what it was."

I told her that my father had shot and killed two grown men when he was a young child, and it was why he had been hounded and harassed right before he died.

"Oh, my God. And how old was he when he did this?"

"Really young. Ten years old. He was so outraged that they got away with it, he shot them both dead. That's his story."

She stared at me. "That's incredible. Do you think it's true? Can a ten-year-old boy even manage a gun?"

"Sure. Some kids are out shooting squirrels and birds younger than that."

"I'm not daft, Michael," she said. "A rifle or a pellet

gun is a different matter than having the hand strength to fire a pistol and kill a grown man. That's a tall order for small hands."

"True, I get that. Sorry. I don't know. The act itself fits him, somehow."

"It would have scarred him," she said, "very badly. Unless a child that age got help, it would profoundly affect them, right into adulthood. I saw enough of it, early traumas, God knows."

Like her niece. Kate had been a teacher before she retired to Ansett and her coffee shop.

"Was he charged with the murders?" she asked. "What would they do with a child back then, send them to reform school?"

"No, this is the worst part. Apparently someone else was arrested and hanged for shooting the two guys. The black kid, the first victim—his father. My dad tried to tell what he did, and they gagged him, wouldn't let him tell the truth."

"Who did?"

"I'm not sure," I said. "I suppose his parents, my grandparents."

"So an innocent man was executed for it? And he wasn't allowed to tell?"

"Appears even the police wanted it kept a secret. They had already executed someone. No one wanted it brought up."

"That's a burden no child should bear," she said.

I looked across the table at her. Her eyes were impossibly blue. "And your ghost yesterday, the child?" she asked. "You think there's a connection."

I stood up to go. She kept her seat and looked up at me, her arms folded on the table.

"I do, Kate. You've always said the island was some kind of doorway, and I have a feeling it's a convenient door for something that's come a long way to find me and tell me something."

I pulled out my wallet, and she impatiently waved it off.

"Then it'll come clear sooner or later. Go with what you're feeling. Ghosts are feelings, after all. Pure emotion. It's why they come here, and why we see them."

That evening I sat on the dock and looked out at the dark. When I had first come here to live, the inky blackness of the nights had nearly overwhelmed me. Darkness in the city was no more than an electric twilight, visible from many miles away as a huge mushroom of light.

When my urban eyes had adjusted after a week or two, I could see fine at night by the ambient light that the surface of the lake gave back. Only the interior of the island was dark enough to need a flashlight, and I never had a reason to go there after sundown. The night was overcast, but there was a hole in the cloud canopy directly above me. The stars over my head were brighter than the scattered lights on the opposite shore.

Molly's dock light was off again. I wondered if she was leaving it dark as a message to me, or if she had left the lake and was somewhere else tonight. It amounted to the same thing.

'*Take your ghosts, and your feelings, your ego, and your fucking...tragedy and bother someone else with them.*'

The cabin's screen door creaked open behind me. After a minute, Blue padded out and put his head in my lap. I scratched the top of his head.

"Deep down, you're a good boy, aren't you?" I asked.

On impulse, I pulled out my phone. I debated a flimsy premise for calling her and then decided to stick to the truth. I missed her. I opened the phone and peered at the lit screen just as it lit with an incoming call.

I pressed the buttons to listen and put the phone to my ear. The voice was instantly familiar.

"I know what you did."

My breath caught in my throat. I pressed the phone hard against my ear. "Arthur?"

"I know what you did," it said again, and disconnected.

I knew the voice. It was the same person, and it didn't sound like Arthur Sutton. Not at all. It certainly wasn't his mother, unless her ghost could use a telephone.

'*I know what you did.*'

"Son of a bitch," I said, and let my breath out.

On cue, the dog sighed deeply and left to go back to the house. He could push open the cabin's screen door to go out, but it swung the wrong way for him to go back in. I knew I'd find him waiting on the porch.

I sat thinking. After a few minutes, I stood up and followed the dog to the cabin and got ready for bed. When I finished brushing my teeth, I looked into the mirror.

'*Take your ghosts, and your feelings, your ego, and your fucking...tragedy and bother someone else with them.*'

I didn't want to see the face in the mirror. I didn't like it. I turned off the bathroom light. In bed, I lay still and listened to myself breathe.

CHAPTER 29

Eli and Roy Tull,
Milton County, Georgia, Tuesday, July 2, 1946:

"Roy?"

"What, Eli?"

The old wood cabin was dark. The two boys lay up in the loft. Their parents slept below, and they spoke quietly.

"Are we going fishing tomorrow?"

"No. I have things to do tomorrow. I can't be fishing with you."

"What kind of things? Can I come?"

"I can't be dragging no little kid with me everywhere, Eli. I have grown-up business, you know."

"I ain't a little kid. I'm near as big as you. Mama says we're two peas in a pod. She cain't hardly tell us apart anymore is what she says."

"Mama always says things like that. You'll never be as big as me."

"Will, too. Bigger, maybe. I might be bigger'n Daddy. You'll see."

There was noise from below, and they heard their father cross to the base of the ladder.

"Hey, peas-in-a-pod, the both of you," he whispered loudly from below. " Go to sleep. Not another word."

They heard him return to his bed. The yellow dog stirred from the floor at their feet, and the bed shifted as his weight landed on their legs. Each boy, in turn, had a warm snuffle in his ear and then the bed settled as the animal lay down between them and sighed loudly.

Their mother's voice carried from below. "Jacob, that dog is on the bed again. I can hear it. I've told them not to let it up on the bed with them. I'm going to put that creature out of this house for good in the morning, I swear."

"Hush, Dottie. You say that every night. Leave it be."

The two boys giggled silently. They both turned inward and put an arm across the dog between them. The old cabin creaked and groaned and settled and finally slept.

 cɔeɔ

Present Day:

The next afternoon, I got a cold drink from the refrigerator and headed outside to sit on the dock.

"C'mon, boy," I said to the dog.

He looked up at me from his sprawl on the front porch and scrambled up. He walked by me and stood patiently at the door. I sighed and turned back to let him in. I had a couple of window air conditioners running inside against the heat, and I closed the door behind him. I could see the blue glare of the lake between the trees as I walked across the forest clearing in front of the cabin. As soon as I came out of the pines, the temperature hit me hard. The large granite pier that jutted from the island was blistering under my bare feet

The day was brilliant. I sat and looked out at the water. The trees on the opposite shore wavered and shimmered. The islands to the west hovered above the lake's surface, like flying saucers uncertain about landing. I took a drink of cold soda, held the bottle up to the light, and wished it was a beer.

My cell phone vibrated.

"Are we better than this?" Molly asked.

Far off, a boat engine revved and I spotted it, red and white, beginning its approach from across the reach. Molly. My heart sped up. "I think we are," I said.

"Good."

I could hardly hear her over the wail of her boat's motor when she hung up.

The heat was forgotten, and I absently set the bottle down beside my chair. For the next couple of minutes, the bow grew larger until finally I could make her face out behind the windshield. When she was near, she cut the engine and drifted expertly to the dock. I caught the rope she flicked at me.

She pushed her sunglasses back on her head and smiled. "Look what I brought us," she said.

It was hard to take my eyes from her face. I glanced at the figure that sat in the other cockpit chair, holding the metal grab handle in front of him.

"Hello, Doctor," I said. 'You keep your promises. Nice to see you."

"That's a fact," he said. "I do. I can now cross Canada off my list of places I never got to. This is beautiful, Mike. I don't know how you can ever leave it."

Roy wore deck shoes, plaid pants, and a high-billed fishing hat. He didn't look like he had spent much of his life outside his office. I was glad to see him.

"When did you get here?" I asked.

"Last night," he said. "Miss Molly was kind enough to drive down to Toronto to pick me up."

I glanced at her. I hadn't known a thing about it.

"Say 'Toronno,'" I told him. "If you pronounce both the 'T's people will know you're a foreign tourist."

Molly burst out laughing, despite herself. "Yes," she said, "and never mind your southern drawl. It's pronouncing all your 'T's that gives you away."

"Someone from Alanna, Georgia isn't worried about it anyway," I said, and helped him out of the boat. "How long can you stay?"

"Just a few days this time," he said. "I can already tell I'd like to come back, though. See it when it snows."

We walked up to the cabin, Roy trailing behind us.

"He's staying with you?" I asked quietly.

"He's seventy five, Mike. You don't even have level ground to walk on here."

"You have room?"

"All we need. Joseph was using the spare bedroom, but he's gone back to the city. I'm by myself."

I was careful to keep any expression from my face. I was relieved, ecstatic in fact, but I knew that Joseph would be back, and that Molly would take him in again when it happened. I was still on the outside looking in.

"I went a little further," she said. "I invited some people to dinner, a get-acquainted thing for him."

"That's a nice idea," I said, wondering if I was invited.

"Of course, you're invited," she said, reading my mind. "I'm having it here. Tonight."

I laughed. "Am I cooking?"

"No, you'd have to open too many cans. You'd hurt your wrist. I have food in the boat. I need you to stay out of my way. You aren't put out, are you? I'm not presuming?"

"I'm just glad to see you," I said honestly. "Attach any strings you want to."

"Kind of glad to see you too," she said. "A little bit."

Her voice was casual, but there was a tiny distance in her manner that made me wonder if I were outside and had lost the keys to whatever parts of her she had let me have access to.

We settled on the veranda. Molly and Roy decided to split one of my beers. On my way in to get it for them, I let the dog out. He pushed by me and greeted Molly as if she were his heart's desire. When I came back out I handed each of them a glass.

"So how was the trip up?" I asked Roy.

He stretched his legs out, looking happy. "I enjoyed it," he said. "It was exciting coming through Canadian Customs. They were a little too nice, though. I would have appreciated more drama, maybe a search of my luggage, to mark the event."

"You've just never wanted to travel?" Molly said.

"Oh, I did. I never had the time. Never had the time for a lot of things, I guess."

He shook his head and smiled, remembering. "In the early years. I was the only black doctor in town. Taking a holiday would have weighed heavily on me. I would have worried the whole time and spoiled it. As I got older, staying close to my practice was habit."

"Well, we'll try to make this a good holiday for you," Molly said. "I'm going to get the dinner stuff from the boat."

She waved away my offer of help and headed to the dock. I noted that Blue followed, eagerly circling her whole way down. The dog's laziness disappeared when she was around.

"How old is this place of yours, Mike?"

"The cabin was built in 1900 or thereabouts. A group of doctors from New York used it as a retreat."

"Colleagues of mine."

"Probably a few years before your time, Roy. They

were Spiritualists. I imagine they used the place for a séance or two. Molly's aunt, Kate Bean, is going to be here
tonight. She can tell you more about that part if you're
interested."

I filled him in on some of the events that had brought
me to the island: the divorce settlement and my own need
for isolation.

"How has all the peace and quiet here worked out for
you?"

Molly raised her eyebrows and smiled on her way by
with an armload.

"It's not as quiet here as you might think," I said.

"Do you still want to talk about your father?" Roy
asked. "Are you ready for that?"

I was uncomfortable. "I think I need to."

Someone across the lake was running a chain saw, and
it snarled faintly across the water at us.

"I told you a little, but not about that day. My mother
had taken me with her to my auntie's house to visit. We
were there when the police came and took my daddy
away."

He pronounced it *On-tay*.

"I wasn't allowed out of my parents' sight in those
days, right after my brother—anyway, we didn't know
my father had been taken until we got home and the
neighbors told us. We went to the jail every day until he
died, but we were never allowed to see him. I only saw
him once, being taken from a police car into the court-
house. He was in a crowd of police, and even though I
hollered for him, he didn't see me."

"Awful," I said.

"It was," he said heavily. "I still dream about it all
these years later. It was the last time I was ever going to
see my father. There was a huge crowd outside the court-
house, trying to get a look at him. The state police were

there to keep it under control. Six or seven police were all around him and ran him from the car to the door."

"Were they worried about lynching?"

He shook his head and leaned back in the chair, arms crossed. "No. I've seen ugly crowds of whites with that evil on their minds, and as a black person, you make yourself scarce. I wasn't worried that day, and plenty of people knew who I was. There wasn't a bad feeling toward my daddy for killing that trash. Those people had white skin, but there were parents in that crowd too, lots of them, and they didn't condone torturing a small child to death, nigger or not." He took a tiny sip of his beer. "What I dream about is that I was never going to see my daddy again, and I yell for him but no sounds come out. I'm mute. I feel like everything will turn out different if I can just get his attention, but I never do."

He turned slightly in his chair to look at me beside him. His eyes searched my face. His voice, normally cultured and without idiom, was lapsing into his childhood's dialect as he remembered. "Course I forgave Sam. How could I not, after all these years? He was thinking about Eli when he did it. It also wasn't a good thing that they got away with it and were going to get a pile of money from a magazine to shit on my brother's death in public. Your father set all that right. I admire the hell out of him, and I know when he got to Heaven, my daddy shook his hand."

"He was sitting where you are now, looking at the water when he died," I said, feeling the sting of sudden tears. "I think he worried about Heaven, at the end."

"No need. God knows our hearts better than we do ourselves. Your daddy was no killer."

He reached down to stroke the dog. Blue got up and wandered away.

"It's a funny thing about that kiss," Roy said. "My

brother didn't kiss that girl, she kissed *him,* and that's what made it so bad. If my brother had kissed her, I think he would of gotten hisself a beating and that would have been the end of it." He turned in his seat and grasped my forearm. "*She kissed him.* Her daddy saw it. He saw his daughter kiss a nigger on the lips. Whether he knew it or not when he came and took my brother, he couldn't let him live. Not when he knew what his daughter was. Elijah was doomed."

It *was* important. I could see it.

"After that," he said, "the evil and lies kept piling up. And you know what else? All the parents of all the kids who were there died that day, even if they kept walking around for a while. All the parents had lives that were over."

"How so?" I asked. "I see some of it, I think, but—"

"Listen," he said. "Wanda's father was shot dead, along with her uncle, by your daddy. Her mother hung herself that winter. Sam's parents, your grandparents were the absolute picture of white middle class stability, but your granddaddy ran off and died badly on the West Coast somewhere. The mother dived into a bottle of booze and never got back out, died destitute and crazy on a ward. Eli's parents, mine too—well, we know my daddy was executed, but my mama was gone to me too. I brought her to live with me when she was old, and that was a good thing, but she had no part of me for many, many years. I reminded her of my dead brother." He was getting visibly upset. "Every family that was involved lost everything. The kiss just got started with my brother, and it's still going on. It's going generation by generation. It's evil. It's just evil, and it still goes on."

I thought about the calls I was still getting. "It's going to end now, Roy."

He nodded, and his face relaxed.

I took his glass and went inside. Molly was standing at the counter cutting vegetables, and I stood beside her to rinse it out. She turned her head and carefully kissed me on the mouth. It was brief, and then she returned to what she was doing. Neither of us said anything.

Her lips were warm, and I could still feel them when I went back outside. The sunlight looked different.

Later in the afternoon, I took Molly aside. I keyed up my messages and handed her my cell phone. "Listen to this," I said.

She pressed the phone to her ear. I could see her body stiffen as she listened. "How do you play it over?" she asked.

I showed her on the phone, and she played it several more times.

"Can you find out where this came from?" she asked.

"The number's blocked."

"Definitely the same voice as on your dad's answering machine," she said.

I agreed.

"Wanda Sutton is dead, Mike. Who the hell is doing this? Why?"

☙❧

Bill and Diane came for dinner, bringing Molly's Aunt Kate with them. When they landed, Kate had immediately taken me aside. "Have you seen the boy in the kitchen again?" she asked.

I shook my head.

"All right then." She dimpled, reminding me of Molly. "I don't see myself putting anything in your kitchen garbage, just the same."

The six of us sat in my kitchen. The door was open, and a warm night breeze brought in soft sounds from the lake. Far away lightning flashed without rain. After dark, the room smelled like mystery—of old wood and apples and dried spices. A metal chandelier hung by a chain from the rafters. Molly had filled it with lit candles, and in their glow, our faces were gold. Summers gone by flickered quietly in the corners.

The evening went well. Molly cooked in an unstudied, casual way, but her results were reliably wonderful. We passed roast beef, corn, and potatoes around the table, and for a while conversation stopped.

"If this is how Canadians eat, I've been missing out," Roy said.

"This isn't really a summer meal," Molly apologized. "If we're going to eat on the water, I suppose it should be barbeque. I just couldn't see it tonight, though. I needed comfort food."

"Me, too," Bill said, looking at me meaningfully.

I tried not to smile. Diane was enthusiastic and hopeless in the kitchen, and Bill and I had suffered through many of her well-intentioned culinary experiments together.

"Sometimes nothing else will do," Roy said. "Years and years ago, my mama always made us stew and biscuits. I cook for myself these days, and that's what I make now when my heart needs someplace to go."

"Exactly," Molly said, putting the gravy boat in front of him. "When your heart needs somewhere to go. I like that." She paused for a moment, lost in thought. "For me," she went on, "it was always that someone cared enough about me to take care of something I needed, something basic, and that they loved me enough to make it good." She smiled at her aunt. "It was always Kate's roast beef on the weekend for me. I remember coming home from whatever I was doing, as a little girl or a teenager—even later coming from college and smelling it when I walked in. It was always home. It always said that I was safe."

"Even now, from time to time," Kate said. "No age limit on it."

"Even now," Molly agreed. "And you never ever forget the smell of it, or how it falls apart in your mouth. It's all about safety, and it's all about home."

"And you made it for us tonight," Bill said, pouring wine into Diane's glass. "We're honored."

"Of course, I did," Molly said simply. "You people are my home."

Over drinks and coffee, the evening slipped into night. I looked across the table at Molly. She leaned forward, her elbows on the table, her tea untouched in front of her. She slowly wound a lock of hair with her finger, her compete attention on the doctor. Her amber eyes were almost black in the candle light. I felt like I could sit quietly and look at her for hours.

Diane brought the coffee pot to the table and topped off her husband. The doctor waved her off, indicating the half-inch of whiskey still in his glass. He looked around the table at us. "I'm so grateful to be here," he said.

It was an odd thing to say, and I was touched. The man had a profound humility, a decency that made me want to be around him. I could see why Molly wanted him as a guest.

Outside in the dark, the loons started calling. It was a night noise that I hated. It sounded like the voices of lost girls. The warbling cries out on the cold water told me that hot tea, candle light, and the faces of my friends were transient. They all might vanish, with me sitting alone in the shadows.

Eventually, drinks were done and dishes were cleared, and I walked my guests down to the boat. Bill kept a firm grip on the doctor's elbow as they went slowly across the clearing in front of the cabin. As we stood out on the dock, the northern sky was clear and full of stars, none of which were reflected in the black water. The night was warm, but I felt like I needed a jacket.

"Getting choppy," Bill said. "Gonna storm tonight for sure."

Molly put her hand on the doctor's arm. "You've got the key," she said. "You're sure you'll be all right by yourself tonight?"

I hardly dared to breathe.

"Actually," Bill interrupted, "he's going fishing up to the Bear Lake falls with me in the morning. You know I leave before the sun's up. We'll give him a bed at the marina."

"I'll be fine," Roy said. "I'm going to teach Bill how to fish. That should keep me busy for at least tomorrow."

"Two old fools," Diane told Molly. "Be a miracle if they don't both fall out of the boat."

We laughed and I shook hands with Roy and Bill. I kissed Diane and then Kate, who stretched up to whisper in my ear. "Take care of my niece, Michael. You both need some healing."

Molly and I stood and watched Bill ease the white boat back from the dock, the engine burbling softly. There was a clunk as he shifted forward and then the exhaust note rose higher and they headed for the reach. There was a gentle series of splashes on the rocks lining the shore as their wash reached us. We stood and watched the craft's tiny red and green lights until they vanished.

"Am I being presumptuous—staying?" she asked.

"Maybe a little," I answered.

She peered at me in the dark and then caught my smile. I caught her wrist as she swung at me, and we walked, laughing, back to the cabin.

CHAPTER 30

Sam and Mike Latta,
Marietta, Georgia, Tuesday, September 6, 1985:

Sam opened his eyes and looked at the ceiling. It was morning, and it felt late. He had a general sense of dread and regret and was in no hurry to identify the reason. His eyes fell on Jenny's side table across the bed. He knew that the drawers were full of her detritus, but he had not opened them in the year and a half since her death. He was careful not to trespass on her side of the bed. Unless the sheets were being changed, her half stayed made, even when he was sleeping. Sam knew that she was dead. He didn't harbor illusions that he was saving the scene for her, but he did it anyway.

The fight with Mike last night came back to him, and his spirit sank. He sat up and swung his feet to the floor. The nearly empty vodka bottle on his own side table accused him. He groaned and went into the bathroom. Then he dressed and went downstairs. He was relieved to hear his son in the kitchen. There were vacuum tracks in the hall carpet. The jumble of mail on the small table by the front door was neatly stacked. It appeared that Mike had set the house in order while Sam slept. It felt like the worst kind of portent. He fought the strange urge to up-end the table, to scatter the contents of the coat closet, to roll the clock back, perhaps to ward off what was happening here.

Mike stood at the sink, finishing up the dishes. Sam leaned in the doorway.

"House looks great," he said.

The son didn't look up from the soapy water.

"About last night," Sam said. "I'm just worried about you. I got pretty upset, and I shouldn't have."

There was long silence. Mike turned the water off and began to wipe the drain board.

Sam took a breath, and persisted. "I'm sorry," he said.

Mike didn't answer and, in one of those strange, rare moments that none of us recognize when they are happening, the course of both lives changed. If he had spoken, everything would have been different, but his hurt was too great, and hope went spinning off into the darkness.

Mercifully, for the rest of his life he didn't distinguish those few seconds for what they were. Ignorance is our doctor, our healer. If we knew what we did, our lives would be paralyzed by regret. We streak like comets, unaware of the wide tails we leave behind.

"You still leaving?" Sam asked.

Mike nodded. The night before, he had announced his intention to move to California. His girlfriend of three years, a sharp and pretty blonde who had always seemed to Sam to be about ten steps ahead of his son, had dumped him. She was attending a university in Paris, France. The decision was sudden and final. Sam suspected that her well-to-do parents had facilitated the change to distance her from Mike and the possibility of a young marriage.

Just like so, she was gone. A bright, glittering future

stretched in front of her, one that included other men. Mike's grief was bottomless. He was going somewhere, anywhere that didn't hold her ghost, the streets she had walked on, the things she had known.

Sam had told him angrily that there were other girls. Mike was an indifferent student and Sam had begged favors from academic contacts to get his admission to Georgia Tech in the fall. If he left for California, a second chance was unlikely. Sam told him that if he got in his truck and drove to the west coast, there could be no coming back.

He told his son that there was an entire world full of girls with cute laughs, clean hair, and shiny teeth. He told him that his youth was magnifying the importance of this girl and distorting his lust into some pretense of love. He told his son that he knew nothing, understood nothing. He was deserting his future to make a wretched gesture to this girl, who couldn't care less.

In truth, there would never again be a first love, this love, for Mike. There would be other loves, but this was a loss that scarred, and Sam knew it. He was a man who kept the ashes of his great love on a shelf in his bedroom closet. He understood the depth of his son's grief. If Mike had spoken, everything would have been different, but Sam's fear was too great, and his son went spinning off to the other side of the country.

The morning passed, and father and son found themselves on the front veranda. They shook hands awkwardly.

"Well, good luck," Sam said. "Call me."

"Thanks, Dad," Mike said. "I will."

Sam desperately wanted to ask Mike where he was planning to go and how to reach him. He was deeply afraid of giving the journey credibility if he did. Better to dismiss it, and perhaps Mike would abandon the idea. He watched the old blue truck turn the corner at the end of the street, and his heart broke. All of the next years would have been different if he had said, "I love you," but he knew that his son didn't want to hear it.

In his truck, Mike thought bitterly that Sam hadn't even wanted to know where he was going. He looked at his childhood home in his rear view mirror before he turned the corner. He felt the loss of his mother and his father both, and his heart broke. All of the next years would have been different if he had said, "I love you," but he knew that his father didn't want to hear it.

ᴄ⁄ᴐᴄ⁄ᴐ

Present Day:

The moon had crossed to the other side of the cabin, and we lay in the dimness, drowsing.

"Do you ever want kids again?" Molly asked.

I was startled awake. "Why do you ask that?"

"Just answer me."

"I'm a little old, Molly. That time's come and gone for me."

"For me, too, maybe. Doesn't mean I can't ask the question." She sat up in bed. "I'll just tell you…" she started.

She was silent again. I saw her jaw working against what she needed to say, and I felt dread wash through me like a strange drug. My face felt cold. I knew that she was ending us.

At last, she spoke. "You told me that you'd never risk another child, not after losing your daughter. Well, you have another one on the way. I'm not going to try to force you, or even ask you to be a part of it." She turned and looked at me, into me. "I decided today to tell you it was someone else's. I knew that would break your heart, but I thought maybe would be kinder to you in the long run. You deserve more credit than that, I guess."

The world around the cabin seemed to slow down and stop. I realized that my own eternity hung in question. Everything about me, no matter how this worked out, was changed in this scene.

"How do you feel about it?" I asked.

"I've waited my whole life for this," she said simply. "Better late than never."

"Part of me died with my daughter. That's never going to heal, not in this world. I said I'd never dream of having another child—but right now I'm wondering what Abby would say if she knew."

"I imagine she does know."

Molly was crying. So was I.

"My answer is absolutely yes," I said. "I feel like I'm alive again."

"Do you really think we're too old for this?" she asked, her mouth moving against my neck.

"We're probably just about old enough, I'd say."

We held each other for what seemed like hours. Outside the screen door, the lake went about its night-time business and we heard none of it. We might have even dozed. After a long time, I spoke.

"What about us?" I asked.

"What about us? We'll figure it out, won't we?"

"We will. Is it a boy or a girl?"

"Don't call the baby 'it.' We have weeks before we know. It's still too early. I think 'Sam' works as a name either way, don't you?"

"It works fine," I said. "My dad would be pleased."

"Have you been thinking more about your father?" she asked.

"Some, yes. I guess I feel closer to him than I did when he was alive."

"What's going through your mind?

"I suppose I admire him," I said. "I admire him for what he did as a kid, and I admire him for somehow living with it afterward. He should have been in therapy after he killed those guys. He was ten years old, and instead of getting help, he had to keep a secret. He was damaged. Damaged for good."

"He went on to get married, though," she said. "He had a career. We both saw your mother in the church, Mike. She came to see you, and to let you know that they were together again."

"Why do you think that?" I asked.

"Not sure. Woman's intuition, I think."

She patted my shoulder and arranged my arm for a pillow.

Her breathing steadied and she got heavier on my shoulder, and I knew she was asleep. I felt myself drifting, and I realized that I felt secure for the first time in a long while. The big dog padded in from the main room, his nails clicking softly on the wood floor. His white shape drifted into and then out of my field of vision as he went to Molly's side of the bed. He sighed loudly as he settled to the floor beside her, and then he was quiet.

There was movement high up in the darkest corner of the room. My eyes slowly adjusted, and I realized that it was a small figure, a child. Eli was back. He sat in the rafters, swinging his feet back and forth, into and out of the moon's shine. My hand rested on the pillow in front of my face. Barely moving my arm, I gave him a small wave. His shape shifted in the darkness and he waved back. I fell asleep.

I woke up the next morning to an empty bed. The air from the open window was cool and fresh, and the early sun through the leaves stained everything green. The day was as weightless as I was. I could see the dock from the window. Molly's boat was gone.

There was a note for me on the bedroom door. She had left early for Huntsville. She taught a summer class a couple of mornings a week and promised to find me later. Out of the shower, I found Blue asleep and sprawled across the kitchen floor.

"Let's go get coffee," I said.

He picked up his head and looked at me doubtfully.

"Might be a donut for you."

He scrambled to his feet.

"Stupid's all an act, isn't it?"

I herded him to the boat. The trip down the lake was fresh and cool. There was no boat traffic at the marina. I knew that Bill and the doctor had probably left to fish in Bill's boat hours before. We walked to the dirt parking area where I kept my truck. Opening the passenger door, I helped Blue up into the old yellow Jeep then went around and pushed him out of the driver's seat.

The lakefront road was empty. I didn't see another car until I left the marina road to join the early highway traffic for the two miles into Ansett. In a couple of hours, the cars would be bumper to bumper as summer residents flooded in for liquor, groceries, and socializing, but this early, the downtown streets carried only a trickle of early shoppers. I had no trouble finding a parking spot near the coffee shop.

I wanted to say hello to Kate. I'd missed her, and with the imminent baby, she was now my family as well as Molly's. She was also the most psychically in-tune person that I'd ever met, and I needed advice.

There was a scattering of early locals at the tables inside. The air was fragrant with baked goods and coffee beans.

Kate spotted me, wiped her hands, and came around the counter. She kissed my cheek. "Congratulations," she said.

I may have looked surprised, because she smiled. "I know you have the news. Your face gives you away. Looks good on you." She went behind the counter. Kate never said too much. "Sit down," she called "Pie?"

"As long as it's not Saskatoon berry," I said.

She burst out laughing. She joined me shortly with a slice of cherry for me and coffee for both of us. "Dinner was good last night," she said. "I enjoyed the whole evening. You and Molly are natural together. You'll make good parents, I think."

"Thanks. I hope so. There's something else I didn't mention, Kate. I wanted your take on it."

I told her about the call I had received while I waited for my plane in Atlanta, and again standing on my dock. It was the same caller from the very beginning. *I know what you did.* I described the silent malice I had felt on the other end of the line.

"Sounds crazy," I said, "but I'm almost wondering if there's something supernatural at work. Seems like all of the major players are dead now."

She shook her head. "Not typical. I'd be surprised. Manipulation of electronics is interesting, but more suited to movies than real life, in my experience. It does sound like spirits aren't at rest, though, especially the old woman who hung herself. You said earlier that she spoke to you even though she appeared to be dead?"

"Wanda *was* dead, Kate. It was her dead body. There's no possibility she was still alive. I could even smell that she'd messed herself when it happened. Then she opened her eyes and talked to me, and it turned into someone else. She was trying to get down, get the noose off. It was hard to watch that and not run over to help. I have a feeling it would have been a horror if I had."

"You said her mother committed suicide in the same spot?' she asked.

"Yes, same spot, probably even the same roof beam. It was in the 1940s, after she lost her husband. I'm thinking it was her I saw right before I ran out, because it definitely wasn't Wanda anymore."

"If there was already negative energy in that store...it's the same store where your dad..."

"Yes, it's where my dad shot and killed the two men."

"Another violent death is like putting fresh batteries in a flashlight. The mother's suicide poisoned the place. Powerful energy."

"Can something like that hurt you? Was I in danger?"

"It's funny how that question always seems to relate to the physical, as if only our bodies can really be hurt." She thought for a moment, looking into my eyes. "Physically, no, I don't think so," she said. "It's a fright show. It's make-believe, in a way. It can't really touch you, can't hurt you or kill you, although I'm sure there are those who dispute that. Mentally is different. It's an enormous amount of negativity, a barrage of harmful energy. How did you feel afterward?"

"Beat up," I said. "Invaded, assaulted. Sick."

She nodded. "That being said, it would make sense for you to actively avoid energy like that for a while. Stay away from the ghosties and the places where they like to go. Make sense?"

"I will if I can."

"Kind of hard, living where you do, but try. More coffee?"

She got up and was busy behind the counter for a few minutes. When she returned with fresh cups, I had thought of something else.

"Kinda funny that three people died violently there,

and there doesn't seem to be a trace of the father or the uncle."

Kate sat very still and rubbed her thumb back and forth on the handle of her cup. She took a sip and looked up at me. "We don't really know why some folks hang around," she said, "and others don't. Some souls are gone on their way before the bodies start to cool down, and others stay here for generations. I can only tell you that the hauntings that I've experienced are pretty consistent. There's always a reason. It isn't random. Hauntings are just delays. A human haunt always moves on eventually. There's a castle in the UK that was reliably haunted for two hundred years, with regular visitations by the same person. They did tours. The sightings stopped forty years ago, completely. Everyone moves on eventually.

"I don't think time is the same over there," she went on, "or matters as much. I lived in a house in Toronto years ago that seemed to be haunted by the spirit of a little girl. Molly saw her, as a matter of fact, several times when she was young. So did I. We heard her from time to time in different parts of the house, always calling for her mother. I looked into it and found an eight year-old girl had died of influenza in…1928, or something like that…in one of the upstairs bedrooms. They found her dead in bed one morning."

"Awful," I said.

"Over time, she stopped showing up. It made me sad to think of her wandering that house for half a century. She was completely innocent, and clearly lost. Eventually I realized that all those years might have been a couple of minutes for her. I like to think her mother came 'round finally to pick her up. Anyway, look at your ghosts as if they were alive, and it might help you figure out the whys. There's always a reason."

"Typically?" I asked.

"All right," she said. "Three main reasons." She ticked off fingers, making a list. "First, unfinished business. The deceased stays around because they feel that they need to control something they've left behind. The emotion, the attachment has to be extreme. A mother who leaves behind young children is a good example. Usually a fairly benevolent presence, not really concerned with living people other than those that are the focus of their concern. Sometimes the unfinished business can involve an unhealthy attachment to a person to a place, though, something that's loved that the dead person is unwilling to part with."

She ticked another finger. "Second reason, guilt. The person doesn't move on, maybe because they're too caught up in their own anguish. The term 'rest in peace' probably comes from this. I don't think any of us rest after we die—be a long eternity if we did. Has to do with agitated personalities.

"Third and last, crazy. People who are lost and confused when they leave this life don't automatically find themselves when they pass on. Those are the ones I worry about. Just as a mentally ill person can be wildly unpredictable, so can a mentally ill ghost. Those are the ones most likely to seek out and interact with strangers and the ones most likely to be angry or hostile."

"What am I dealing with?"

"You have more than one ghost, Mike." She smiled. "You've told me about three of them. The little boy has appeared several times. We think it's Elijah Tull, the little murdered boy. He fits the description, and you say he's manifested his injuries."

"Not guilt, surely. He didn't do anything wrong."

"No, I think we give him the first category. He has unfinished business. He's not attached to a place. You've seen him in the Atlanta graveyard, and now more than once at your island. Nor is he attached to a person. He's clearly interacting with you, and he never met you in life. He's even gone to some effort to change his appearance for you, so you know who he is. What's his business, and where do you come into it?"

I thought about the little boy's sunny smile and invariable wave to me. I felt a surge of affection for him. "I wonder," I said, "why he'd crawl out of the garbage can in the first place?"

"Sounds just like the kind of grand entrance an eleven-year-old boy would choose." She smiled slightly. "Then you have the hanging woman, who we assume is Wanda's mother," she continued. "She's in the old store, but she's not following you anywhere else. I suspect lots of people have run into her over the years. I think, as scary as she is, that she's just an example of insanity. She'll resolve and move on eventually. If they ever tear down the old building that may force her to."

"Who's the third ghost?" I asked, momentarily confused.

"The black woman you saw in the house you were visiting. Molly told me about her when the two of you got back from your first trip down there. You both saw her then, and you said you saw her again, standing in his office. She closed the door when you came down the hall."

"That's easy," I said. "She fits the first reason. She was the doctor's *de facto* medical receptionist; very attached and possessive. I think she died in the house."

"How long did she live there?" she asked.

"A couple of years. I'm pretty sure she went to live with the doctor pretty late in her life and found her calling at his reception desk. She was a bit of a dictator with him and his patients."

"Was she very close to him?"

"Maybe at the end, I don't know. I think they were estranged most of his life. She sent him away to live with a relative when he was young. Roy said he reminded her too much of his dead brother. She couldn't take it. The brother, Eli, was apparently her favorite. Poor Roy."

Kate waved and called out to a pair of older men who were leaving. They promised to see her the next morning.

"I don't like it," she said. "It doesn't make sense. If they were estranged, I can see her living with him if the alternative was a nursing home, but after she died, why did she stay behind? She may have answered the phones for his medical practice, but it wasn't ever really her house, by the sound of it. Why stay after death, when she could go to the son she loved? She stayed so no one else would answer her phones? Doesn't add up."

"So you'd put her in one of the other categories? Guilt? Insanity?"

She shrugged, palms up. "If there's still something funny going on...I don't know, she catches my attention, that's all."

"Molly saw her too, when she visited the house. She thought the woman was warning us."

Kate nodded. "Unfinished business."

"Warning us about what, though?"

"Don't know," she answered. "Maybe there's no way left to ever know." She shook a finger at me and pointed to my plate. "Eat your pie."

CHAPTER 31

Dorothy Tull,
Milton County, Georgia, Sunday, January 1, 1950

P astor Walker, I need to ask you something."
"Of course, Dottie. Can you wait for me? We'll go
back to my office."

George Walker continued to greet the Sunday parish-
ioners leaving the church. It had been a good service, and
there were smiles and laughter. The pastor often thought
that when the Spirit was truly present in the congregation,
no Broadway show or gin-soaked gala could produce the
kind of high spirits he saw in his church.

He often preached that you'd want Jesus at your party.
"Look at the marvelous first miracle, water into wine, for
no other reason than that the booze was running low and
people were leaving early. He didn't tie strings to it, either. He didn't say, 'Here's a drink, now listen to a ser-
mon,' he just did a nice thing. The bride had her day and
the guests had a good time. How were you going to make
something grim and serious out of that? 'God was good,'
he said, and people shouldn't forget that."

He watched Dorothy Tull out of the corner of his eye.
She was probably barely past her thirtieth birthday, but

she looked fifty. A hard fifty, at that. He said goodbye to the last of his flock. Rusty sedans began to thread their way through those people headed out to the road on foot. He sighed and turned his attention to the woman.

"My office, Dottie?"

This first day of the year was warm, but she stood with her arms crossed as though she were freezing cold. She stirred herself and followed him back inside, up the central aisle to the front. He went through a door at the side. His office was in the area that had been the sacristy when Catholics had worshipped here. The card table and painted kitchen chairs sat in contrast to the rich stained glass in the windows.

When they were seated, Dorothy pulled out a worn Bible. She didn't open it. She could read and write, but it was a trial to her, and she relied on her memory for verses.

"Pastor, I know that the sins of the fathers get passed down for four generations. Stands to reason that applies to the sins of the mothers, too. I need to know how to make that shorter than four whole generations. It isn't right it should be so long."

He leaned back as best he could in the hard chair. "Dot, that verse isn't meant to be taken literally. God doesn't curse us. It doesn't mean God is punishing us. It means we punish ourselves. It means it's hard to change a bad example once it's been set, you see? Our children learn from us and pass it along to their children in turn."

She looked determined. "It's in Ezekiel, chapter five," she said. "It's there."

"Yes," he sighed, "it is. But it isn't to be taken literally. If you go a little deeper into Ezekiel—may I?"

He reached a hand out for her Bible. She parted with it reluctantly. He leaned forward, elbows on knees, and looked down through his bifocals.

The only sound in the hushed church for a minute or two was the turning of the thin pages.

"Here we go," he said. "It isn't Ezekiel, it's Deuteronomy you're thinking of. 'Punishing the children for the sin of the fathers to the third and fourth generation of those who hate me.' If you skip ahead a little way, Dot, to chapter twenty-three—" He shook his head. "This contradicts what you're thinking. Listen. 'Fathers shall not be put to death for their children, nor children put to death for their fathers.'"

He realized he was talking to the widow of a man who had been executed by the State of Georgia for avenging his son's murder and mentally kicked himself. "I don't like any of this much, I'm a New Testament fellow," he said quickly, "but that clarifies it a little bit, I think. You see?" He looked up, and was startled to see her crying. "What's this really all about, Dottie?"

"And the sins of children, Pastor? Do those get passed back? My child suffers because of me, and I suffer because of what my child done?"

"Eli?" he asked, incredulous. "Eli didn't sin. Not in any way."

"Not Eli." She shook her head vigorously. "The other one. I sent him away, but I don't know if that's good enough." Suddenly, she stood up and headed for the door. "Only answer is to make sure there are no more generations. Someone got to stop it. How do you get rid of it? I guess I can tell you it's true about parents put to death for their children. When the parents and the children sin, it just spreads out, like…like…"

She threw her hands up, and walked out.

"…ripples in a pond?" he thought, and shook it off. He followed her out. The front door of the church was already banging shut, and he hurried to catch her. Outside, she was already halfway to the road.

"You left your Bible, Dot!" he hollered.
She didn't turn around.

అంబం

Present Day:

I turned the calendar on the kitchen wall from June to July. Most months were half gone by the time I remembered to do it, but I liked July first. I looked forward to it more than any other day in the year, and always remembered the calendar change. The doctor had gone back to Atlanta, and Molly and I had resumed our routines.

Canada Day opened the summer. Fireworks splashed against the night sky like prayers of thanks for the trees, water, lush grasses, and the chirp of frogs, blessings on the holiday traffic, and the warm, lazy days when everything was still possible. Hot morning suns and torrential afternoon rains surrendered to inky darkness, full of colored lights that promised every romance would last a lifetime, that death was a lie, and autumn would never come.

Molly and I had made no decisions about our future together, save that we would be parents. I had asked her to marry me. She'd thanked me sweetly and said it wasn't the right time to think about it. She was sure that a marriage couldn't be built on a baby, or we would all suffer, and that we would make a good decision together, in time.

Practical, sensible, Molly. I wondered how much her ex-husband Joseph, ever-present in her life's background, had to do with her deferral. Disappointed and hurt, I tried to concentrate on the child.

Molly had instituted a morning ritual on days that the weather was decent. We swam a circuit around the island in the early morning and watched from the eastern end, treading water as the sun came up over the trees. "Kind of new-agey," she said, "but there you go."

I pulled on a pair of shorts and padded barefoot down to the dock to wait for her. When I opened the screen door, Blue got to his feet and followed me. The dark morning was humid and overcast. I could smell the water, giving up its essence to the air. A half-mile or so across the reach of water that separated our houses, I heard an engine start and Molly's navigation lights came on. I watched as they got larger, and then the dock lifted under my feet as her boat washed in.

She leapt up onto the boards before I had her tied off. Blue caught her excitement and danced around her, barking. Even in the near-dark her eyes were shining. "I was sick this morning!"

"Oh no," I said. "What's wrong?'

She grabbed both my hands. "Morning sickness, you idiot! Oh, my God, I'm so happy. It makes it all real."

"Well, forget swimming," I said. "Can you handle tea? Maybe try some toast?"

She had kicked off her sandals, and she quickly shucked her shorts. She shot me a sideways scornful look and dove in. I followed her. The water was cold. I surfaced and looked back at dock. Blue sat watching. He had shown a herding propensity, and I was worried he might follow us into the water, but he seemed content to wait on the dock. I followed Molly.

We swam steadily along the north shore. The goal was to go around and then come back along the southern edge to greet the rising sun in the east. I knew Molly would stop and wait for me under the cliffs at the western end.

The far side of the island looked as though it had split and tumbled into the water. The vertical rock face rose thirty or forty feet from the surface to the only spot that wasn't treed.

There was a large clearing carpeted with low blueberry bushes at the top.

Molly usually stopped at the end of the island, over the Hole, to tread water and catch her breath, before starting back up the other side. I hated the interlude and usually tried to hurry the break. This morning I stopped under the cliff face where I expected to find her. It was darker than usual because of the overcast, and it was hard to tell gray water from black sky. I didn't see her. The water always seemed much colder over the deep part beneath me. The lake currents were active, tugging and pulling at my legs.

"Molly?' I called. "You here?"

There was no answer. I only heard the lake lapping at the rocks off to my right. I turned around, treading water, and saw nothing. It seemed odd that she would have changed her routine, and I felt the first scratching of fear in my chest. Suddenly I sensed a change in the water pressure beneath me.

Three feet away, a head silently broke the surface. My breath stopped, and I fought the urge to swim madly for shore.

"Molly?"

"You're slow, Mike," she said. "The winter off didn't do you any good at all."

"I wish you wouldn't do things like that," I said. "Really."

"Do what?" she asked innocently. "I was trying to touch the bottom. Had to do something while I waited about an hour for you to paddle your way here. I need to get you one of those floatie things that you blow up."

"The bottom is four hundred fucking feet beneath us."

She blew water at me and laughed. "Doesn't mean you can't try."

"I'm going."

"Wait a second. I forgot to tell you," she said. "I got a call. An 'I know what you did' call. Definitely the same sort of breathy voice as your dad's answering machine. Hard to tell if it was a man or woman if we didn't already know it was Arthur."

"Are you kidding? Kind of an important thing to forget to tell me, Molly. Was it a message, or an actual call?"

"It was a call. I answered when it rang."

"When was this?"

"Last night, close to ten," she said. "I was in bed, reading."

"Did you say anything?"

"I laughed," she said. "I laughed and hung up." She looked suddenly solemn. "It has to be Arthur Sutton. I probably shouldn't have laughed. The poor guy just lost his mother. It's so stupid, though."

"The poor guy may well be dangerous," I said. "Try not to laugh at him if he calls again, okay? He's dangerous. He's unbalanced and has a history of assaulting women. There's no telling what he might do. I don't understand how the hell he got your number. It's unlisted."

"C'mon, Mike, it doesn't matter. He's dangerous in the suburbs of Atlanta. Can you really picture him finding his way up here? A foreign country? And actually locating this lake if he ever got here? It's almost impossible to give someone directions to my house when I *want* them to find me."

The sky over the trees was lightening. I could tell we weren't going to see a sunrise in today's overcast.

"I think I'm going to stop by the police station, anyway," I said. "I'll feel better. I'll call Sydney Cotton down in Atlanta, too. I want to see if she can get the law down there to warn him off."

"You worry too much."

"Let's move on. I hate being over the Hole."

We swam more slowly back along the south shore, side by side.

"Have you thought about us?" I asked.

"Thought about us? We're right here."

"I mean what we're going to do? What our plans are."

"Our plans are right now, Mike. Our plans are happening to us. I don't know why you can't see that. Why force things into some agenda?"

"I guess a kid on the way makes everything between us seem…loose. Vague."

"You're looking for a perfect love story, Mike, and there isn't one. Wait a second, my mother's love story was perfect, and I don't think you'd want it."

"Why?" I asked.

"She met the love of her life when she was a teenager, and he felt the same. He died in a car crash after the best summer of their lives. She never recovered, never loved anyone else, and I think she was glad when she was able to join him. In fact, I think the rest of her life was all about trying to die."

"You never talk about her."

"It makes me too sad," she said simply. "Kate was my mother in every way that matters." She went underwater for a few strokes, as if to wash away her sadness. When she surfaced again, she went on. "They never had moments when they hated each other," she said. "They didn't get old, or have to go on a diet. They didn't embarrass each other in public. They never flirted with someone else, they never stopped wanting sex for a while, they didn't disappoint or humiliate. No one said something so unbelievably stupid or hurtful that it took months to get over it. No one found drugs in the other's coat pocket." She reached out a hand and stopped me in the water.

"You know why?" she asked. "Because they didn't

have time. That's all. They didn't have time."

We started to swim again. The dock came into view as we rounded the final point of land. We were almost done. Blue stood at the end and barked at us.

"Love that lasts is messy," she said. "Sometimes you don't get what you want right when you want it. This isn't perfect, and I'm sorry I'm putting you off. If you love me enough, you'll wait for me. I don't blame you if you don't, but that's what we have."

I thought about it. She was climbing out of the water, and I spoke to her back. "I'd rather wait for you always and not get you, than have someone else. I'll wait."

She turned and looked at the gray sky. It was getting light enough to be sure we wouldn't see a sunrise. I looked at her standing over me, and thought she was the most beautiful woman I'd ever seen.

"No show today," she said. "Let's go get dry."

She left me and headed to the cabin to start coffee. I toweled off and was just about to follow her when I spotted an early fisherman gliding by in a wooden canoe. He was about thirty yards from the end of the dock. His craft was green, long, and appeared to be very old.

He wore a snap-brim fedora. His face was shadowed and indistinct, but the long red hair that reached his shoulders was a startling splash of color in the dim early light. He paused in his paddling and touched the brim of his hat. It was a curiously old-fashioned salute. I gave him a small wave in return and went inside.

CHAPTER 32

Sam and Jenny Latta,
Atlanta, Georgia, Sunday, August 7, 1965:

She rolled onto her stomach and propped herself on her elbows. It was the first really warm day of the year, and the bedroom window was open.

"You don't look pregnant," he said. "How can I tell?"

She kissed his forehead and smiled. "You can't. Not yet. I can feel the difference, but you won't see anything for another month."

He rolled off of the bed and padded over to the dresser to retrieve his cigarettes. He looked back at her and waved the package. She looked at him over her shoulder and shook her head.

"I'm quitting those. I read somewhere it can give the baby a lower weight at birth."

"You believe that?" he asked.

"More and more people are saying smoking isn't good for you. I'm not taking the chance."

He tossed the pack back on the dresser and came to her side of the bed and sat beside her.

"I'll quit, too," he said. "No more for me."

"Just like that?"

"Just like that. Do I usually do what I say I'm going to?"

She turned into him and pulled him down into a kiss. Eventually, he broke it and stroked her belly. "I thought we'd have five kids by now," he said.

Her face clouded for a moment, then cleared. "We've been busy. Better late than never."

"What are we going to name it?" he asked.

"Don't say 'it.' We should call him Michael."

"What if he's a girl?"

"He isn't," she said. "He's a boy. I like Michael. He's the angel that killed dragons."

"Not dragons, I don't think. He fought demons."

"Killing demons is good, too." She giggled. "It would be very handy to have a little boy around who can kill demons."

A shadow passed across him. He stared at the curtains moving gently in the open window. His face was empty.

"Sam?" She touched his cheek. "Where did you go?" she asked.

He shook it off and looked down at her and smiled. "I'm right here."

"What's wrong?"

"Nothing. I hope he never has to fight dragons or demons or anything else, at least not while he's a little boy."

"You look so sad," she said. "Why does that make you sad?"

"He has me to protect him."

"Of course, he does." She smiled. "Anyway, I'm sure he won't have to, at least not until he's older, but it will be nice to know he can if he has to. You never know when you're going to run into a demon, do you?"

He stroked her belly. "Michael, then," he said. "God help him. I hope he really wants to be an angel."

ఌఄఄ

Present Day:

My cell phone vibrated. I answered, but the caller was silent.

"I've walked away from you, Arthur," I said. "Do yourself a favor and do *not* push this. I'll make sure you're stuck in jail until you're so old they have to wheel you out. Now fuck off."

I snapped the phone closed and tossed it on the seat beside me. As soon as it hit, it started to vibrate again. This time Sydney's number in Atlanta was displayed.

"You didn't just call me, did you?"

"No, why?"

"I've been getting odd calls, and Molly actually had the caller say 'I know what you did.' She's positive it's the same voice as on my dad's answering machine. With Wanda gone, we're sure it's Arthur. I'm debating how to handle him."

"If you just now got a call, I can tell you it's not Arthur," she said. "Arthur Sutton is dead."

The shock I felt was physical. "Hang on a sec." I said. "Let me pull over."

I was driving through Ansett. It was raining, and traffic was even slower than usual. Cottagers were kept off of the water and, tired of being cooped up inside, were inventing reasons to come into town.

I squeezed the jeep into a corner of the liquor store lot and shut it off.

"He's dead?" I asked. "How? When?" I had a sudden dreadful vision of the big man hanging from a rope in the old general store.

"Someone shot him. He was watching television in his living room last night. Someone walked into the front yard and emptied a gun into the room. Shot him right through the glass."

"Shit. I was going to call you today. I was about ready to lay this out for the police."

"Wanda and Arthur may have been the blackmailers— but as for the callers, I don't know. That theory's falling apart. You better put a timeline of when these calls came into you and Molly, but if you just got one now, it wasn't the Suttons, unless they were calling from the afterlife."

I hadn't ruled that out, but I kept it to myself. "The caller and the blackmailer have to be the same person," I said. "Makes no sense otherwise. Could his death be tied in somehow, you think?"

"No. His shooting doesn't seem related to any of this. There was a witness. Neighbor heard the shots and saw a black male, alone, coming out of the yard. He saw him under streetlights when he went on the street. Not much a description. Black guy, dark car. This sounds like a drug thing."

She paused, and I heard her lighting a cigarette on the other end.

"How's the quitting smoking coming along?" I asked.

"Great," she said. "Persistence is the key."

I could hear the smile in her voice.

"Anyway," she went on, "small-timer like Arthur selling drugs? He probably stepped on someone's toes. Suspect pool's an ocean. They won't arrest anyone."

"How did you find out so fast?"

"Aha. Very good question. You'd be good at my job. Cops called me for a different reason—because the medical examiner in Fulton raised some questions about Wanda. Seems she had some bruising and scratches consistent with one hell of a fight. She might have had some help hanging herself."

I thought about the figure in the old store, swinging at

the end of the rope, kicking and trying to pull herself up. I shuddered.

"One of the slippers she was wearing was found in the store. She kicked it off when...you know. The other was in her house."

"Arthur told me that himself," I said. "He found it in the front hall when he came home. He thought someone killed her."

"Interesting. He could have been blowing smoke, if he did it. Trying to divert you."

"So now they don't think it was a suicide?" I asked.

"She definitely died from hanging, they say, and they don't think she was hoisted up there. She may have hurt herself, but the condition of the body has them curious. She wasn't light, and even though Arthur was strong, it would have taken more than one person to do that. She might have climbed the ladder herself, under duress."

"What kind of duress makes you put a rope around your own neck?"

"Gunpoint?"

"Wouldn't be enough to make me hang myself," I said. "I'd rather get shot."

"You'd probably do anything to buy you one more minute. It's human nature. If someone holds a gun on you and says, 'I'll shoot you right now, or you can do what I say and climb that ladder and have a few more seconds to live', you'd do it. Anyone would climb, and hope something might happen to save them."

"Whether she chose hanging in the old store, the same death as her mother, or someone chose it for her," I said, "there's a symbol there. Same as my dad. This is all connected to Eli Tull."

"That occurred to me." Her voice changed. I could tell she was feeling some strain. "I called for two reasons, really. The first was to let you know that the police may be in touch. Don't worry about that, but they're re-interviewing everyone, which is why they called me. We found her body, so we're on the list. The second is this. Your dad dead, now Wanda and her son—that's almost everyone connected in any way to the main players in the Eli Tull story gone, except you—"

"And Roy Tull," I finished for her. "You think there's a connection here?"

"It's just too weird," she said. "You hire me to find out what happened to your dad, and the more we pull on loose threads, the more the Tull story seems to be at the center of it. It's like every member of every generation is gone now, except a couple of loose ends. You and Roy Tull."

"Someone's making these calls," I said. "But if every-one connected to the story is gone, who's left to be doing it? And why?"

"I've been trying to reach Roy Tull all morning. No luck. I'm worried about him."

"I'll try him later," I said.

I was worried about him, too. It would just about kill Molly if anything happened to him.

❧❧

I met Molly at the Echo Island Pie Company. I spotted her in the baking area behind the counter with a mop in her hand. Kate was at the cash register.

"You see how I treat family when they come in here," she said, nodding at her niece. "Your days of eating up all my pie are almost over. This baby gets here, I'll be hand-ing you a broom before you get a crumb."

I laughed and headed for a table. "Let me know when the time comes. I'll enjoy my status in the meantime."

In a few minutes, both women joined me at the table. I

felt enveloped in their easy familiarity. The baby had made me an intimate. We busied ourselves for a few minutes with rituals of cups and spoons and small talk. Finally, I broke in.

"I've got some disturbing news," I said.

The two of them watched my face while I recounted the circumstances of Arthur Sutton's death, and the new suspicions surrounding Wanda's suicide.

"I hate to say it," Kate said, "but in a sense isn't that good news? I'm sorry about the people, but it puts an end to all of this, doesn't it?"

I shook my head no. "Not necessarily. We assumed it was Wanda making the calls, then after she died we figured it must be Arthur. The last call couldn't have been made by either of them."

"So you're back at square one?" Kate asked.

"The thing that disturbs me most," I said, "is that Arthur accused me, the last time I saw him, of harassing his mother. He said that I was phoning her at all hours. What if she was getting calls from the same person?"

I absently played with the silverware on the table, arranging it like my thoughts.

"My father was terrified when he ran up here and died. We know he went to Wanda and Roy, told them about the men he had killed. He was trying to heal things, but did he end up stirring someone up? Who else did he tell? Did he get someone angry enough to kill? Is someone taking the people connected with this, out, one by one?"

"There are a couple of things that don't make sense to me," Kate said. "Why call Molly with this warning? Or you?"

"Whoever it is, they're crazy," Molly said. "They probably don't have to be logical. The thing is, only Wanda had both of our phone numbers. They were written down in front of Arthur, so I can also see him as the caller, but now you say he was dead when at least the last call came in to your phone."

"I want to ask you both something, and it'll seem crazy," I said.

I took a deep breath, really not even sure what I was asking.

"Eli Tull is central to this whole thing. The kiss and his murder are central to all of it. I keep seeing him. He *wants* me to see him. He's joined me on the island. I want to try to talk to him. I can see these...spirits, sometimes, but I've never been able to communicate really. You guys can."

"You want us to try to talk to Eli?" Kate asked.

"Yes," I said. "On the island."

"I'm not doing a stupid séance," Molly said, shaking her head. "On the island? No way. You have no idea how much this stuff messes me up, Mike. We have a baby to think about."

Kate also shook her head at me. "I don't know exactly what the island is, Michael. It's a busy place, though, in the spiritual sense. Enough happens there without looking for trouble."

"I'm not asking you to play with a Ouija board," I said. "I just think that Eli has something to say, and I can't hear it. All three of the children who were behind that store are dead now. I tried to walk away from this, and it won't let me."

Both women were silent.

"Roy Tull may be in serious danger," I pleaded.

Kate looked at her niece for a long moment before she turned to me. "Molly stays out of it," she said. "There's a baby to think about now. I'll come out tonight. I'll be out there late. Meet me at the dock, please. I have no desire to stumble around your woods in the dark."

She stood up and headed back to her ovens. "Don't

make me tell you," she called back over her shoulder.

"I know, I know," I muttered. "eat my damn pie."

I smiled at Molly. She didn't return it.

CHAPTER 33

Dr. Roy Tull,
Hollow Lake, Canada, Saturday, July 2, Present Day:

Roy thought he was lost. For the last hour his head-lights had revealed nothing but endless trees, bro-ken by vast pools of blackness that were lakes. Lights twinkled on the far shores. Twice he had seen eyes glowing from the shoulder of the road. A deer or a moose, he supposed, or worse, a bear.

He was no stranger to the pines of Georgia and had lived many of his years away from city lights, but the huge expanse of the wilderness here was unnerving. The forest pressed in on both sides of the road. It went on and on. It was summer, when the region was at the height of activity, full of city-dwellers escaping to cottages and camps, but he saw other vehicles only occasionally. He could hardly imagine the loneliness of these forests in the winter, when everyone had left.

He shuddered, thinking that he wouldn't live in Cana-da for anything in the world.

Finally, the green-and-white exit sign for Ansett ap-peared to his right. He found the gravel turnoff for the marina road. The small rental sedan slid a bit on the loose surface. It was well after midnight, and meeting another vehicle was unlikely, so he was able to stay in the center of the road.

So close to his destination, he began to feel a sense of urgency. Time was short, things were wrapping up, and this whole sorry mess was coming to a close. He had travelled all day, and he was tired. He felt every one of his seventy-five years.

The road weaved and turned, since it had been laid according to the contours of the land rather than blasted straight through. He had a moment of anxiety when he thought he had passed the marina, but then the sign appeared in his lights. He remembered Bill and Diane fondly. He didn't think that he would see them again. He had set himself against a great evil, though, and in the greater scheme of things he was paying only a small price if he didn't survive.

As it was, he was sick, and had been for several months. The curse of being a member of the medical profession was that knowledge allowed none of the false hope that sustained most people who were in his position. His time was limited, regardless of the events that were about to play out on the lake.

He turned onto the lake access road just past the marina, and he was on the last leg of his trip. Hollow Lake appeared on his left, looking like an immense, dark sea. The moon was bright and the water sparkled with white light. If there was more time, he could have stopped the car and watched the lake's slow currents at work in the pattern of illumination on its surface. After he had seen Molly, he was going to have to make his way out to Echo Island. He knew that Mike's cabin was a straight shot north from Molly's dock, but the thought of finding a single small tree-covered rock in this vast body of water, in the dark, was frightening.

There was something about the island that called to him, and he knew that his brother's story was going to end there, over a thousand miles and more than sixty-five years from where it had started. The kiss had come to this.

He looked forward to seeing Mike and Molly, the woman especially. She had confided in him from the beginning of their acquaintance. He wished that he had been permitted to have children. She seemed like the daughter he might have had. Michael, Sam Latta's son, was also connected to him by something deeper than blood. He thought of Molly's baby. Had he ever been a father, he would have recognized the peace that a man finds in his grandchildren.

Six or seven miles along the lake road, Molly's small white house appeared, on the shore below the road. Her dock light was on, and he saw her boat tied up. She had taken him out on the water numerous times when he visited her, and small craft's controls were easy and familiar. He hoped she wouldn't mind when he borrowed it.

He pulled the rental car as far to the side as the narrow road allowed. Molly was going to be surprised to see him.

"We're here, daddy," he said. "We made it."

There was no answer from the back seat of the car. The doctor waited a moment and then shrugged. A long package wrapped in cloth sat on the passenger floorboard and rested against the seat beside him. He collected it and got out of the car.

⁓♋⁓

"You see things," Kate said. "I almost never do. I get impressions, and sometimes I hear things. Almost like a blind person can tell that someone else is in the room with them, and even give an uncanny description of them."

"Example?" I asked.

"Well, a blind person might tell you that a person is a man wearing a heavy winter coat, because they smell a slight trace of pipe tobacco and wet wool. Sort of like that."

"Gotcha. And sometimes their observations might be more informed than someone who just sees them."

"And I hear voices, sometimes," she said. "But what they say doesn't always make sense."

We sat in my kitchen. I was going to put her up for the night, so that she didn't try to navigate either water or roads in the dark. The candles were lit in the wrought-iron chandelier over my kitchen table. The cabin was otherwise dark.

"You're getting used to seeing Eli?' she asked.

"Yes, I saw him at the church where he's buried, and several times here. Might sound strange, but I like him. He seems like a good kid. He has a killer smile."

"If you see him tonight, don't say anything. Don't muddy the water, so to speak. Just see if I pick up on him, and what my impressions are."

"Tea?" I asked.

She nodded, and I busied myself at the counter.

"If, on the other hand," she said, "you see something that is *not* Elijah Tull, I want you to tell me. I am not here to engage with anything else on this island, are we clear?"

"Clear, Kate. Are you sure you're okay with this?"

"It's fine. I don't think it's a crazy idea, really. I've never deliberately tried to do it, and this island is the last place I would have picked. If it's where Elijah is getting through, we're stuck with it, if you want to talk to him. If he shows up, I have a feeling he'll let you see him, so don't tell me he's here."

"Anyone else, I'll warn you off," I said. "You can shut it down, what you're picking up?"

"Somewhat. About the same as you can ignore the sound of a radio playing if you don't want to listen to it."

I brought tea to the table. It was a warm night, and the screen door was open, but the cabin felt cold to me. Kate must have felt it, too, because she warmed her hands on her cup.

"Last year, we talked about why there seems to be so much activity here," she said. "We know it was a group of doctors from New York that built this cabin in 1901, and they were Spiritualists. It seemed likely they started something here, with whatever they may have been doing. I don't know if you remember me wondering why they came here at all to build a holiday getaway. It's brutally hard to get here, and they would have passed hundreds of equally lovely spots on the way."

"I remember," I said. "You wondered if the island called to them, if it was already a spiritual hot spot before they ever got here."

"Exactly. I've found some things since we talked. Done some research. It's spotty, but interesting."

The candles flickered. I listened to Kate, but I was looking for Eli.

"The earliest maps I've found call this Squaw Island," she said.

"Really? I thought this was Echo Island since forever."

"At least a hundred years, yes," she nodded. "I'm talking about a lot older than that. I needed some help with this. It's taken some digging to find out why it was called that. I had an old academic contact in Ottawa do some archive diving for me, and he came back with a hell of a story, if you want to hear it."

I nodded. I knew some of the story already, but I wanted to hear it in detail.

"One of the indigenous tribes in the area...Algonquin, I think, I have it written down at home...anyway, they sequestered their women and children here when they went off to battle. It was a safe place for them to camp, in case the men lost and their village was raided. If they didn't make it home, the women could hide here until it was safe to go and join a friendly tribe, or whatever they did in a case like that."

"This was strictly a temporary camp, then," I said.

"A hiding place, yes. No one could live here for long. There's no game, and it's too small for crops. It was home for short periods during battle. Anyway, they seem to have been betrayed. Someone told the Iroquois war party where the Algonquin put their families. They came here. The men of the tribe were off looking for the enemy, and the enemy was right here, raping and killing. They slaughtered everyone on this island."

"Nice story for late at night, Kate," I chided. "I have to live here. I wish you hadn't told me that."

"Really?' she asked.

I thought about it. "No," I said. "I'd rather know. So you think it's the women and children that were brutalized here that made it into some kind of doorway?"

"Not quite. I get a sense of something else. I think it was the men."

"The men?" I asked, confused. "How so?"

"It's just a feeling I get. I think the warriors came back from the battle that never happened, and found out they'd been tricked. I think they found the brutalized bodies of everyone they loved here, everyone they were supposed to protect. None of those men would have been spared. The hiding place was literally a death trap, and they had been off running in circles while it happened. Their grief would have been utterly unspeakable."

"And their rage," I murmured. "Think of the rage."

"I think they must have cursed this place, Michael. Cursed the very ground."

Just then, Eli appeared in the room, standing behind Kate's chair. His skin shone in the candle light, but his eyes reflected no light. Kate stopped talking and looked puzzled.

"He's here, I think," she said. "Someone is, anyway."

She looked frightened. I could see no advantage in that, so I nodded. "Yes, he's here."

She swallowed visibly, and her voice was strained when she went on. "It's a big day. I think it's his birthday."

He smiled at me, a lovely impish smile, as if we were in together on a colossal prank.

"Of course it's a big deal," I said. "Happy Birthday, Eli." I smiled back at him.

"Where is he, Michael?" Kate asked, alarmed.

"He's behind your chair," I answered. "Don't be afraid of him."

"I'm not afraid of him. There's a darkness…something near him. He has dark news."

She leaned over the table and rubbed her temples. Her eyes were closed. "He's worried for you. Someone's coming. He says you have to watch out for…a man. It's a man…hurting people, Elijah? A man? Who is the man?"

Eli looked at me, his expression very serious. Blue had been in the corner, watching us. He went to the screen and began to bark. I shushed him, but he paid no attention.

Suddenly, he bolted against the door, which flew open. He was gone, and I could hear him barking outside. It sounded as though he was headed for the dock.

"He says you have to watch out for the man, Mike." Her voice was rising. "He says be careful of the man. The man thinks he's with his father. Their father. He thinks it's their father with him, but Eli says their father isn't with him, he's gone, he's dead…"

Behind her, Eli had changed. He was covered in mud, and his features were bloated and unrecognizable. He was excited. He jumped up and down and seemed to be yelling. In unconscious parody, Kate's face twisted and her voice rose to a shout.

"I don't understand…the man is coming here now. He's coming in a boat. The man is angry…the man says it's all your fault. You hung his daddy, all you people hung his daddy and his daddy didn't do anything, you all hung his daddy, Eli says, 'Watch out, he's coming here!'"

Suddenly, she stood up, grasping the table. Her face was white. She was choking. "Oh, my God. Molly—he says Molly—"

I was out the door, running in the dark, running for the boat, with Kate behind me. Even before I reached the dock, I could see red and blue lights flashing and pulsing on the opposite shore. I had the engine on my boat started and was untying the lines when Kate hurried onto the dock. Blue had jumped onboard with his usual clumsiness. He fell and yelped. I didn't have time to see if he was hurt. I jammed the lever into reverse, got us away from the dock and spun the wheel hard over.

"Hang on!" I screamed back to Kate and shoved the throttle forward.

The bow pointed up and the stern tried to bury itself in the water as the boat struggled to come up on plane. I knew that we were flying across the surface, but the pulsing lights on shore didn't seem to get any closer. It only took a minute or two to cross the reach. At about the halfway point we passed another boat. It was a white blur to my left. I realized in some vague way that we were lucky not to have collided, as we were both running on the black water without lights.

There was a popping flash of light. I realized it was in my own head, like the retinal image from a migraine. I saw the bare skeleton of a dead tree against a violet sky, and I knew who was in the other boat.

My cell phone vibrated almost constantly in my pocket. I ignored it.

A cop was waiting for us under Molly's dock light. I recognized John Park. We were friendly. On the rise by her house, at least three police cruisers and an ambulance sat with whirling colored lights. The forest on the other side of the road looked like it was burning with red and blue flames. I got out of the boat while John was tying it off and ran for the house. He leapt for me, and latched on to my arm as I passed him. I dragged him like an anchor. He was shouting at me, but I couldn't hear the words. After a moment, he gave up and let me go.

At Molly's back door, I saw her in the kitchen. She was on the floor, lying on her back. Only her bare legs were visible under the long T-shirt she wore to sleep in. My view of the rest of her was blocked by the backs of the paramedics working on her. There were bloody towels on the floor beside her. I threw the outer door open and was suddenly grabbed by multiple hands, all of them belonging to strong policemen. Gradually, as I struggled, I became aware of the shouting in my ear.

"She's okay—stop—she's okay—take it easy, she's going to be fine—stop it—" John Park's voice was in my ear. "Don't make her more upset than she is, Mike. She got cut by flying glass. They haven't found a bullet wound. She's going to be okay, they're gonna deal with the bleeding."

"What the hell happened?" I shouted.

Molly's soft voice cut through the hubbub in the room. "Mike, come here."

I went to my knees. The paramedics let me shoulder

in, though they stayed busy. I had never seen so much blood. Her face was mostly covered in towels. Kate slid in on the other side and stroked her matted hair.

"It looks worse than it is," one of the ambulance people murmured in my ear. "We're just trying to clear out glass so we can get some pressure on before we move her."

The eyes that looked at me were only Molly's. She ignored what was being done to her and seemed to will me to her. I brought my face as close as I could. She grabbed my hand. Hers was sticky with blood.

"He's looking for you now, Michael," she said softly. "You have to let him find you. I think he's on the island. If these people confront him, they'll kill him. It has to be you."

"Who is it, Molly?"

"It's Roy." She sighed. "It's Roy. I came in the kitchen for water. When I turned on the light, he shot through the glass. He can't help it. He thought he could make things right. He thought he could bring his father back. He was so sad, so sorry. He says everything that happened is all his fault."

"Why, Molly? Why?"

"He came in and called the ambulance. He's talking about sin. He said he did something bad to Eli, and he's being punished. He has to get rid of the sins of all the fathers. He said a lot of people got Eli killed, and…I don't know…he has to kill them to get rid of the sin."

"I don't understand. What did he do to Eli?"

"He isn't responsible, Mike. I don't know. He says he killed Eli. He says that ever since your dad came to see him, he thinks everyone will know what he did. Everyone will know his secret."

She was getting tired and drifting. A gurney had been brought in, and they prepared to move her onto it. I started to get out of their way, and Molly's grip tightened.

"'I know what you did. *I know what you did.*' His mother knew what he did, the secret he was keeping. The poor little boy. The poor, poor boy, Mike."

Her voice broke, and I found myself moved back. The paramedics and one of the cops positioned themselves and lifted her onto the stretcher in one smooth motion. They fussed with straps, and then lifted it up onto its wheels.

"Just half a second," I said and moved in close again. Her hand was trapped under a strap. I found it again with mine.

"What did he do, Molly? What did he do?"

"It wasn't Eli who kissed that little girl," she said. "It was Roy. They were peas in a pod." She was crying openly now. "Those men took the wrong brother. They took Eli. He died without even knowing why they killed him. Roy said Eli was terrified of white people; he thought monsters were taking him, and he never even knew why."

"Oh, God," I said. "They were monsters." I was crying, too. "All those people died, all those families broken, and he blames himself because he stood and watched them take his little brother and he was too scared to say anything. He was just a baby, just a little kid."

"They all were, Mike. Your dad, Eli, Wanda, Roy. When your dad came to Roy and Wanda, to ask for forgiveness, Roy finally fell apart. He says his mother hates him."

"He's sick," I said. "He's terribly sick. His mother's been dead for years."

"We saw her, Mike. We both saw her when we were in his house."

I remembered the figure standing behind the sheer curtains of his office doors. Molly and I had seen her the first time we were in the beautiful, crooked house. I remembered the tree with bare branches that had appeared in my vision both times.

"You know it's true," Molly said. "She hated him his whole life. Eli was her favorite, and Roy let him die."

"Why you, Molly? Why would he hurt you?"

"Because I told him I was expecting," she said. "Back when I first knew. I talked to him, Mike. I confided in him. He was my friend the minute I met him. I'm carrying your baby. Another generation."

One of the paramedics touched my shoulder. "We need to get her in to hospital now," he said. "She's going to be fine, but she's lost a lot of blood. We can't risk a blood pressure drop if she's pregnant."

"Can I ride in with her?" I asked.

"No, Mike," she said, almost inaudibly. "Kate will come with me. You have to find him. Remember, he called for help after he shot at me. Be careful, but Mike—" She pulled me down so close that her bandages were against my cheek. Her breath was warm in my ear. "I don't think he's going to live through the night," she said. "Find him. I don't want the police to kill him, and I don't want him to die alone. No one should die all alone."

"I'll try to find him. I promise."

"Mike…" She was fading, and I could hardly hear her. The paramedic tugged my sleeve, and I shrugged him off. "Mike, Eli was here. The little boy. I saw him…I saw him." Her breath was warm in my ear. "He was standing in the kitchen when I turned on the light, looking at me. He ran to the door and stood in front of the gun when it went off. He saved me, Mike. Eli saved me. And one more thing…"

She was almost asleep. I could hardly hear her. "Roy called the police and left," she whispered. "I was so scared. Eli held my hand and told me about the baby. He said it's going to be a boy. He told me while we were waiting for the ambulance. Isn't that sweet?"

I finally allowed myself to be pulled away from her and watched as they carried her out.

CHAPTER 34

Sam and Jenny Latta,
Atlanta, Georgia, Thursday, March 31, 1966:

He looks like a Michael, doesn't he?" Jenny asked. "Not a Mike, or a Mikey. A Michael."

"I imagine he might be a Mike by the time he's in school," Sam said.

"Well, he's just perfect. A perfect boy."

The baby lay on the bed between them. The room was warm. Summer was coming in early this year. Sam got up and went over to the electric fan in the corner.

"Don't you dare turn that on, Sam Latta," she said. "I won't have this baby getting chilled."

"Really?" he asked.

"Really. You have no idea how delicate these are, so young."

Chastened, he came back over to the bed. Looking down at his infant son, he thought that he did have an idea of his fragility. He had never seen a baby so new and had been unprepared for how small he actually was.

The baby looked up at them. He waved his tiny fists and kicked at nothing for a moment, and then he was still. He looked impossibly solemn.

"How come he smells so good?" he asked, looking at

Jenny's face. "Did you put something on him?"

"Brand new babies just smell good, silly," she said.

She kicked off her high heels, smoothed her skirt, and settled herself on the bed. She lay on her side, head propped on an elbow so she could watch her son. A red-faced yawn made her laugh delightedly. She cooed as the baby fussed for a minute or two and then dropped into sleep.

Sam hadn't known, all through the pregnancy, how to feel about being a father. He was older, at thirty-three, than he had imagined he would be when it happened. He still didn't know what to think, or how to act. He did know that this tiny face was perhaps the most perfect thing he had ever seen. He leaned down, almost fearfully, and kissed his baby son.

"You might be a Michael, but you'll never have to fight dragons," he whispered. "Not as long as I'm around."

Sam and Jenny lay facing each other, their sleeping baby between them. It was a moment that was enough, and it never ended, not really.

℘℘℘

Present Day:

Sergeant John Park stood with me in Molly's driveway. We watched the ambulance turn onto the lake road and head toward the highway. The splash of red lights was visible up against the pines for a long way.

"You following them?" he asked.

"They'll be working on her for a while, I imagine. I'll be there by the time they put her in a room." I was fighting my emotions. I felt exhausted and nearly overwhelmed, but the night wasn't done for me.

"I can't tell you how lucky she was, Mike. He fired through the glass part of the screen door; she'd left the inner door open for some air. He used a shotgun. It must have been a light load. The pellets blew out the window and then deflected all over the place. She really got hit by a cloud of glass and not much else."

"Bad enough," I said.

"Tell me about it. It's a miracle she has two eyes left. Her face got cut to shit. She's gonna have some trouble with this, maybe. There could be scars. Most women would. You know the guy, right?"

"I know him. He's an old man, an American."

"And he has something against Molly?"

"Something against me," I said. "My family, more like it. He knew my dad."

"So he takes it out on Molly?" he asked angrily. "What am I missing here?"

"He's a bit crazy, John. The situation's crazy. Molly just got in the middle."

"Whatever you're not telling me now, you'll tell me when you can? So I can do my job?"

I nodded.

"If he's an American, how did he even find you on a map? This isn't the beaten trail."

"He was our guest here last week. He was visiting both Molly and me. She met him in Atlanta, when she came to my dad's funeral. Now, I have a question. How the fuck did he get a gun up here, John?"

"No idea," he said, jerking his chin at the small car parked across the road. "That's his rental car. He picked it up at the Toronto airport. He couldn't legally buy a firearm in Canada—but in the small towns between here and there? This is hunting country, Mike. Ask nicely, and someone would have a rifle or shotgun they'd take a few bucks for. No one would worry much about selling to an old man, if his story was good."

He shook his head, disgusted. "Come to think of it, he could have walked into just about any bar on the way here tonight," he said. "A drunk needing a few bucks for his next round would probably sell his sister, and for sure have an old shotgun in the basement he'd part with. He couldn't be fussy about ammunition though, and I imagine that's what saved her life tonight."

He looked at his cruiser, anxious to get going. "Let's lock her house," he said, "and get out of here."

"I have a key. I may clean up a bit before I leave. She can't come back home to this."

"Fine," he said. "Our man left the keys in the ignition of his car over there. Don't let me forget them, okay? I'm happier with him out there on foot. We'll tow it in the morning."

Headlights turned into the drive. I saw that it was Bill. He got out, leaving his door open, and came toward us. In the wash from the headlights, his face was ghastly. Molly was like a daughter to him. I met him halfway and filled him in. He stared at the ground, shaken, while I spoke.

"Should I head to the hospital now?" he asked.

"No, I don't think so," I said. "Kate's with her. By the time they get her fixed up, she'll be asleep. I'm sure she'll be doped up. She's going to need sleep as much as anything. She's had a terrible night."

He looked utterly bereft. He nodded a hello to John Park, who had come up beside me. "I saw all the police lights go by the marina about an hour ago," he said. "I thought maybe there was a drowning on the lake tonight. I got up and sat by the window and then decided to drive by here and make sure Molly was asleep. My God—I'm glad Diane didn't wake up. We'll head over there in the morning."

"I hate to ask you this, Bill," I said. "I still have some running around tonight. Can you keep the dog for me? Until tomorrow?"

He nodded absently. "Sure."

"I didn't bring his leash; I'm sorry."

"He won't be no trouble. He never is. He's a good dog, so he is a little hairy, but what can you do about that, eh?"

He took Blue's collar and started for his vehicle. Blue resisted and looked back at me. I crouched in front of him and spoke softly. In a moment, he shook Bill's hand off his neck and led the way to the truck.

"Lock up good, Bill!" John called. "I'll have cruisers patrol all night, and get a boat in the water at first light, but until we find him, remember—he's an old man, but he's crazy, and he's got a gun."

Bill waved back at us without turning around. He backed the truck out and left.

"He isn't going to hurt anyone else, John," I said. "He needs help."

"We hope so," he said. "Where you headed?"

"I'll pick up a few things and go on to the hospital," I said. "I want to be there when she wakes up."

He looked up at the woods across the road. The tall pines were black against the night sky. His eyes roamed the dark, a cop's restless look that missed nothing. "Watch yourself," he said. "Seriously."

His brake lights flashed once, at the curve in the road, and then John was gone. I looked at Molly's empty house and was unspeakably sad. I trudged up the driveway to shut the lights off, and lock up. I stopped in the back entrance. The empty kitchen was a brightly lit horror. The floor was a bloody mess. Footprints tracked everywhere were just beginning to dry. Bandages and wrappers lay in sticky pools. It seemed impossible to me that Molly had survived this, and I fought the urge to race to the hospital.

I found a mop, bucket, and garbage bags, and got to work. I changed the hot soapy water twice. By the time I was done, I was glad to get out of the house. It felt strange and unfriendly, not like her space anymore.

I left the kitchen light on, and locked the door behind me. The night was winding its way onward. It was just after three when I walked down to the water. I had inadvertently shut off the dock light when I hit the switches by the back door. I wished that I hadn't, but I wasn't going to go back. I got into the boat and switched on the running lights. I missed the stupid dog.

Before I switched on the engine, my cell phone vibrated, as if on cue. I answered, and was greeted by complete silence. There was flash behind my retinas, the branches of a dead tree against a pale purple sky. I sat down in the pilot's seat, the silent phone held to my ear.

"Mike," he finally said.

"Hello, Roy."

"Is Molly going to be all right?"

"She'll be fine."

"You know where I am?"

I looked across the dark water. I had left the island without turning my own dock light on. I was two-for-two on dock lights tonight.

"You're on Echo Island, Roy," I said. "When I came over, you passed me going the other way. No one thought to wonder where Molly's boat was. Since there's no phone reception there except out on the dock, that's where you are. You're standing on my dock. If you look across the water you can see my lights. I'm sitting in my boat. Might help if we look at each other while we talk."

"I can hear you fine," he said. "I don't need to look at you. Can't see you a mile away in the dark, anyway."

"You can look across the water and see me all you

need to. If you look over here where I am, it might keep the bad things away." I could sense him considering it and I waited quietly.

"Might," he finally said. "She was the only girl I ever kissed, you know. Wanda. I guess now that it's over, I'm saddest about her."

"She didn't do anything, did she? I suspected her all along of the phone calls and the blackmail, and she never knew a thing about it."

"She was as guilty as we all were."

"Why, Roy? Why all this?"

"They killed my daddy," he said heavily. "I might've been responsible for Eli, but all the rest of you got my daddy killed."

"Why Molly? Why me?"

"Sins of the fathers," he said. "Some things don't ever go away, 'less you make them go all the way away."

"I've been wondering, Roy. Arthur Sutton got shot in his living room. Neighbor saw a black guy walk out of the bushes in the front yard right after. Everyone assumes some gangsta rapper was protecting drug turf. It's almost funny. It was you, wasn't it?"

His silence was assent. "Poor Arthur," he said. "He suspected that his mama didn't kill herself. He thought it was you did it. I guess sooner or later he'd of figured out the truth, but what did I care if I got caught? Just self-preservation kicking in, I guess. Stupid."

"Here's what I want to know. How the hell did you get Wanda Sutton up a ladder to hang herself? Would some-one really do that if they had a gun pointed at them?"

"She wanted to," he said.

"She *wanted* to? You expect me to believe that?"

"I pointed a gun to get her into the car and out to the old store," he said. "She put up a fight, for an old woman, the whole way there. I tell you. Once we were inside, I thought I'd have to shoot her, but she went up the ladder and stepped off, with no prodding from me. She wanted to be done with all of it, too."

"That's hard to swallow, Ray. Why would she do that?"

"Tired, I expect. Like me."

"And my dad?" I asked. "Why the blackmail. You didn't need the money, did you?"

"I didn't blackmail him, Mike. I didn't. He came up with that notion on his own, and I played along with it."

"What the hell does that mean?"

I glared across the reach, gripping the phone so hard my hand hurt.

"I think he needed to be punished. He came to Wanda and he came to me, a few months ago; just an old man crying about what he did. He shot her daddy and her uncle, and my daddy got hung for it, and he was never taken to task. He was looking for a clean conscience, so he came to us and confessed. Shit, Wanda knew all about it sixty-five years ago, and never saw fit to tell me about it. Let me believe my own daddy did it, when it was yours the whole time."

"He did it for your brother," I said. "The men he shot tortured and brutalized your brother, and got away scot-free. He did it for you—and he was ten fucking years old."

"I know that," he said softly. "You think I don't know that?"

The evening was taking its toll. I felt my chest grow tight from tears and anger. "Then why blackmail him?"

"I didn't," he said. "I just said that. Do you know your own father less than I do? He would have spit in anyone's face who tried that. He would have faced a firing squad before he paid someone a nickel for their silence. Do you not get it?"

"No. Tell me."

"I called him, and I wanted to see him suffer. I didn't have a plan beyond that." His voice rose. "Blackmail. He made that up in his own head. He decided that that's what I wanted and delivered me every penny he had. Once he got the idea that's what my calls were about, I just didn't say different."

"You're blaming him for being blackmailed?" I asked, incredulous.

"It shocked the hell out of me. I thought he had dementia at first, but then I decided he just needed to be punished so bad that he was making it up for himself. I told him where to drop the money, and he did it. I wasn't going to deny the man some misery before he died, if that's what he wanted."

"He died before you could kill him, though," I said.

"He did do that," Roy said. "I would have hung him, same as my daddy, same as Wanda. He didn't give me the satisfaction. I have to respect that, I guess."

"I do, too. I respect the hell out of him."

"Mostly, he was tired, though. Like Wanda. Like me."

There was the sound of a marine engine from far off, and lights in the passage between Duck and Long Duck islands grew larger. Eventually the boat passed between us. At this hour, it was either a provincial police launch looking for Roy, or a group of drunks on the way home to bed. I watched its lights get smaller.

"I know what you did, too," I said. "Molly told me about Eli."

"My mama never forgave me," he said. "She didn't figure it out until after my brother got found and they buried him. One day she recollected that Eli had been moping around the house all day, because I was supposed to take him fishing. I had better, more important things to do. He was home and I was out, on the day it happened.

Peas in a pod, they took the wrong one. They came and took away the wrong pea."

"They were evil men, Roy. That wasn't your fault."

"I don't know if they were evil," he said. "They were scared. Scared of what that kiss was going to do to Wanda, to their family. Ironic, isn't it? They let the genie out of the lamp. They killed my brother and gave the kiss all its power."

"Doesn't make it your fault."

"I think they honestly intended to scare him, scare him so bad he'd never tell anyone that he kissed a white girl. Eli never knew what they were talking about, so he couldn't cooperate. It made them so mad they lost control."

I realized he was crying. The words were coming hard.

"If I would have spoken up," he said, "if I would of said something when they came to our house, they would have taken me. Maybe they would have just slapped me around some and let me go. Maybe none of this would have happened."

"That does no good now, Roy. No point in thinking about it that way."

The lights from the passing craft were nearly out of sight when the small waves from its wake finished their half-mile journey to me. They gently rocked me and slapped the hull of my boat.

"You know the hell of it?" Roy asked. "The thing that makes me sad still, all those years later? I had nothing to do that day. I just left the house so that I could get rid of my younger brother, and his pestering me with questions about everything he saw. You never saw a kid like that for questions all day. The last day of his life, and I wouldn't take him fishing."

"Kids, Roy. Big brothers, little brothers. What can you do?"

"What can you do?" he agreed. "I never felt bad about the kiss, though. Never kissed a girl before that, or since. Black, white, or any other kind."

"Never?" I asked, startled.

"Never. Not what you're thinking, either. Mama made a big deal when I was older about sins of the fathers, and I shouldn't never have children, but I also never had the time. I was married to medicine. Never thought much about it 'til I was too old. I always remembered that kiss, though. She planted it on me, but I didn't mind. I still think about it sometimes; that day seems close enough to touch."

"What now?" I asked.

"Just goodbye, I guess. I'm done. I'm not coming after you."

"You think the kiss is going to stand for that?" I asked. "You think it'll just let you walk away?"

"I'll take care of the kiss," he said. "I'll take care of the kiss. It's done with everyone else but me."

His guilt and grief had driven him crazy, and my father's confession had driven his insanity out into the open. I felt tremendous sorrow for him.

"Everyone's gone now Roy," I said. "All three kids behind that store, all of their families. Just you and me left."

"And now your baby."

Hearing it said out loud in that way made the baby more real to me. It was a good feeling. "I can't let you go on," I said. "The baby means I can't risk it. You understand that?"

He didn't answer right away. "Does it matter?" he finally asked. "Would it ever matter in a court of law?"

It was my turn to have no answer.

"Do one thing for me?" he asked.

"If I can."

"Tell Molly to have a happy baby for me. She isn't going to want to hear it, but give her my best. She'll never forgive me. I understand that."

"She already has forgiven you," I said. "If you think different, you don't know Molly. She sent me to you, as a matter of fact. Why don't you stay there and meet me on the dock?"

"I don't think so, Mike."

"I'm coming out there, Roy. Molly made me promise. Whatever happens from here, I'll stay with you. You won't be alone, okay?"

For a long moment, he didn't answer, and I wasn't sure he was going to. Finally he spoke. "Thank you for that. I appreciate it. Come on ahead, but come slow."

I went back to the island. I had only been gone for a few hours, but the night seemed endless. Maybe it was always dark, and the sun was something that I had dreamed once. As I came close, I saw Molly's boat tied up there. Even without lights, I could tell that the dock was empty. No one was waiting for me. I nosed in, opposite her red-and-white bowrider.

Walking through the trees and up to the dark cabin, I saw the faintest trace of gray begin to lighten the sky. On the far side of the lake, a murder of crows told each other the news that another day had come.

I sat at the kitchen table, too tired to make coffee. I didn't know where Roy Tull was, and I was far too weary to look for him. He would turn up in his own time, and I believed his promise that he was no longer a threat. In many ways, I thought he was one of the best people that I'd ever known.

There were two small outbuildings nestled into the pines behind the cabin, which I could see out of the back kitchen window. As the early morning brightened imperceptibly, I saw that the door of the old icehouse hung ajar. I used it to store tools and odds and ends. I normally kept the door closed. I stood up and went out. It was strange not to be followed by the dog.

In front of the icehouse door, twin tracks had been scraped into the dirt. I looked inside and confirmed that my ladder was missing. I knew where Roy was. I went back to the cabin for a flashlight and then headed for a path I rarely used. I was so tired that my breathing ached as I walked up the north side of the island. When I reached the place, it was light enough that I didn't need my flashlight.

Roy hung against a purple sky. The dead oak spread its leafless branches above him. The ladder lay on its side beneath. Even in the half-light, I recognized my bright yellow clothesline. I was too late, and I had known that I was going to be, but a promise is a promise.

"Good bye, Roy," I said. "Travel safe."

Back on the dock, I pulled out my cell phone and called the provincial police barracks in Ansett. They were able to put me through to John Park, and we spoke briefly. I sat on the end of the floating dock, took my shoes and socks off, and soaked my feet in the cold water. I watched the day brighten and then the sun burst over the trees. I wished Molly was with me to see it.

When my feet got cold, I took them from the water and lay back on the boards. The morning sun was warm by the time I heard a marine engine approaching. I saw the police launch coming a long time before it got to me.

CHAPTER 35

Elijah Tull was finally going home. He left the old churchyard for the last time, followed closely by his yellow dog.

We are, each of us, born knowing our own stories. We enter the world in a state of perfect possibility. Only a heart understands the eternal, and hearts weren't designed to think, but to know. A small child and a dog walked along a dirt road, carrying more knowledge between them than all of the majesties in human history.

Eli finally came to the place he knew, though he had never been there before. Up ahead, he saw small figures, waiting. He broke into a smile as bright as any sun that ever was.

"Roy! Roy! Roy!" he shouted and started to run.

Love ran through everything, a perfect golden line, through all of those who came before us and all of those who were yet to be. There was no end and no beginning. There was only now, and only love. Simple.

ᘓᘐᘓ

"Are you still going to love me if I have scars on my face?" Molly asked me.

We sat on my front veranda. She was still bandaged. There was a steady warm breeze off the lake and the canopy of leaves that shaded the clearing in front of the cabin played with the light on the ground beneath them. Through the screen of trees in front of us, the lake was a brilliant blue, waves dazzled by the sun.

"I'll always love you," I answered.

From the island, we watched Hollow Lake go about its summer business all afternoon. Mostly, we were quiet, absolutely content to be together. Blue dozed on his side on the boards. Periodically he lifted his head to look at us. Every time that he was reassured we hadn't moved, he went back to sleep.

"You're perfectly beautiful," I said. "Any scars you come out of this with will just make you look hot. I'm going to fantasize that you're tough."

She looked at me steadily. "I am tough," she said.

I thought about it. "I guess you are."

"You are too," she said.

We smiled at each other.

"A little bit," she amended.

She got up and went inside. Blue scrambled to his feet and went after her, neatly catching the screen door with his nose before it swung closed. He tossed his head to open it and followed her in.

"Stupid's all an act," I murmured. "Stupid dog."

Molly came back out and handed me a glass of ice water before she sat down. "You'll wait for me?" she asked. "No matter what?"

"No matter what."

We heard the lazy buzz of small planes overhead, the shouts of water-skiers, and an occasional song on the radio from a passing boat. I wished the summer would never end.

There was the unmistakable sound of children playing.

They shouted, whooped, and laughed, high voices giddy with the excitement of the day.

Molly and I looked at each other.

"That's here," she said. "That's coming from here on the island."

We stood up and went around the corner of the cabin. The little girl stood on the footpath, looking at us. Her hair was long and blonde, and her eyes were a gray that seemed to hold many colors, like water in a glass. She was so completely still that I began to doubt what I was seeing. She was a reflection, an image imposed on the forest behind her.

Finally, she moved. She turned and began to walk away from us, up the path that led to the blueberry plants on the western end of the island.

After a few steps, she broke into a run. She ran like wind blowing through long grasses, water flowing over rocks. My eyes followed her as she joined three young boys, two black and one white, farther up the trail. They were playing with a yellow dog, throwing a stick into the trees, and cheering him when he returned with it.

Elijah spotted me and waved enthusiastically. His smile warmed me, and I waved back. I glanced at Molly. She was gazing into the trees, rapt. She saw what I was seeing. Blue sat at her feet. He whined softly at the other dog's play, but made no move to join in.

All four children stopped moving at the same time. They looked away from us to a point farther up the path, out of our sight. They seemed to be listening to something I couldn't hear. The light in the forest became gradually golden, as if the sun had come up for a second time, and I felt a warm wind on my face. I saw it stir Blue's long hair.

Three of them broke away, ran up the dirt trail, and were gone. The yellow dog ran after them. Only one boy remained. He walked a few steps closer to where we stood and then stopped, looking at me. He was about ten years old, dark-haired and perhaps a little bit small for his age.

He had a curious gravity, a solemn weight for a child so young. He held my gaze, and after a few moments, he tried a tentative smile.

I returned it as best I could.

Very slowly, he raised his hand up from his side, reaching toward me. I stood with Molly and Blue, looking at him, and then all at once I understood and raised mine toward him.

From more than a hundred feet away, I felt my father's touch.

For a moment, he held my hand, and I felt the generational river that flowed through all of us, fathers and mothers, sons and daughters, brothers and sisters. It was a current that flowed through time and made years and centuries insignificant. It was music that vibrated and echoed, over and over, until the end became the beginning.

He dropped my hand and turned to go. He looked back at me over his shoulder, only once, and walked away, growing dimmer with each step.

On impulse, I blew a kiss at his back. It was a strange, desperate gesture, but the only thing I could think to do. He stopped, looked back, and returned it. I could still feel it on my face after he was gone.

Molly and I stood looking at the empty forest for a long time.

"They were finally all together at the end, weren't they?" I murmured. "Eli, Roy, Wanda, and my dad. Together at the end. I think that's what it's all about."

"I think you might be right, mister."

I put my arm around her.

"Let's go in," I said. "Show's over."

She looked up at me. Her smile was gorgeous. "The show," she said, "is never over."

The End

About the Author

When he was little, Bob Bickford haunted the library. It was his favorite place. He hunted for good stories, got lost in pages, and daydreamed about becoming a writer. When he got older, real life got in the way and paychecks became more urgent than classes or degrees. The dream was filed under 'impossible things,' and nearly forgotten. After years spent in various corners of the United States and Canada, he dusted off his imagination and became a writer-by-night. He hunts for good stories once again, and he still haunts the library.

P Rot 3/18
GT Rot 7/18
TR MN 1/19

CPSIA information can be obtained
at www.ICGtesting.com
Printed in the USA
FSOW02n1342170117
29748FS